# Escorting the Billionaire

# Also By Leigh James

The Liberty Series

The Bad Judgment Series

The Escort Collection

Romancing the Alpha Boxed Set

# Escorting the Billionaire

(The Escort Collection, Book 1)

Leigh James
CMG Publishing, LLC

Cover Design by Cormar Covers.
Interior Design & Formatting Angela Quarles, Geek Girl Author Services

Sign up for Leigh's mailing list at: www.leighjamesbooks.com.

*For My Mother,*
*Otherwise Known as Cha Cha the Great*

# JAMES

All I wanted was a date for my stupid asshole brother's wedding.

Not a girlfriend. Not a relationship. A *date.*

No strings. No ties. No games.

No sex.

So when I called Elena at the escort service, I was very clear.

"I want someone beautiful. Who can function at high-society events," I said. "She needs to be able to use her silverware properly and to be discreet. I can't have someone who gets drunk and falls down in public. Also, no one who looks cheap. I don't want a lot of makeup and big, fake boobs."

"I don't have any cheap-looking girls, Mr. Preston," Elena said. "Unless the client is into that. Then I have plenty." She laughed.

I waited for her to finish. "I need her to be available for two weeks. I have cocktail parties, lunches, brunches, the rehearsal dinner, then the wedding. And then for some ungodly reason, my brother wants us all to go on his honeymoon to the Caribbean with him. It's going to be the wedding from hell."

I sighed and rubbed my temples; two weeks with my family was going to be bad enough. And now I was going to have to babysit a hooker the whole time.

But it was better than going alone. I hoped.

"She'll need a passport. And a drug test. I don't want any users." I winced, remembering the last time I'd hired an escort. It had been over ten years ago, but I still clearly remembered waking up and finding her in the bathroom, shooting up in between her toes.

I went on a penicillin and no-whore diet after that.

"All my girls are drug tested," Elena said smoothly, "and they all have passports. They have to travel frequently. It's not a problem." She paused for a beat. "Speaking of tests, you're going to have to be screened for STDs. I'll need those results emailed to me before we make the final arrangements."

"I'm not planning on actually sleeping with her—" I said.

"Excuse me?" Elena asked.

"I don't want to sleep with her," I insisted. "I need her as a buffer from my family."

"Whatever you like," Elena said sweetly. "But she will be young and gorgeous. And completely at your disposal."

I exhaled and stalked around my living room, my footsteps bouncing off the hardwood floors. I was dressed in a suit and ready for work. I looked out at the sun rising over Los Angeles, the light flooding my house. I didn't want to leave here. I had everything I needed, including my favorite leather couch and an enormous flatscreen television, and nothing I didn't, including a prostitute and my family.

I didn't argue with the madam. Still, I had no plans to sleep with the girl I was hiring—I wanted to keep her at arm's length, just like everyone else. I didn't want any messy emotional entanglements. I just needed a fake relationship to keep my family at bay. No more questions about why I was alone, no more wondering or whispers. The whispers that I was gay. Or worse, that I was lonely.

The truth was that I preferred to be alone, left to my own devices. And it was nobody's damn business.

"I'll have my doctor send you the test results. Tomorrow. I need to get this wrapped up—I fly in on Friday, and I need her then." All the events and the wedding were happening in Boston. Then we were all flying to Providenciales together, one big happy family.

*Fuck me,* I thought. I needed a drink just running through the itinerary in my mind.

"What sort of look do you prefer?" Elena asked. "I gave you the code to look at the girls online…"

"I already did," I said. "They all look decent. Find me one that won't embarrass me. Find me one that's smart. Not some hick. And no strippers. My brother can pick out a stripper from a mile away."

"Do you have a preference for hair color?" She asked. "Build? Anything? Because you're going to be around your family, you'll want it to seem natural."

I thought of my last girlfriend, Logan. She'd had stick-straight blond hair and not an ounce of fat on her toned, lithe body. And she'd been a total, complete, unending pain in my ass.

"Dark hair," I said. "Curvy. I want someone who isn't afraid of a steak. And who looks good in a bikini—but not *too* good, if you know what I mean. I don't want someone who's going to have their ass hanging out in public. *Tasteful*, Elena. I need classy."

I rubbed my temples again. I was hiring an escort as a date to my brother's wedding. Classy probably wasn't a reasonable request, all things considered.

"I've got that," Elena said confidently. "In fact, I think I have the perfect girl. I'll send you over the contract. Send me that test result and your deposit."

"How much is it, again?" I asked. The fee was astronomical, if I remembered correctly.

"The total for two weeks, including the travel, is two hundred thousand dollars." She paused for a beat. "Half paid up front. And we're cash-only."

"Don't you think your services are a bit, umm…overpriced?" I asked. "I'm not prepared to pay investment prices for a rented date."

"You're paying for a luxury product," Elena said, not missing a beat. She'd heard this a thousand times from rich men who doubled as cheap bastards.

"The cost breakdown, per hour, is five hundred and ninety-five dollars. You pay your lawyer more than that, I'm sure. And he doesn't always bend over when you tell him to."

If I'd been capable of it, I'd be mildly chastened by that. I let her continue.

"That being said," Elena continued, "the price I'm charging you is our standard rate. I'm not gouging you just because you're a gazillionaire. But *do* feel free to tip generously at the end of your arrangement."

I snorted.

"Your escort is going to be the most beautiful woman you've

ever met. She's going to fulfill your every fantasy—which in your case, is being the perfect date for your brother's wedding. If you had any other fantasies"—she paused for effect—"she could fulfill those, too." She laughed again. "But of course, you're not interested in that."

"Ha ha," I said. "For that price, I might just *have* to fuck her." *Six ways from Sunday.* I made myself stop from forming a mental picture.

"Of course," she said. "And once you get a taste, you'll really understand why you're getting your money's worth. By the way—all of our escorts are on birth control. We test them regularly to make sure they're in compliance. So condoms are optional. Her test results are part of the contract. We guarantee healthy, clean girls. So if you're clean, too, you can both relax and just enjoy each other."

She paused and I squirmed, my cock stiffening at her words. It had been a long time.

*Down boy,* I thought.

"We'll see you soon, Mr. Preston. I'm looking forward to working with you."

We hung up and I shook my head, laughing to myself a little. Two hundred thousand dollars. But the promise in her words would make any man's dick hard. That was the point. That was why Elena's escort service was the most successful, the most exclusive one on the East Coast. She was good at sales.

And based on the pictures she'd sent me, her employees *were* pretty hot.

I willed the stirring of my erection to go away. I was using Elena's service because I was in a bind, not because I couldn't get laid. I needed the perfect woman to bring to my brother's perfect wedding.

So that everybody would leave me the fuck alone.

# AUDREY

A hot shower wasn't going to be enough to wash the date off me, but that didn't stop me from trying.

My skin was practically raw when I finished. I didn't look at it closely, just like I didn't look at the dirty clothes I'd thrown in the corner. The John had cut my bra apart.

With a switchblade.

I shut my eyes tightly and made myself block it out. It was over, and he'd managed not to cut me. He'd paid me. And that was all that mattered.

I was just drying off when my cell phone rang. "This is Dre," I said formally, knowing full well that it was my almost-former boss, Elena.

"How are you, Dre?" She asked. She was being fake nice to me, I knew. She was still pissed about that thing I'd done.

I was pissed at her, too. Elena hadn't been giving me any work lately. That's why I'd spent the afternoon with Mr. Switchblade, who I'd found online.

"I have a top assignment for you," she said. I immediately perked up. "James Preston. The real-estate mogul. Have you heard of him? He's been in the tabloids—one of those *Hottest Bachelors* lists."

"No," I said. I wasn't exactly up on my real-estate moguls or my tabloids. Outside interests were luxuries I couldn't afford.

"Even better," Elena said. "I need someone who can be genuine with him. This is an extended assignment, Dre. Two weeks. Incredible money."

My mind flashed immediately to my brother, Tommy. I got a lump in my throat. "I'm listening," I said over it.

"Mr. Preston needs a date for his brother's wedding. There are related functions as well—including a family trip to the Caribbean the day after the wedding. He wants you to pretend to be his girlfriend. His family needs to believe that you're a couple."

"Why isn't he bringing an actual date?" I asked.

"He's not seeing anyone right now. He said his family was difficult. They've been giving him a hard time about his bachelor status—so he wants a date as a buffer."

"Huh," I said.

"He also told me he wants this to be a business transaction, no strings attached," she said. "He's a professional, and he needs a professional. He wants you to attend these functions with him, pay you afterward, and then say goodbye with a clean slate. If you perform per the terms, you'll receive a third of the full fee. In this case, that's over sixty-five thousand dollars for two weeks' worth of work."

My mouth dropped open, gaping.

"Do you understand?" Elena asked.

"Hell yeah," I said, because money I understood. What was less clear was why a billionaire real-estate mogul had to hire an escort for his brother's wedding. If he'd made a "Hottest Bachelor" list, *someone* must want to date him…

But really, it didn't matter. There was no way I was letting this assignment go to another girl. Not a real-life girl and not another escort. Sixty-five-thousand dollars would be life changing for me.

"You can do this, Dre. Be polished. Your best self. Just like that girl you were when you first came to me," Elena said.

I peered at myself in the mirror. My hair, long and brunette, hung wet and dripping over my shoulders. My face was red and blotchy from crying in the shower.

I was a wreck.

But if I let myself block out everything that I'd done—including the things I'd done earlier today with Mr. Switchblade—I could see myself the way I used to be. Before this. What I'd become.

"I'd love the assignment. Thank you so much for thinking of me," I said quickly. "That money will help out so much."

"I know it will," Elena said. "That's why I know you'll do a good job. This needs to seem natural. No fuck-ups. If there are any problems, that's it—you're out for good. And I know how much you need this."

"I won't let you down, Elena," I said, trying to sound upbeat. "When do you want me to come in?"

THE GOOD THING about working as an escort was the money. And the clothes. The bad part was the guys who cried, or who hit you, or who were just plain-old weird.

There was a lot of weird.

Elena hadn't given me any assignments for a whole week, so I'd been taking in strays I found on an online "dating" site. The money wasn't enough to cover my rent, let alone Tommy's, and there were plenty of weirdoes out there. Mr. Switchblade was Exhibit A of that.

So I was relieved to go back to AccommoDating, Inc.'s South End office the next morning. Located on Tremont Street, the office was airy elegant. It was also easily accessible from the Financial District, where most of our wealthy clients came from.

AccommoDating, Inc. was a mostly legitimate business. We were registered with the Massachusetts Corporations Division as a high-end dating service, which at heart we were. All of our other services were strictly off-the-record. Sometimes Elena had us give the necessary politicians free services, so they were happy and we were left alone.

This morning I had to get tested again, both for STDs and to prove that I'd faithfully been taking my birth control pills. I also had to get prepped and packed for my trip. Mr. Preston was picking me up this afternoon. I had butterflies in my stomach. I was curious about my new John.

Usually the clients chose their escort via our pictures and a brief description on the private AccommoDating website. James Preston, however, had left it to Elena.

"He said he wanted someone brunette, curvy, and smart," she'd told me. "I immediately thought of you, even though you're on probation. He also said he wanted classy."

I wasn't sure about that part. I'd been an escort for over a year, and any classiness I might have had was long gone, rubbed away by more hands than I liked to count. But for this kind of money, I would fake the classy. Maybe wear a turtleneck or something. In the Caribbean.

I would do just about anything.

Elena greeted me at the front desk, all business in a cream pantsuit.

"Dre. We missed you around here," she said, air-kissing me on each cheek. Her hair was spiky with mousse, and her maroon lipstick was applied flawlessly, as usual. She was what someone would call a *handsome woman*; she was tall, six feet, but she still always wore heels. As for what had gotten her into the escort business in the first place, no one knew.

"Elena," I said and forced myself to smile. It wasn't that I disliked her. But she'd sucked me into this life, with the shining promise of money. True to her word, she'd delivered, and now I was on the verge of making more in the next two weeks than I'd ever thought possible.

"This assignment is first-class. You'll have to pack all Louis Vuitton luggage," she said, getting right down to business. She led me to the back room, where we kept closets full of clothes, shoes, and accessories. We all picked clothes for our assignments from here. Elena kept everything we needed—whether the John liked his escort to look like a buttoned-up accountant, a glittery cowgirl, or a French maid, we had it all.

"You have to dress tastefully for the duration of the next two weeks. Not flashy. No boobs." She looked at the T-shirt and jeans I was wearing and scowled. "And no T-shirts."

She went through the racks of clothes and handed me a conservative blue dress. "Wear this today."

I went and changed as she bustled around, packing and giving me instructions.

"The Prestons are an old Boston-Brahmin family. They have more money than God," Elena said. "You need to fit in with them, and by that, I mean that your clothes have to be impeccable and outrageously expensive. I've been shopping, and I've gotten you all the essentials—cocktail dresses, skirts, blouses, jewelry, and handbags. A lot of it's from a luxury rental service—so don't spill anything on any of it. I have to send it back."

I came out in the dress and she smoothed it. Then she examined me, playing with my hair, running her gel-manicured fingertips through it.

"You're so naturally pretty. He'll be pleased." She smiled at me approvingly and went to another one of the wardrobes, pulling out clothes in dry-cleaning bags.

"I picked out a couple of dresses for the wedding," Elena said. "Do you like red?"

"I think yellow would be better, actually," I said. "It looks good on me. And no one wears yellow when they're trying to look slutty," I offered.

"I like that," Elena said. She pulled a pale-yellow lace dress from one of the racks and handed it to me. I turned the delicate fabric over in my hands. I recognized the label; the dress cost well over a thousand dollars.

I tried it on, and we both liked it. Then we went through lots of other outfits, picking out dresses for brunches, lunches, and cocktails. The bathing suits for the trip were the hardest to choose. I looked like an escort no matter what I wore. I had boobs and a round ass that I couldn't hide.

"Your body just screams sex," Elena said and laughed. "Maybe you should just wear a cover-up and not swim the whole time. Hmm," she said, pulling out another suit. It was pink and covered in flowers. "How about this?"

"A pink *tankini*?" I asked. "I think that's a little too soccer mom for a Hottest Bachelor."

Elena frowned. "You're right. Let's just stick with black bikinis. But no jewelry except for a watch and diamond studs. No body chains."

"I'm not sure what a body chain is, so that works for me," I said.

"Perfect," Elena said. "Now, for your background. You're going to tell the Prestons that you're in school still—graduate school for design at a little school in New Hampshire they've never heard of. I've had other girls use this bio before—it works like a charm. Nobody knows how to talk about graphic design. Plus, everyone in James Preston's family is a lawyer, so they'll have no idea what you actually do.

"Tell them you met James at a PR event in California while you were interning out there. Easy. He doesn't stay in touch with his family, so they don't know what he does on a regular basis.

"They don't know that he's dating someone—because he isn't. But for the fake record, you two have been together for a few months. It's getting fairly serious. Serious enough that he's bringing you to his brother's wedding, to meet his family."

"Why *isn't* he dating anyone?" I asked. *Please don't let it be because he's totally weird,* I thought. A lot of the Johns were. And two weeks was a long time to be on a date with someone who was obsessed with peeing in your face, for example.

That would be a lot of pee.

"He broke up with someone recently. And now he doesn't have the time, he said. Doesn't want the commitment, the games, the issues. He wants no strings." She paused. "He says he doesn't want sex, either."

I looked at her, stunned. "Huh?" I asked.

"I said, he's not interested in having sex with you."

I raised my eyebrow at her. "I beg your pardon? Isn't that, like, the whole point? I am an *escort*, after all. That's what I do."

She shrugged. "I'm still having him get tested, and he still has to sign all the waivers," she said. "Because once he takes a look at you, he's going to change his mind."

I smiled at her. "We'll see," I said. I sort of hoped he wouldn't. Two weeks without having sex with a stranger would be a *real* vacation for me.

"So, back to James Preston," she said. "He's extremely wealthy. As in, the top one percent in the country wealthy. He's into real estate, like I told you. But don't worry about that, and don't talk about his business unless he brings it up. If he does, just ask questions, be polite, and listen. Men like James have women after them all the time. He has a fixed arrangement with you. This should be relaxing for him. A break from what his real life is like."

Elena turned to me. "I want you to make this the best two

weeks of his life," she said. "A client like James Preston only comes around once. If he likes us and uses us again—or recommends us to his jet-setter friends—I'll be able to put my girls through college. And you can get your brother into a single room for the rest of his life. Don't fuck this up for any of us."

# JAMES

Being a billionaire had lots of perks. Two of them were that you never had to pack for yourself and you never had to shop for yourself. Nita, my personal assistant, had bought me a new tux and a bunch of new suits for the trip. My housekeeper had ironed all my clothes and packed them all perfectly.

These things did not suck.

What did suck, however, was that I had over one hundred emails that I had to answer on my flight to Boston. It also sucked that I wouldn't be able to bark into my phone at the various directors who worked for me. I was flying commercial for the first time in years. I thought it would be good practice—to be around people that I didn't particularly care for, and to try and maintain my manners.

Because that was the real suck of the moment. I was going home, and that meant I had to deal with all the people who drove me crazy. I was going to have to behave, because it was my family, because my stupid brother was getting married, and because that was the decent thing to do.

I hated decent.

At least the escort would be there, and that would be my private little joke. My *fuck you* to my oh-so-proper family. I really hoped that she was nice, and that she had a sense of humor.

She was going to need it.

I finished making sure that my things were assembled and went to get some cash from my safe. As I grabbed the bills, I brushed the worn edge of something familiar, something I'd touched a thousand times. It was an old photograph.

I pulled it out, wishing that I could stop myself. It was of me and Danielle, from our senior year of high school. She was wearing a black dress, her dark-brown hair pulled back in a ponytail, and she was laughing. In the picture, I was looking at her and laughing, too.

It was the only picture I had of her. Of us. And for all the times I'd wanted to cut myself out of it, I couldn't bear to.

I put the picture back into the bottom of the safe. And then I cursed the day that I'd entered this world, along with the day that she'd left it.

MY DRIVER EXPERTLY maneuvered my BMW in and out of traffic on the way to LAX. *Goddamn traffic,* I thought, but I really didn't mind. Los Angeles had been good to me, and I was used to the traffic just like everyone else. It was a part of the landscape, just like the smog, the rolling hills, and the built-out horizon.

I hated to leave. I hated Boston—except for my sports teams. No matter how long I'd been in California, I would always be a Red Sox, Patriots, Celtics, and Bruins fan. I'd loved those teams since I was a kid. I didn't miss the New England winters or my family, but I missed my teams.

I'd left Boston for grad school, and I went back as rarely as I could. But this time there was no way out. Todd was probably getting married just to spite me. In a classic dick move, he'd also asked me to be his best man. He had me then. My mother insisted that the best man had to attend every event, including the trip to Eleuthera, to fulfill his duties.

"Who takes their family on their honeymoon?" I spat out at her when she'd told me there was no getting out of it.

"Someone who loves their family," she'd said icily. "But I guess you wouldn't know too much about that."

IT WAS THE FLIGHT from hell. I'd grabbed a window seat, ordered some coffee, and was reading the *Wall Street Journal* on my tablet. The other passengers were filing in, taking their seats. I took no notice of them until a frizzy-haired forty-something parked her kid next to me. "Be good," she told the boy. "I'm in the row right behind you with the twins."

She looked at me and pointed to the boy. I noticed that her mascara was smeared a little under one eye and that she had a little something that looked like jelly smeared on her cream-colored blouse. "This is Liam," she said.

I looked at her blankly. She sighed and turned back to her son. "Don't ask the fancy handsome businessman for anything. He's useless. Just like Daddy. But I'm right behind you. Just call me if you need me." She kissed him on the nose and then gave me a fiercely dirty look.

"Can I pway with that?" Liam asked, pointing his grimy little hands at my tablet.

"No way, kid," I said and put my earbuds in.

THE TWINS SCREAMED the whole flight. The earbuds did nothing to block out their wails.

"It's their ears," I heard their mother telling the flight attendant.

Their fucking ears had been hurting for six straight hours. If I were her, I would have given them both sleeping pills to knock them out.

I wasn't her, and I was thinking about trying it.

"Poor things," the flight attendant said while everyone in first class glared.

Liam was looking up at my tablet again, longingly.

"Oh, just take it," I said. I opened up the Flappy Birds app and practically threw it at him.

"Miss?" I called. "I'd like a double bourbon."

I also sent the frizzy-haired mother a glass of Chardonnay. She clearly needed it, and despite what people say about me, I am not a complete prick.

Not always.

A DRIVER IN A SUIT was waiting for me at Logan with a *Preston* sign. I raised my hand in greeting, and he gave me a pleasant smile and took my bag.

"Mr. Preston, I'm Kai. A pleasure to meet you."

"Get me the hell out of here. The flight was full of screaming kids."

"Of course, sir. You can wait in the car while I get your luggage."

A Mercedes SUV was parked at the curb, hazards flashing. Once inside the cool, dark interior, I leaned back and tried to relax. The memory of the screaming twins didn't help. The fact that I had to go see my mother and then pick up my prostitute/wedding date didn't either.

Kai came out shortly with my luggage, and we sped away from the airport. "Where can I take you, Mr. Preston?"

"I need to go to my parents' house in Beacon Hill." I gave him the address. "Then to the South End to pick up my...girlfriend." The word felt foreign on my tongue. But I might as well start the facade now. "I have a dinner tonight, a brunch tomorrow...you'll be driving me to all sorts of annoying shit all week."

I grabbed my phone and called my office assistant, Molly. She answered before the phone even rang. "Yes, Mr. Preston?"

"Where is the Mueller report?" I asked. "It was supposed to be sent to me during the flight."

"There are a few problems with it," she said. She was using the tone I mentally referred to as the *Don't Make Mr. Preston Scream at Me* tone. "The inspections didn't come back the way we hoped. The EPA's going to have to be involved."

"Are you kidding me?" I yelled into the phone, because (a) this was bad news and (b) I was trying to toughen Molly up. She'd been working for me for ten months, and she'd already cried twice. But this was real estate. If she kept crying, I was going to have to replace her. I didn't have time to emotionally babysit anybody—especially not the hired help.

She took a deep breath. "No, Mr. Preston, I'm not kidding you. They found traces of contaminants in the soil. Not exactly ideal for a retirement community."

"I disagree," I snapped. "It's not like it's a school. These retirement people are on their way out, anyway."

Molly paused for a beat. "Mr. Preston, what would you like me to do?"

"Deal with it and buy me some time. Hire some independent analysts and get them out there. Today."

I hung up as we pulled up to my parents' townhouse. I found myself in serious need of another drink. I needed to be home, managing this land deal that was derailing. Business deals gone wrong were easy for me.

Families gone wrong were an entirely different matter.

"Wait for me here," I told Kai. My father would be at work, so it would just be me and Mom. Even though I hadn't seen her in over six months, I hoped I could make a hasty exit.

I braced myself and hit the buzzer.

"James," my mother said to me, warmly, as I went into their stuffy townhouse. There was floral wallpaper covering the entire entryway, a white background with dark-green jungle-like vines. Looking at it made me feel short of breath, as if the vines were wrapping around my neck.

But then, I always felt like that when I saw my mom.

"Mom, the eighties called—they want their wallpaper back," I said, hugging her stiffly.

"Wallpaper happens to be very stylish right now," she said with a sniff, and pulled back to take a look at me. At least I knew I looked good. I had on an expertly tailored Armani suit, Hermes tie, and my plain-old ruggedly handsome James Preston face.

"You look good," she said. She sounded slightly surprised. She probably thought I'd be drunk already, like at Thanksgiving.

"I always look good, Mother. Just like you."

My mother did always look good. She'd been a knockout when we were younger—naturally blond, thin, smiling a large, fake smile. She currently maintained a regimen of just the right amount of plastic surgery, Botox, and tennis to keep her looking refreshed.

"Honestly, Mom. I don't know how you do it."

"Yes, you do," she said tightly. "It's all the boards I chair. Keeps me on my feet and dressing up."

I snorted. "You know that's not it," I said.

"It is if I say so," she said. That was a classic Celia Preston statement if I'd ever heard one.

I decided to pace myself and not give my mother and all her charitable activities a hard time right away. She'd run around for decades for her boards, pretending to be a saint, while one Guatemalan nanny after another had raised us.

Oh, the irony of my mother's charities. The Boston Public Library Children's Room. All that crap she'd done for the importance of healthy meals and fresh vegetables for kids. The woman had never even cooked me a processed chicken nugget. The nanny was the one who taught me the words to *Goodnight Moon*.

"So," said my mother, clapping her hands together and breaking my brief reverie. "I'd ask you how your flight was, but I couldn't care less. Tell me about your new girlfriend!" She slipped her arm through mine and led me to the formal sitting room. In typical Preston fashion, she poured a before-lunch bourbon for me and a larger one for herself.

I gripped it as if it was one of the few life preservers left on the *Titanic*.

"Tell you what?" I asked.

"To start with, I'd like to at least know her name," my mother said. "So that we can let Todd and Evie know."

I winced at the mention of Evie—she was Todd's fiancée. She was just like my mother. Thin as a rail, all collarbones and wrists, with a perfect outfit for every occasion. I was not looking forward to seeing her.

I took a sip of my bourbon. *Oh fuck,* I realized, *I don't even have the escort's name.* "You get to meet my girlfriend tonight. All secrets will be revealed then," I said.

"James, don't be ridiculous. Tell me about her. We're all going to be spending the next two weeks together. I'd at least like to be prepared. And since you neither call your family nor return your family's phone calls," she sniffed, "this is the one opportunity I've got. So stay right there. Don't look like you're going to feign an important phone call and run out of here."

*Shit,* I thought, and took my hand off the phone in my pocket.

"She's young, and very pretty," I said, making an educated guess that both of these things were true. "She's…in school, still," I said, trying to remember the story that Elena had come up with. "Grad school."

My mother raised her artfully waxed brows at me. Grad school was a pretty amorphous category.

"How long have you been seeing her?" she asked.

"A few months," I said. *I'm picking her up on the way home from here,* I thought, *and making a one hundred thousand-dollar deposit with her madam. And signing a waiver that says I won't sue the service if I happen to contract chlamydia, genital warts, etcetera, even though they've signed a contract that states my escort's vagina is pristine and sparkling.*

Not that I was going to sleep with her.

"So, her name?" my mother asked, expectantly.

Just then, my phone buzzed. I smiled at my mother in triumph. "I have to get this," I said and picked up. "Molly. Wait one minute." I knocked back the rest of my bourbon and leaned down to give my mother's papery cheek a quick kiss.

"See you tonight. I gotta take this."

Then, happier than I'd ever been to get bad news from Molly, I hustled out of the house without a backward glance.

# AUDREY

My luxury wardrobe was packed and ready to go. I was sitting in the office, crossing and uncrossing my legs, waiting for Mr. Preston to pick me up.

Elena clicked around the corner in her heels and frowned at me. "You look nervous—don't be. It's going to be fun," she said.

"I really appreciate you giving me this opportunity, Elena," I said. I sprayed my mouth with breath freshener for what was probably the tenth time in the last fifteen minutes.

"Well, you're perfect for this job. Beautiful, smart. You're able to hold your own in a conversation. And I have a guarantee that you'll behave this time." She gave me a look that I understood instantly.

"That guy was a creep, Elena," I said defensively. "If I hadn't run, I would probably still be his sex slave, shackled up in his scary basement."

"We're lucky he didn't press charges against us," Elena said. "And I don't blame you for wanting to get out of there. But if there's ever a problem, you call *me*. You don't pepper-spray a client, handcuff him to a wall in his underwear, and then run away."

"What if he was going to kill me, huh?" I asked.

"He wasn't going to kill you," she responded, rolling her eyes at me as if I were being dramatic.

"Elena, he told me I was going to be his lifelong prisoner. And he'd already done some scary stuff to me at that point," I said. "All I kept thinking was, who was gonna help my brother? Who was going to take care of him if I never came back?" I was traumatized more by the memory of that worry than by the creepy John himself. I could handle *him*. But Tommy being left all alone?

That I could never handle.

"There, there," she said, coming over and rubbing my shoulders.

"Don't get all blotchy."

I knew she was being nice and cooing over me because I was her prized show pony of the moment. But I smiled at her anyway. She'd given me this assignment, and I was going to be able to set things up for Tommy now. So that if a John ever did decide to keep me as a permanent-resident sex slave, my poor brother would at least have a roof over his head.

She cupped my face in her hands and clucked her tongue in approval. "You're perfect looking even when you're upset," she said. "And all your body parts are real. James Preston is going to love you. And then he's going to love me, too."

After staring off into space for a second, probably counting all the money she was going to make, Elena came back to earth. She looked at me. "Back to the pepper-spray incident. I do not want my girls getting hurt. Not ever. You call me if there's a problem. If it's bad, I'll have you call 911 immediately. *After* I screen the issue. But that guy telling you that he wanted to lock you up and hate-fuck you every day for the rest of your life? Honey, you haven't been around that long. That's nothing. Really, that's not so bad."

I looked at her, indignant. "He had a basement filled with handcuffs and shackles, permanently affixed to the walls," I said. "It seemed pretty bad at the time."

She squeezed my face as if I was an insolent child. "I forgive you for running," she said, even though I wasn't asking for her forgiveness. "But I want you to make this James Preston thing your triumph. Your return to good graces. You remember that you owe me for giving you another chance. If you make him happy, I'll be sure that you only get the best clients from now on. The normal ones, who just want to pretend that you're the perfect girlfriend. And maybe jerk off in your face."

"I'd take that over being chained up and hate-fucked by that fat, hairy dude any day," I mumbled.

"Duh," said Elena. "Who wouldn't?"

ELENA WENT BACK to her office, and I started pacing, intermittently misting my mouth, waiting for Mr. Preston.

"Dre. *Dre!*" my friend Jenny called. She burst into the room, breathing hard.

"Omigod, *Dre.* James Preston is out front! And he's frickin' gorgeous! Can I switch with you? Please? You can have Fat Vinnie, and Loopsy, and all my other regulars, but I'm not kidding you, you're gonna die when you see him—"

"Jenny, I'm gonna die if you don't stop talking so fast." I said, laughing. I grabbed her hand and squeezed it, trying to calm her down. Even though we were about the same age, Jenny was like my little sister. I was always trying to soothe her and keep her out of trouble.

I smiled at her and shook my head encouragingly. "Okay? You okay?"

She exhaled a shaky breath and nodded. "But I am not kidding you, Dre, you're gonna frickin' *die*. He's that hot. I cross my heart and swear to God. My underwear are soakin' wet just from looking at him."

I laughed and held up my hand to stop her. "Okay, Jenny. I get it. He's good looking."

She looked at me expectantly. "Aren't you excited?" she asked. She sounded disappointed.

I looked at Jenny, her sweet, open face. Jenny was my friend, but she was not the brightest of bulbs. The fact that my new client was *frickin' hot*, as she put it, was not enough to get me excited.

"Of course I'm excited," I lied, and pulled her in for a quick hug. "I'm just nervous." This, at least, was the truth. "I'm worried about being around his whole family for two weeks, for starters. And going to all those brunches and cocktail hours. Then a vacation. That's a lot of family time...and I'm pretending to be someone else. Someone normal. Educated."

"Dre, you *are* normal. And smart. You're the smartest girl I know!" She hugged me again, her dirty-blond curls bouncing against me. "He's gonna love you. He's gonna love you in that blue dress you got on. You look good, girl. He might even try to *buy* you."

I laughed out loud. "*Buy* me? Like a sweater?"

"Yeah, like his own personal sweater. Don't be silly—you know what I mean. He might really like you. Enough to not want to just rent you." She slapped me on the ass. "Although he's gonna enjoy renting you!"

I laughed and swatted her away. "I don't think it's going to get that serious. Elena told me he said no sex," I said.

"Shut the fuck up," Jenny said. She sounded crushed.

I shrugged. "It wouldn't be the worst thing," I mumbled.

"Oh, Dre, when you see him? You'll know that would be the absolute worst thing that could happen to you. I'm telling you, he is—"

"Frickin', panty-liquefying hot," I finished her sentence for her. "Thank you. I'm glad you approve."

I grabbed her hands again. "Listen, I'm not gonna be able to talk to you for the next two weeks. I'm gonna miss you. You have to take care of yourself—don't let Loopsy push you around. I mean it."

Jenny had a bunch of regular clients who saw her weekly, but I still always worried about her. She was blonde, round faced, and twenty-one, with pillowy, Angelina Jolie-like lips. Men always told her she had a mouth that was built for shoving a cock into. That's what she told me the day I met her. And she'd laughed about it. She didn't let things like that bother her, which was good, because they happened to her a lot.

There was a knock on the door, and Elena poked her head in. "Dre, Mr. Preston is here. Jenny, Loopsy's called for you. Twice."

"Tell him I don't want to see him and his nasty, saggy balls," Jenny said, smiling wickedly and inspecting her nails.

She looked up and saw the madam frowning at her. "Just kidding, Elena! Tell the squirrelly little bastard I miss him—and his nasty, saggy balls."

She turned to me and gave me one last hug. "If Loopsy ends up buying me, and James Preston ends up buying you…I'll be frickin' hurt. I mean it."

I shook my head at her in mock disgust, but suddenly I realized

I was close to tears. "I'm gonna miss you, Jenny...be safe."

"I'm gonna miss you, too...but don't be such a baby," she said, tossing her curls over her shoulder and winking at me. "And if he lets you get in there...suck it hard, girl! Let him know what it feels like to have a *real* woman."

"Okay," I said, laughing. "I will suck it. Hard."

"That's a relief," said a man's voice, from near the door.

Jenny and I just looked at each other, eyes wide. Then she let out a whoop of laughter, and we both looked toward the door. And there stood a man, the most gorgeous one I'd ever seen. He had steel-blue eyes, dark hair, and massive shoulders underneath his suit.

He was exactly my type, and I didn't have a type.

He was my worst nightmare, and I had to pretend that he was the best thing that had ever happened to me. For two weeks.

"Mr. Preston," I said and forced myself to smile at him. "It's a pleasure to meet you."

# JAMES

I was going to go out on a limb and assume that the brunette in the tasteful blue dress was my date and not the blonde with the semi-exposed breasts and the big, honking laugh. *That* girl had a round, pouty face and luscious, full lips surrounding a mouth that begged to be...put to use. She was beautiful and voluptuous, but she was not my type.

The brunette next to her, however, was exactly what I liked.

And what I usually avoided.

"Ladies," I said, smiling at them tightly from where I was. "One of you is coming with me."

The blonde looked as though she was going to hurl herself at me for a second. She must have had some loyalty, though, because she held back. She took her friend's elbow and brought her forward a little bit.

"Mr. Preston, this is Dre," the blonde said.

"Excuse me?" I asked.

"Dre," the blonde repeated. Dre herself came forward then and shook my hand firmly. She was shorter than most of the women I dated, and curvier, with breasts, hips and...I wanted to ask her to turn in a circle for me so I could check out her backside. But I figured that would have made her feel too much like livestock being eyed for the slaughter. Her dark brown hair was thick, falling in waves down past her shoulders, and her eyes were a sweet, liquid *Bambi* brown.

*Sweet, liquid Bambi brown?* I seethed at myself. *Where the fuck did that come from?*

"Pleasure to meet you," I said, relieved that no one could hear my ridiculous thoughts. "I'll have your bags brought down now."

"Okay," she said and smiled at me. Her smile was lovely and revealed two dimples. She put her hand on me, and I felt as if I'd been electrically shocked. My cock actually twitched, as though it was trying to get closer to her.

This Dre was trouble. I inwardly cursed Elena for picking her, my mother for having me, and my stupid brother for getting married. Then I cursed Dre for being drop-dead gorgeous, having hips, a lovely smile, and eyes like fucking *Bambi.*

*Fuccccck,* I thought, and I knew that word was going to get me in trouble over the next two weeks, one way or another. It would certainly get me in *something.* Or maybe someone. I hoped that it would and wouldn't all at the same time.

My cock twitched again. *Traitor.*

"Are you ready, Mr. Preston? Or do you want me to call you James?" Dre grabbed my elbow, and I stiffened—several parts of me stiffened, actually, and I cursed myself some more—as I tried to smile at her as if I was a normal person.

"James is fine," I said, leading her through the door.

"Bye, Jenny," she called over her shoulder. "I'll see you soon."

"Bye!" Jenny called, clapping her hands together. "Have fun!"

Elena was waiting for us at the front desk; she beamed at me over her glasses. "I see you found her, Mr. Preston," she said. "Everything to your liking?"

I might have imagined it, but I thought Dre winced a little.

"Everything's perfect," I said smoothly. I decided I did not care for Elena. "We'll see you in two weeks."

She smiled at me and nodded at Dre. "Have fun," she said to her, sounding like a mom trying to convince her shy daughter to dance at the prom.

We got into the elevator, and Dre released my arm.

"What sort of name is Dre?" I asked. "I've never heard it before."

"My name's Audrey," she said, looking up at me from under all that luscious hair with those big brown eyes. I felt myself stir again, and I bit the inside of my cheek, hard, just to bring myself back down to earth.

"But I go by Dre for work," she continued, and shrugged. "It's more street. Audrey's too prim."

"Why would you want to sound street?" I asked her.

"Because I'm a streetwalker," she said and laughed. "So I figured, if the shoe fits…"

"You're not a streetwalker," I said. "You're an *escort.*"

"Aw, James…are you complimenting me?" She gave me that smile again, and I realized that it was practiced, that she was using her dimples against me like she had used them against hundreds, maybe thousands, of other men.

"No," I said. "But I'd prefer to introduce you as Audrey to my family. Prim is fine with them." *As long as prim has a trust fund and a penchant for vodka at midday,* I thought.

Technically, under that narrow definition, *I* was prim.

"Whatever you prefer, James," she said smoothly, the pleasant smile still on her face like a mask.

"Which do you prefer?" I asked.

"Audrey," she said. She gave no further explanation.

We reached the ground floor, and this time, I took her arm. From now on, I was going to initiate all contact, stay out in front and in control of every interaction we had. I'd hired her, and I needed her to fill a specific function.

If I changed my mind about the things I needed her to fill, or what *I* needed to fill, that was fine. But it was going to be a choice, not some stupid reaction to her doe-like eyes and my mystifying, painful erection.

Kai was waiting for us at the curb, a wide smile on his face.

"Mr. Preston," he said, nodding politely at me, and smiled at Dre. Audrey. She went into the car ahead of me, and I finally saw her glorious ass. It was one that you could grab on to with both hands.

"Don't smile at her," I said to Kai as soon as she was out of earshot.

He nodded and dropped the smile immediately. I slid inside the car.

"Why don't you want your driver to smile at me? We're the hired help, after all. We should stick together," Dre said as soon as Kai closed the door. She'd heard me after all. She crossed her toned legs and smiled at me playfully.

"I'm a divide-and-conquer kind of guy," I said. "I don't want to get ganged up on."

"I won't do that. I promise," she said.

The car pulled out, and Audrey suddenly laced her fingers through mine. Heat shot through me at her touch, and I winced. I looked at our hands and then at her, my eyebrows raised in a question.

"We're supposed to be in love, right?" she asked me. "We should probably be able to hold hands. We need to look legitimate. That's what I'm getting paid for."

She waited a beat. "Is that okay?"

With no small amount of indignation, I felt my palm begin to sweat.

"Maybe later," I said. I pulled my hand away and wiped it on my pants. Audrey had the grace to not watch me while I did it.

"Elena tells me you're a student," I said, desperately trying to start over.

She looked shocked. "Really? I'm totally not. I'm hooking full time."

We just looked at each other for a beat.

"Oops. I mean, Elena probably meant my cover—so yes. I'm a full-time graduate student. New England School of Graphic Design."

"Why'd Elena pick graphic design?" I asked.

My hand was still hot where she'd touched me, but I wasn't going to think about that.

"She said it was perfect because it's too boring to talk about. We were going to do law school, but she said your family had a bunch of lawyers in it."

"She's right. My brother, Todd—the one whose wedding we're going to—is a corporate lawyer. His fiancée, Evie, is a lawyer too, but not for long."

"How come?" Dre asked.

I snorted. "She was just waiting to marry into a pile of money. You know the type, right? Just goes to law school to meet a rich guy?"

A look of distaste crossed her face, but she stifled it immediately. Almost immediately.

"Trust me. She deserves every bad thing I say about her. She's a twat," I said and desperately wished that I'd just hired this woman to fuck me senseless. For the first time in years, I felt self-conscious. Every word I said made me sound like a bigger and bigger jerk.

Usually, that was the idea. In my business ventures, it worked to my advantage for people to think I was unpleasant and difficult to deal with. But right now? I had to stop talking

"Okay then. The sister-in-law-to-be is *bad*," Audrey said, her voice soothing and agreeable. She probably thought I was upset because I'd called Evie a twat. But she would learn, as we went on, that I *always* called Evie that. Because she was one.

I grabbed a decanter filled with bourbon from the side of the car. "Would you like some?" I asked.

"Sure," she said, accepting the small tumbler I poured for her.

I poured myself a drink that was significantly larger and took a sip. Something about Audrey unnerved me. She seemed like a whole person, not someone broken that wanted to get fucked up and then fucked hard, just to shut the world out. Which is to say, she was not what I was expecting. She seemed like somebody's sister. Like a graduate student.

Like somebody's girlfriend.

"So…tell me about this wedding. The more details you give me, the better prepared I'll be," she continued, all soothing efficiency.

"I'm dreading the wedding—I don't have a great relationship with my family," I said. I could hear the tension in my own voice. I always sounded like that when I spoke about them, which was one of the reasons I never did.

"James." She put her hand on mine again. "None of the guys who come to us have good relationships with their families. None of the girls at work do, either. You have nothing to be embarrassed about. Trust me," she said.

The fact that she understood put me at ease. Until I thought about it some more, and then the fact that it put me at ease made me uneasy.

"So," she said, "back to the wedding."

"I'm the best man," I said. "I think Todd did that to make sure I'd show up. My mother informed me that I had to come to every non-stop event. Evie really wants this week to be a big lead-in to the wedding. There's a dinner tonight and an endless series of brunches, cocktail hours, and photo shoots that we have to attend. Then Friday night is the rehearsal dinner at Il Pastorne. And Saturday the wedding is being held at Trinity Church. Then we're off to Eleuthera for a week with the happy couple, my parents, some cousins, and some friends."

"It all sounds very proper," Audrey said. She sounded impressed.

"It's going to be a complete cluster fuck," I said.

She nodded at me. "I have a family. Mine's probably messed up in a different way than yours, but I get it, James."

I swallowed the rest of my bourbon, hard. "I hired you because I didn't want to deal with questions from them about why I'm still single," I said. "I broke up with someone a few months ago. I've decided to take a break from dating and just concentrate on work. My family's beside themselves that I'm almost forty and not married. They're worried about not having any heirs." I smiled at her grimly. "So I hired you to bear the brunt of the misery with me."

"I'm on it," she said, upbeat and optimistic. "I'll do whatever you ask. You tell me how you want me to be. This is all about you. Your comfort. Your experience. I'm a buffer."

She was a pretty hot buffer, but the fact that I thought so was something that I was going to keep completely and solely to myself.

There was a reason I stayed away from women I liked. And I'd learned it the hard way.

# AUDREY

James was quiet for a minute after he told me about his family. We were stuck in midday traffic on Massachusetts Avenue. I watched the brownstones crawl by as I sat, lost in my thoughts.

I couldn't figure out whether it was good luck or bad that James Preston was gorgeous. And that he had feelings and people he was worried about dealing with. It made him seem too human.

Family made him vulnerable, and we had to deal with his family. I didn't know what he was normally like, but right now, he seemed nervous and quite possibly afraid of the next two weeks.

I couldn't have that, for a couple of important reasons.

First, we had to win this. We were going to be the perfect couple. His family was going to be completely fooled, and I was going to be paid lots of money for exactly that. I believed, like Elena, that James Preston was my golden ticket. I was going to make him happy these two weeks, and I was going to play my part perfectly. Then he'd recommend me to all of his jet-setter friends, and I'd be sucking rich cock for the rest of my life. And then I could make everything okay, at least for my brother. For me? I could survive just about anything. The fact that I was here, right now in this hired car, was living proof of that.

Second, I didn't want to care about James Preston. He was a John. The Johns were a nameless, faceless group of men that I preferred to block out. I'd cultivated only a fuzzy memory of the men who'd rented me, and I liked it that way. That was the only way I could sleep at night and meet my own eyes in the mirror each morning.

"So, is graphic design something you did?" James asked me, breaking my reverie. "You know, before?"

"Before hooking?" I asked. "Nah. I never went to school."

"Too excited to jump into your chosen profession?" he asked.

I gave him a quick look: he didn't appear to be kidding. I supposed he thought he was being kind by being blunt, but really, he was just being an ass. Nobody hooked because it was exciting.

You hooked because you had daddy issues. *Duh.*

"Something like that," I said. I decided that every time I found him insulting, I would just look at his head and see a big dollar sign there instead. I hoped he kept saying unattractive things. It would certainly help combat the unwieldy urge I had to check out what he had going on under that suit.

"So, where are we going first?" I asked.

"To my apartment. It's in the Back Bay. I'm not here much, but I like to have my own place when I am. We'll get you settled, change, and go meet my family for an early dinner. And drinks. There's always drinks when you're with my family." He paused. "So it'll be my brother Todd, Evie, and my parents. Celia and Robert. And probably a few cousins, aunts, friends, business associates..."

"Are your parents lawyers, too?" I asked.

"My father is a partner at a major law firm. Has been for years. He moves corporate money around. My mother does charitable work and goes to lots of lunches where she doesn't eat. She's really..."

I raised my eyebrows at him and waited.

"Thin," he said. He turned to look out the window. He was quiet for a beat. "My parents are very proper. They're into Boston society. They also have family money." He almost sounded as if he was apologizing.

"Family money?" I asked. "On top of major-law-firm money?"

"Yes, and lots of it," James said, still looking out the window. "It's very much a part of who they are."

I swallowed hard. I had probably never met people as rich as this before. Most of my Johns were wealthy, but all they wanted to do was have sex. Not parade me around for their families. I looked down at my blue dress; it was getting wrinkled in the car. It wasn't going to do.

"Well, we'll tell them we met when I was out in California

for my internship. You couldn't resist my…charms," I said, trying to be brave.

I looked down at my chest in a push-up bra. I was charming, all right.

I continued, "We've been dating for a few months, doing the long-distance thing. My family's from New England—I'll tell them they're dead. They can infer that I'm living off my inheritance. And no, I don't have any other family. So, no one for them to look up, no one for them to ask to meet."

James snorted. "I doubt they'd bother with all that."

"Why's that?" I asked.

"Because they aren't going to be that interested in you once they figure out that you're not society. You will just be a blip on their highfalutin radar. And they don't think I'm ever getting married, anyway."

"So I'm doomed. They're going to hate me," I said in a wave of real nerves. "They won't even know I'm a whore—but I'm still not good enough for you."

James shrugged. "They would hate you a lot more if they knew you were a whore—an *escort*. But yes, they'll hate you anyway, or at least dismiss you, because you're not from their world."

"Your world," I said.

He shook his head at me. "That's not my world. My world is self-made. I didn't use their money for what I've built. I did it myself. And I'm not interested in what country club anyone belongs to, or what boarding school they went to. My parents are more invested in society than they are in anything."

"Maybe we should say my family was really wealthy," I said, shrugging.

"Wealthy isn't good enough. It's about the *right* people, Audrey, not how much money the people have. It's who your parents knew and where they went to school and what boards they sat on. If just money was good enough, then *I'd* be good enough."

I was quiet for a second, wanting to remember every word he said. He was a puzzle I had to piece together. One part was clear: his family sucked. I was sure about it, and I hadn't even met them yet.

He must have seen the look on my face because his own face relaxed into a smile. "It won't be that bad, Audrey. They're civilized. They won't say anything bad to your face—they have manners. They'll stab you in the back instead. It shows how well-bred they are. They adhere to that rule no matter how many vodkas they've had."

"Awesome," I said, dreading it all now almost as much as he was.

"Don't say 'awesome' in front of Celia," he said. "We want you to stay off her radar. The further off, the better."

"Okay," I mumbled quickly. I hadn't even met her, but I already knew that Celia Preston was not someone I wanted to mess with.

James went back to looking out the window, and I regarded his handsome profile. I was starting to sweat, and it had nothing to do with how hot he was.

"So how do we win this?" I blurted out.

James laughed and turned back to me. Instead of seeing a large dollar sign where his head was supposed to be, I saw his gorgeous face, the lines next to his mouth deepening. "How do we *win*?"

I nodded at him, mentally kicking myself for my mouth that never seemed to stay shut when it should. "What is it you want from these two weeks? What's your best outcome?" I asked.

James shrugged as he considered me. "Let's see how it goes this afternoon. I'll tell you after that."

"Fair enough, James."

"Fair enough, Audrey."

The car went down another street into Back Bay and smoothly pulled up to a curb in front of The Stratum Hotel. The hotel was new to Boston and very chic, way outside my pay range. I'd had a couple dates over here, though. Two hedge-fund managers and a music producer. No one I wanted to remember.

I hoped no one on staff would remember *me*.

"I thought you said we were going to your apartment," I said, confused.

"I have a condominium here. It makes it easier. The hotel handles everything, and I don't have to worry. Plus, it has housekeeping and room service."

A hotel doorman appeared and opened the door for James.

He got out and held his hand out for me; I forcibly ignored the shock waves that his touch sent through me. If he changed his mind about the sex, that would be more than fine with me.

In fact, it would probably be for the best. Every man I'd ever slept with had now become a John. They all blurred together. Maybe it would be better if James wasn't quite so...special.

Kai rolled down the window, and I nodded at him. "See ya later," I called, and turned to find James frowning at us.

"Have the bags sent up," James snapped at Kai.

"Easy, buddy," I said. "We won't gang up on you. I promise." I reached for his hand again and twined my fingers through his; he immediately tried to pull back as we went through the doors to the opulent lobby of the hotel.

"Uh-uh," I said, gripping his hand more tightly. "We need to practice. Gotta look natural." I turned and looked at the grand room: it was just like I remembered it. Marble floors, marble columns, teak woodwork accents in unexpected places. It was beautiful and pristine.

I needed an apartment with a lobby like this.

I would have to suck a *lot* of cock to be able to afford it.

That thought made me burst out laughing.

"What?" James asked, wrinkling his brow at me.

"You don't even want to know." I laughed some more as the desk clerks nodded to us. "Mr. Preston," one of the female clerks said. I might have imagined it, but she seemed to be sticking her chest out at him.

James pressed the button for the elevator.

"What floor are you?" I asked, sticking my chest out at him.

"The top."

I rolled my eyes at him. "Of course you are."

"Of course I am, is right." He squeezed my hand. "Don't be fresh, Audrey. I thought we were in love."

"Part of being in love is calling people out when they act pretentious," I said as the elevator rose silently.

"I'm not in love with you, so I won't tell you you're stepping outside your pay grade," he said in a warning tone. "Stop being so honest. You're about to hurt my feelings, and I don't have any."

"You're the boss," I said, laughing a little. Being alone with him in the elevator wasn't helping my attraction to him, or my curiosity. I hoped he couldn't hear my stupid, wildly pounding heart.

This was the thing. The thing that I was working through in my head, as I held hands with my newest, sexiest, richest John in the history of all my Johns—and there were a lot, mind you. James was gorgeous. Any breathing heterosexual woman would instantly agree to that. He had huge shoulders, a square chin, and steel-blue eyes. On top of all this, he was tall, and from what I could guess was going on under his thousand-dollar-plus suit, he appeared to be devoted to working out, damn him.

None of this would have me all that excited. Although I did like his hair, too…it was steel-colored, neither brown nor black, some in-between color of thick, wavy, glossy godliness, gelled back just enough to keep it off his face.

*But wait!* I was getting off track here, again. Nothing about his looks, not even that glossy hair, was that thrilling to me. I'd been with lots of good-looking men, and while it sometimes made the job a little easier, I'd found that the good-looking ones were just as likely to be assholes as the plain-looking ones. In my experience, they were actually a little nastier. Maybe because they'd had everything handed to them their whole lives, and it still wasn't working out for them.

His looks weren't what was troubling me.

The fact that when he touched me my body responded with heat didn't bother me, either. That was one good thing about hooking, aside from the money: I usually enjoyed the sex, as long as the John was decent and relatively kind.

I also liked good-looking men with big shoulders and big… hands, which James had. Not that I'd been studying them in the car or anything, wondering if he was going to break down eventually and let me see what else he had that might be big…

*I was getting off track again.* What I wanted to say, in one complete and uninterrupted thought, was what worried me about James, and what was going to happen over the next two weeks, was that he seemed almost normal. Like someone I could talk to. Like someone I might need to help.

I needed a lot of things. Needing to help someone else was not one of them. In fact, that was probably the last thing I needed, on a long list of last things. I was going to have to watch my back with him. Not let him get under my skin. I had enough people to take care of.

We were both watching the numbers on the dial go up, not saying a word. I wondered what he was thinking, and whether or not he felt the same heat between us that I felt.

I wanted to un-feel it. It would just be so much easier, all things considered.

We reached the top floor, and James punched the code in for his unit.

"Holy shit," I said, knocked out of my inner monologue by the stark beauty of James's apartment. "This is gorgeous."

The space was massive, with enormous floor-to-ceiling windows letting in a flood of warm sunlight. Dark hardwood floors gleamed beneath a huge couch packed with colorful throw pillows, and colored clay vases dotted the various tables in the room. It was a stunning but comfortable space, a place where you wanted to pick up a huge book and curl up on the couch.

Given James's intense attitude, comfortable was not what I was expecting.

"I'm glad you like it." He released my hand and motioned for me to follow him in. "Thank you. I don't like being back up here, so I wanted the space to feel like my house in California. Lots of light. Comfortable."

"It's definitely not classic Boston," I said, "but I love it."

"Where do you live?" he asked, and I could tell he almost didn't want to.

"New England School of Design campus housing," I lied, easily.

He smiled at me again. "Where do you really live, Audrey?"

"Southie," I said, and he nodded, not surprised. "It's getting really yuppie, though."

"I bet." He paused for a beat, and we stood there, awkwardly. The escort and the billionaire, all chatted out. He looked at his watch. "I'll show you your room," he said, heading down a hallway. I followed close behind, marveling at how enormous the apartment was, wanting to stop and ogle at the view of the city and the Commons below.

James threw open a door, and I stepped into a beautiful bedroom with a king-sized bed. I went and sat on the bed and looked up at James.

"Thank you. It's lovely," I said.

He nodded at me, and a flicker of something—I didn't know him well enough to recognize it—crossed his face. He started backing out the door.

"You don't have to go, James," I said in a low voice. "If you want, we can just do this now. So we seem natural around your family." I patted the bed.

*What are you doing?* I asked myself. *He told Elena no sex. You were happy about that. So what the hell, Audrey?*

The thing was, I only sort of wanted to fuck him. It was more that I wanted to get it out of the way. It was more that I wanted this just to be a regular job, a regular exchange—money for sex.

Not money for I wasn't sure what.

I wanted to make him a John.

James smiled at me and held up his hand. "I'm sure it would be…a pleasure," he said. His eyes took me in hungrily but only for a moment. "But I already told Elena. That's not what you're for. You're here to play a public role. So try to keep your legs crossed, and keep your eye on the ball. *The ball*, Audrey. Not my balls."

He closed the door, hard, and I tried to ignore the inexplicable fact that I wanted to cry once I was alone.

# JAMES

*Fucking women,* I thought as I marched down to my bedroom and slammed the door.

You never knew what they wanted. First, it was sex, then it was money. Right now it was sex for money. Or something.

I couldn't figure this Audrey out, and I didn't want to.

My cock was hard and throbbing; it didn't want to figure her out, either, but it wanted to get in there and pound her, hard. I didn't blame it.

I went into the bathroom and locked the door. *Go back in there and get it over with,* I thought. I wanted to. I wanted to fuck her, to watch that long brown hair spill down her back. Grab her breasts and suck on them, greedily claiming her body as mine.

So. Fucking. Inconvenient.

I unzipped my pants and grabbed myself, a little roughly, imagining her writhing beneath me, arching her back, and calling my name.

It only took a couple more images like that to make me come, hot, stupid liquid spurting out of me. It was easy.

Too easy.

I groaned, spent but still unsatisfied, and leaned against the counter. Clearly, I wanted to fuck her. She was beautiful, sexy, and she actually seemed smart. I was surprised by that and angry at myself for being surprised—I prided myself on not underestimating people. Underestimating people was how you got stabbed in the back, or got an ice pick to the back of the head, *Trotsky*-style.

*So you should just do it,* I thought, cleaning up the mess I'd made. But that was just it. I didn't want to clean up another mess. When I'd gone to Elena, I'd said no sex because I just wanted this to be a business transaction. I wanted it to be another item on a list that I could control and check off.

*Attend Todd's wedding*. Check.

*Appear to be successful personally as well as professionally.* Check.

*Not have to deal with so many questions and nagging about having an heir that I want to kill everybody in my family.* Check.

If Audrey hadn't been nice, and smart and funny, I'd be back there banging her right now, as soon as she'd asked. I was very particular, but I was not a man that said no to sex with a beautiful woman easily. I was not that controlled, even though I desperately wished I was. It would make the messiness of life a lot easier.

But she *was* nice. And smart and funny. I didn't need this to be any more complicated than it already was. I didn't need to *like* her. In fact, liking her would work against me in the long run.

So no sex was going to stay no sex, but for a different reason than I'd planned.

I grabbed my phone, thinking about calling Elena. I could return Audrey and ask for a different girl, I reasoned, someone more like that Jenny. Someone more obvious. She wouldn't work as well with my family, but I wouldn't need to pay any attention to her, either. She would literally be a no-brainer, ha ha.

A few minutes later, there was a knock on my door.

"What," I said as Audrey came through the threshold. She looked twitchy and troubled.

"I'm sorry about before," she said nervously. "It's the escort in me. I guess I thought you didn't mean it. What you told Elena."

I raised my eyebrows at her.

"About the no sex thing," she said, explaining. "So I figured I'd be the one to break the ice."

"I appreciate that, Audrey," I said and smiled at her. "You thinking of me."

She sighed and rolled her eyes. "You don't have to be sarcastic. I just wanted to say that I'm sorry. I crossed a line. Now that I know how you really feel, it won't happen again."

She looked at the phone in my hand. "Please don't fire me," she said, and I could hear real worry in her voice.

"I wouldn't do that," I said. I dropped the phone onto my bed, secretly guilty as charged. Once again, I'd underestimated her. I didn't know why she needed the job so badly, and it was a failure on my part not to have considered it. "I told Elena I didn't want to sleep with who I hired. That's mainly because I'm trying to keep my distance from these two weeks. I don't want it to get complicated—I want to be on auto-pilot," I said. I figured I could be honest with her, at least partially. What did I have to lose?

She looked at me with those big beautiful brown eyes. "I won't try to seduce you again, I promise. But if you decide you want to fuck me, just speak up. We can do it on auto-pilot." She smiled warmly at me.

She was nicer than I was used to, and certainly nicer than I deserved.

"I'll keep that in mind. We need to get ready for the dinner," I said, adjusting my cuff links. "I'm going to change into a darker suit. Elena said she'd been shopping for you. I'd recommend a dress, something relatively conservative, if you have it."

"Okay," she said. "James, can I ask for a favor?"

"Sure," I said, a feeling of relief flooding me. This, at least, was familiar territory for me—someone asking me for something.

"Can we eat something and have a drink before we go? I don't want your family thinking I eat like a hippo, and I'm..."

"Nervous?" I asked, and smiled at her in spite of myself. "You should be. My family sucks."

"Starving," she said, embarrassed. "I'm starving."

"Of course," I said. The unusual sensation of sympathy flooded me. "I'm hungry, too."

I led her into the kitchen and opened the enormous refrigerator. I'd never been grocery shopping in Boston. I had no idea where the housekeeper bought the food I'd had Nita request. Someplace organic and expensive, I was sure. I pulled out olives, cheese, grapes, and a bottle of wine. Dre opened up a cabinet, pulled out a platter, and got a knife, wine opener, and cloth napkins.

"You seem right at home," I said to her.

"You can tell the hired help organized the kitchen," she said. "Everything makes sense. Do you come here a lot? It seems a little...sterile."

"It is," I assured her. "I don't spend a lot of time here. I prefer Los Angeles. I've always hated the winters up here." I poured two glasses of Chardonnay and handed one to her.

"Plus, your sucky family doesn't live in L.A. That makes it better, too."

"Cheers to that," I said, clinking her glass.

She grabbed an olive, and I tried not to watch as she put it into her mouth. I also tried not to look at her skin, which was smooth, perfect porcelain.

"So...what do you want me to do at this thing tonight?" she asked.

"For tonight, just smile and look pretty. Feel free to drink as much as everyone else, as long as you can handle your liquor."

"I'm an escort. I can drink with the best of them," she said.

"Then you should fit right in."

# AUDREY

My clothes were delivered while we were eating. I excused myself and headed to my room. I selected a black lace cocktail dress and small, black, kitten-heeled sandals. Fortified by the wine, I also wore a tiny thong and a gorgeous black bra. Just in case James changed his mind.

Back at headquarters, I'd been thoroughly waxed within an inch of my life. I'd had a manicure and a pedicure; my nails glittered like jewels in the fading afternoon light. Elena had packed some really beautiful clothes for me to wear over the next two weeks. I ran my hands over them. Dresses, suits, handbags, lingerie, and swimwear that surely cost more than all of the clothes in my closet put together, along with my rent for a year. At least I would look the part. I tried to find some confidence in that.

I wore my hair down, in waves around my shoulders. I kept my makeup reasonable, like what I imagined lady lawyers wore on days when they went to court.

That seemed appropriate. I sort of felt like it was Judgment Day.

James had rejected me, and I still felt stung by that. I'd wanted him. I'd wanted to take his clothes off, check out his hot body, and get it over with. Then he could be a John, and this would be a normal assignment.

I looked at my reflection in the mirror. No matter how much I sometimes despised myself, I could still see that I looked beautiful. I was young enough that I always looked good, no matter what I drank or the crap food I ate. But these clothes made me look special.

*It's easy to be special,* I thought. *If you have money.*

I put the expensive watch Elena had lent me around my wrist and enormous cubic zirconia studs in my ears. I hoped that the Preston family was so rich that they'd never seen fake diamonds before. I figured I was probably safe.

The final touches of lip gloss were applied to my lips, and I shook my hair out again. I nervously sprayed my mouth with mint spritzer. Part of me really wanted James to think I looked beautiful, and I chose to steadfastly ignore that part. That part was asking for trouble—gorgeous, intense, and distant as he seemed.

*Steady girl*, I thought. Unfortunately, I felt anything but.

JAMES DIDN'T STARE, or even really look at me, on the ride to the restaurant. Kai averted his eyes as well, which I took as a good sign.

"Are we going to stay together?" I asked James. He was staring at his phone, tapping out messages on it impatiently.

"We should," he said. "That way, we can hear each other's answers and stay on the same page."

"Okay," I said. I was feeling almost sick with nerves, and I realized it had to be worse for him. "Are you normally affectionate with your girlfriends in front of your family?"

"No," he said, reaching over and grabbing my hand. "So we should be."

Kai pulled the car expertly up to a street in the North End and double-parked out front. He opened the door and smiled without looking at me.

Apparently James had given him another talking to.

"See ya later," I said to him anyway, smiling at him warmly and flagrantly violating the rules.

James grabbed my hand and squeezed it. "Behave," he said.

"That's what I'm here for," I said innocently.

He pulled me to the front of the restaurant: Le Ciel, read the sign, in fancy script.

"French?" I asked.

"My family's old school," he said, stopping to adjust his tie.

"Let me," I said and fixed the knot. "Remember, we're in *love*."

He gave me a small smile; behind it, I thought I saw his temples pulse. He was stressed. I reached for his hand again and squeezed it. "Let's go have a drink," I said.

"Let's stay drunk for the next two weeks," he said and led me through the door.

*Then maybe we'll end up in bed,* I thought, ignoring the clench of desire that tore through me at the thought. I looked at James as we walked through the door: tall, steel-grey hair, powerful shoulders, a square-cut chin. He was expensive looking.

He was also totally clench-worthy.

I heard him suck in his breath as he took in the restaurant; it was wall-to-wall fancy people, probably all related to him in one way or another. I suddenly wished I wasn't wearing cubic zirconia. A waspy-looking woman with a white-blond bob was already heading for us. She was wearing a classic Chanel pink suit and a string of pearls.

"Is that your mom?" I asked James through the fake smile I'd plastered on.

"Yep."

"She's petrifying," I said.

"Absofuckinglutely," he said, and I saw that he'd plastered on a smile, too.

She reached us before we were ready for her, before we'd even had a chance to catch our breath.

"James," she said, reaching out and giving him a hug, careful not to get makeup on his suit coat.

"Mother," he said, and he did not sound friendly, even though the fake smile was still in place. He pulled back and grabbed my hand. "This is Audrey Reynolds."

"Mrs. Preston," I said, holding out my hand to her.

She didn't take it. Instead, she looked me up and down, and looked back at James. "Very nice, James. Very nice." She turned back to me and beamed. I could almost hear her buzzing, a bundle of sharp edges, nerves, and plans.

She finally took my hand. "It's a pleasure to finally meet you, Audrey," she said. "James never lets us meet his girlfriends. It's lovely to see that you not only exist, but that you aren't designed to embarrass his family."

I looked at her, shocked and wondering what she meant by that. I shook her hand limply. I noted that my plastered-on smile was intact; if the rest of his family was this bad, I was going to need a steady supply of alcohol to keep it in place.

"It's so nice to finally meet you. I've heard so many wonderful things," I said.

"Oh, nonsense. You don't need to bother with that, dear—I know what my son really thinks of me," she said without bothering to look offended.

"Enough," James said. He sounded defeated, and we'd been here for less than five minutes. "Let Audrey at least think we're civilized for the first night. Can you show us to the bar? And where's Dad? And Todd and his bitch-ass fiancée?"

Mrs. Preston stopped inspecting me and turned to him with a glare. It must have been the way she normally looked at him—her face relaxed into it. "You watch your mouth, James. And here's a waiter—be sure to take your medicine. Just make sure it's not the kind that has you hurling the c-word, or any other of your trash talk, at your new sister-in-law."

"Yes, ma'am," James said.

She rolled her eyes at him and turned to me. "You better order a double, young lady," she said, nodding her head toward her son. "You're going to need it."

*Funny,* I thought, *James said the same thing about you.*

Except that it wasn't funny.

I ordered a double anyway. I really wanted a martini, but I was too worried that I wouldn't be able to balance it while running away from James's scary mother.

"What did your mother mean by that?" I asked. "The 'designed to embarrass your family' thing?"

"I have no idea," he said, and I didn't believe him.

James took a big sip of his bourbon and grabbed my hand. He leaned over to me. "My father, Robert, is straight ahead," he said. "He's talking to Johnny O'Mara, the city councilman. Probably dreaming up new ways to pillage the city. And there's Todd and stupid Evie." He pointed to a slightly taller, thinner version of himself that must have been Todd. He was next to a young, reed-thin woman with a blond bob. She looked like a Mrs. Preston Jr. except that her teeth were a little horsey, and when she laughed, her bony shoulders shook aggressively.

"Why do you hate her so much? She looks nice," I said. Actually, she looked exhausting, her laser-like ice-blue stare piercing every person who came within range.

"Let's go meet her. You'll see what I mean."

I held up my drink. "Let me finish this first. Your mother keeps looking over here. I'm worried she's gonna talk to us some more."

I leaned up in my kitten heels to whisper to him, keeping a playful smile on my face. "Let's pretend we can't get enough of each other. Maybe your mother will leave us alone, then."

James leaned against me. "That sounds great, Audrey."

We were pressed against each other, and suddenly it felt as if it had gotten very, very hot in the restaurant. "Don't you have any friends here?" I asked. "Anyone helpful? We need another buffer besides me."

"My best friend will be here later tonight. Cole. He'll probably try to steal you from me." He slid his hand down my back, into the curve of my spine.

"You can't lend me out. It's in our contract," I said, even though the contract said nothing of the sort.

"I might make you my newest venture," he said, leaning down to talk into my ear. He rubbed my lower back slowly, his hand lowering down to graze the top of my ass. Every nerve ending in my body was on high alert.

Daring him, I turned my face to his. "I'm not for sale," I said, our lips close. Too close. I brushed my nose against his so that we looked like the happy couple we weren't. "I'm like a timeshare, baby. No one gets to own me. You just get to stay a while."

My words hung in the air as he looked at me darkly. "That's a horrible thing to say about yourself, Audrey," he said.

His words cut me, and my back stiffened. But I didn't have the right to react to him like that.

I knew what I was.

I didn't let any emotion show on my face, but I pulled back and took another long sip of my drink. Now there was hurt mingled with the heat between us, and I was unsteadied by it, almost a little dizzy. I stood there and absorbed it, letting my shame mix with my other wild emotions.

It was nothing I didn't deserve.

James took a deep breath and pulled me against him. I stood there, stiffly, wishing the floor would swallow me up. "I'm sorry," he said in a rush, into my ear. "I shouldn't have said that. I didn't mean it the way it came out."

I took a steadying breath and looked up into his eyes, a pretend loving look on my face. If nothing else, I was going to do my job right. "Yes, you did," I said. "But it's okay. I know exactly what I am, James. You should, too."

He stared down at me, his eyes intense. "You're not a timeshare, Audrey. You're a beautiful, kind woman. You're way too young to give up on yourself."

I simultaneously loved and hated the fact that my body was on fire beneath him, and that I wanted to remember every word he was saying.

"I'm not giving up on myself. But I also don't lie to myself," I said, giving him a tight smile that betrayed none of the wild emotion that was going on inside me. At its core, being an escort was just like being an actress, and that had never been more true for me than right now.

"Not lying to yourself is good—we should all try that more often," James said. "But you've said some negative things about yourself this afternoon. Don't. Don't talk about yourself that way."

I hadn't realized I'd said anything bad about myself. I didn't want to think about it. Instead, I put on my actress mask and changed tactics, quickly. "Are you lecturing me?" I asked, suddenly playful.

He watched my face, trying to read me.

"No," he said, "I'm trying to help."

"Is trying to help a thing with you?" I asked, teasing, trying to break the tension. "Are you one of those do-gooder sorts of billionaires?"

He gave me a small smile then, following my cues. Even though the vibe between us had changed, his powerful arms still gripped me. My body was still molded around his. I tried not to think about that—because if I did, I might try to climb on top of him right here.

That was ill-advised for several reasons.

"Hardly. And I don't have *things*," he said.

"Maybe you do," I chided, trying to keep my voice even. "You just don't have anybody to point them out to you."

"Well, then please, over the next two weeks, be the pointer-outer of things," he said, and I could tell he was relaxing a little. He was holding me close, and I could feel him stirring against me. Still, he didn't back away, emboldened by the crowd. I wanted to climb up on him and wrap my legs around him, to find out exactly what he had going on underneath that suit.

I could feel his mother's eyes on us. At the very least, we were successfully convincing her that there was *something* between us. What that something was, I wasn't sure. It was more complicated than I'd thought.

Even though my body was on fire, I shivered against him.

"Now finish that drink," he said commandingly. "We have to go meet the rest of the firing squad."

"I'm ready when you are," I said, and even though he made me feel off balance, I was sure that I meant that for a lot of different things.

# JAMES

Putting my hands on Audrey in the middle of the restaurant might have been the stupidest thing I'd ever done. But telling her to stop saying bad things about herself was much, much more treacherous.

She was just supposed to be a date. Not a girlfriend. Not a relationship. A *date*. No strings. No ties. No games.

I hadn't even been planning on fucking her.

And yet here I was, my aching erection pressing up against her thigh, my entire family within spitting distance. And it wasn't the erection that was the problem, although it was certainly uncomfortable and inconvenient given the present circumstances. The problem was that I felt protective of her. The problem was that when she called herself a timeshare, it cut me. And when I said something that hurt her feelings, I felt like shit. I felt *sorry*.

So. Fucking. Inconvenient. Feelings were for the weak, or for those who didn't know any better. And that wasn't me.

*Maybe it's because I'm around my family and I'm unsettled,* I mused. But that didn't make it any better, or any safer.

Still, I pulled her to me and almost kissed her, right there. I could feel her body through her dress, hot to my touch. But I stopped myself. I didn't need to give Todd and Evie any ammunition against us.

"Let's do this," I said tightly. Audrey exhaled loudly, and I couldn't help but smile at her. I felt exactly the same way—that is, if she felt both frustrated at not getting closer and relieved that we were finally apart.

I grabbed her hand and headed to my brother, grabbing two glasses of wine from a passing waiter. We were probably going to get piss drunk, but that was okay. Given the curious, icy stare Evie was giving Audrey, we were going to need to.

"There he is," Todd said. He pulled me in for a quick, strong hug.

"Best man, reporting for duty," I said.

Todd clapped me on the shoulder and beamed at us. "My big brother. It's been too long."

"I know," I said. I almost felt bad. "I've been—"

"Swamped at work," Todd finished for me. "We've all been swamped at work. You could still make some time to come home and see the little people sometimes."

He turned and smiled at Audrey and Evie. He was younger than me, but taller by about two inches. I was wider than him from years of lifting weights, and he was thinner, with a runner's build.

"I had to ask your boyfriend here to be the best man," he said to Audrey. "Because otherwise he might not have shown up."

"Of course he would have shown up," Audrey said. "He's been talking about the wedding for weeks."

Todd laughed so hard he almost spit out his drink. He looked at me. "She's a keeper. Loyal *and* a pretty decent liar."

He turned back to her and held out his hand. She took it warily, but he smiled at her. "It's a pleasure to meet you. I'm Todd Preston," he said, giving her a firm shake. "Younger brother of Mr. Hot Stuff here."

"Audrey Reynolds," she said. "Girlfriend of Mr. Hot Stuff." She dropped his hand but smiled back at him.

"This is my betrothed," Todd continued, motioning to Evie. "Evie Walton."

"Always a pleasure, Evie," I said, not bothering to try and sound enthusiastic. I chugged some wine.

She gave me a mean smile and turned her laser-like eyes to Audrey, who was far more interesting than me. She knew she'd never win me over. Not after the first night that I met her, when she'd tried to get me to take her to bed. She'd just started dating Todd then. We were at a bar, and he'd run into some friends; Evie and I were drinking and waiting for him to come back.

"Todd's nice, but I've been really wanting to meet you," she'd said to me. To her credit, she was more than a little drunk.

To her discredit, she'd rubbed her flat chest up against me while my brother was a stone's throw away.

"Really?" I asked. "Why's that?"

"'Cause you're his hot, successful, *big* brother," she said. She eyed my crotch.

I took a huge step back from her. "Really, Evie?" I'd asked, disgusted. Todd had already told me that he was quite taken with her. "I'd thought that someone who went to Smith would have a little more tact."

"You should know better," she said in what she might have thought was a sexy voice. But Evie was bony, and she was dating my earnest little brother. Maybe she'd thought the combination was something that I couldn't resist, but she'd been dead wrong.

"Thanks but no thanks, Evie," I'd said. Todd showed up then. She'd turned her horny eyes on him and probably took him home and fucked his brains out to drown her disappointment. But he'd bought her a five-carat diamond ring a few months later, and as far as I knew, she hadn't looked back.

But now Evie was examining Audrey, the girl who'd gotten the larger prize. Audrey smiled at her, pretending not to notice the scrutiny she was under.

"It's nice to meet you, Evie," Audrey said. "Congratulations."

"Thank you," Evie said. She fake-smiled at Audrey, and her collarbones moved up and down when she shrugged. "Congratulations to you, too."

Audrey smiled back at her blankly. "For what?"

"For landing your boyfriend," Evie said. Her laser-like stare looked as if it was micro-analyzing Audrey's every pore.

I might have imagined it, but Todd seemed to shift uncomfortably next to me.

"He landed me," Audrey said, grinning back at her. She grabbed my hand and pulled me closer. "The lucky bastard."

"That's me," I said, smiling and shrugging. "The lucky bastard."

Evie looked at us suspiciously, and Todd swooped in to rescue Audrey. "What is it that you do, Audrey?" He asked. I did refer to him as my stupid asshole brother, but he was actually a nice guy. He was just stupid and an asshole because he was still marrying

Evie, even after I'd told him what had happened.

"I'm a graduate student in graphic design," Audrey said.

"How interesting," Todd said, still being kind.

"Not really," Audrey said. "But with a studio-art undergraduate major, what else are you going to do?" With that, she and Todd started chatting about art, teaching, and Audrey's fake dead family from New Hampshire. Audrey didn't miss a beat, and she managed to hold onto my hand and engage Todd all at the same time.

"She's something," Evie said, watching her with a wrinkled brow.

"Yes, she certainly is," I said.

"I GIVE YOU an A-plus," I said ten minutes later. I'd finally inserted myself into the conversation and swiftly killed it. I needed another drink, and I needed to get away from Evie.

"I see why you don't like her," Audrey said when we were finally in a quiet corner of the bar. "But why do you *hate* her? And your brother...I don't want to make you mad, but he seemed really nice."

My jaw clenched. "Todd *is* really nice," I said, motioning to a passing waiter. "That's the problem."

The waiter brought us over more wine, and I took a long swallow. A look of concern crossed Audrey's face, but fine actress that she was, she buried it quickly. I didn't bother to tell her that I could handle my liquor just fine. She'd experience that firsthand over the next two weeks.

"I don't want Todd to marry Evie. That's the problem," I said. "She hit on me the first night I met her. It was right after she started dating Todd. She made it very clear that she was after the richest man who would have her, even if that man was her boyfriend's brother."

"Gross," Audrey said.

"Absolutely," I said. "So the reason I refer to Todd as my stupid asshole brother is because I told him about it, and he chose not to believe me. And now he's chosen to marry her."

"I'm sorry," Audrey murmured.

"Not as sorry as he's going to be," I said and rubbed my face. "It's just that he could have done better. And now she's in between us for good. Todd was the one person in my family that I could still stand, and that's all over now. She'll never let us be close. And he probably hates me for what I told him."

"He asked you to be his best man," she said, "so he apparently doesn't hate you that much."

"Todd's a pleaser," I said. "He's trying to make it up to me that he's still marrying her. He's always trying to make something up to somebody. He probably proposed to Evie to apologize for not being me."

I finished my drink and immediately wished I could have another. "We have to meet my father now," I said, dreading it.

"I'm not ready just yet," she said. A waiter walked by with crab cake appetizers, and she grabbed one.

"Eat," she said and fed me a forkful. "You need to keep yourself fortified against all that booze."

I found crab disgusting, something akin to what I imagined cat food tasted like. But I didn't say a word. I watched her as I chewed. "You're taking good care of me," I said. "I'm actually really glad you're here, Audrey. It's nice to have an ally."

She smiled up at me. "That's what I'm getting paid for, remember? I was just supposed to be taking care of you in a different way." I saw that she was starting to blush underneath her makeup. It just figured—the one escort in the world who was capable of blushing was my date.

My traitor cock stirred again.

She fed me another bite, and our eyes locked.

"Waiter, we're going to need some more wine. Stat," she called, and I think I might have fallen a little bit in love with her right then, if I'd been capable of doing such a thing.

"Well, aren't you two just adorable," a voice boomed out from behind me. A hand clapped me on the back, hard, knocking me back to reality.

"Ow, Cole," I said, grinning. "You don't have to hit me that hard." I turned to greet my best friend.

"Yes, I do," he said and pulled me in for a quick hug. "It's been too damn long since I've seen you." Cole Bryson came into view, all six-foot-five of him, a shock of black hair hanging over his brow, a huge grin of his own on his face. We'd been best friends for almost twenty years. We'd met at Wharton, where we consumed an infinite number of beers and planned to take over the world.

"It's not my fault you're so busy with your stupid hockey team," I said. Cole was a venture capitalist. He usually invested in new companies and let them be, but since he'd become part owner of an NHL farm-team, he'd become obsessed with the industry. We hadn't seen each other in months.

"It's not a stupid team, and you're right, it's not your fault we haven't seen each other. Maybe it's hers?" He asked, motioning to Audrey and simultaneously checking her out from head to toe.

"It's lovely to meet you," he said, taking her hand and beaming down at her predatorily.

Audrey shot me a quick look, as if to ask a question, and smiled back at him tentatively.

"I'm Audrey Reynolds," she said. "It's a pleasure to meet you, too."

"Cole Bryson. And the pleasure's all mine," Cole said.

"Down boy," I said, moving closer. "Audrey's mine. She's agreed to be my date through these two horrible weeks."

"So she's beautiful *and* brave," Cole said, reluctantly dropping her hand.

"Yes. She is." I took another step protectively toward Audrey and wrapped my arms around her side. Cole was my best friend, but he loved women, and more importantly, women loved him. He'd been my staunchest competitor in grad school for hot dates; I had no intention of losing my current one to him.

I squeezed Audrey a little tighter to me.

She turned to me and laughed. "I'll give you two a minute to catch up," she said, pulling away from me. She handed me the plate of half-eaten crab cakes and, continuing to play the game, kissed me gently on the cheek.

"I'll be right back," she said and was gone before I could process the fact that my cheek was burning where she'd just kissed it.

We watched her head down the hallway to the ladies' room.

"I thought I'd never see the day," Cole said, turning to me with wide eyes. "You're in love with that girl."

I came back to earth with a thud and scoffed at Cole. "You just got here," I said. "Don't start being an asshole already."

"I've never seen you look at a woman like that before," Cole said. He motioned to the plate I was holding and stared at it, aghast. "And you ate crab. You hate crab. You must be totally in love with her."

"Oh, fuck off, Cole," I said, exasperated with either myself or with my best friend, who knew me better than anyone.

I put the plate down on the bar and turned back to him, irritated. "I'm not in love with her," I told him in a low voice. "I only ate the crab cake to be polite."

"You're never polite," Cole said. He grabbed a pint of beer meant for someone else from a passing waiter.

I sighed and glared at him. "She's been very good to me," I said, wondering how much I should tell him. Cole was the only person I was almost always honest with. Still, he didn't know everything about me. No one did.

Cole drank some beer, waiting. "Out with it," he said. "Tell me everything and make it quick. She'll be right back, just like she said."

I glowered at him. I didn't want to tell him the truth, but I also didn't want to deal with his nagging. Cole could be a relentless pain in the ass when he wanted.

"I *hired* her to be my date," I said, keeping my voice low.

He looked at me, his handsome brow furrowed, not comprehending.

"She's not your girlfriend?" he asked.

"No," I said.

"She sure seemed like it," Cole said.

"I just met her this afternoon. I picked her up from an escort service," I said.

Cole almost choked on his beer. "Shut the fuck up," he said.

"It's true. I couldn't face my family alone, and I broke up with

Logan a while ago."

"Logan sucked ass," Cole said.

I nodded at him, my exasperation deepening into chagrin. "You don't have to tell me that. I'm the one who broke up with her."

"So this one's just for sex?" Cole asked.

"She's not even for sex," I said. I felt a headache coming on. "I'm not going to fuck her."

Cole looked at me as though I had three heads. "She's a fucking *escort*, bro."

"I know," I said. "But she's just for show. I don't want to get involved with her any more than that."

"You can still fuck her. That's why you're paying her. It's about as clear-cut as it can get," he said.

"It's not clear-cut," I said, running my hands through my hair.

We watched as Audrey emerged from the hallway and smiled at me.

"She's gorgeous," Cole said. "It's a fucking waste, James."

"I'm making it worth her while," I snapped. "Now please, finish your beer and come over to see my father with us. I've put it off long enough."

"You're the boss," Cole said.

I watched as he watched Audrey come closer, and I bit the inside of my cheek on purpose to remind myself of just what an asshole I was.

# AUDREY

I finally made it to the bathroom. Relieved to be alone for a moment, I splashed cold water on my wrists. I would have shoved my whole face under the faucet, but my makeup would run. I needed to keep my game face on—for James, for his family, for his buddy Cole, for myself. *Easy girl*, I thought, willing my racing heart to slow down. *It's just another date*, I reminded myself. *He's just another John.*

Except he wasn't.

I looked up in the mirror and fixed my hair. I put some lip gloss on. I sprayed breath freshener into my mouth five times and straightened my shoulders. *Think about Tommy*, I reminded myself, and that calmed me down. My brother needed me, and no matter what I felt about James, no matter how hard and how fast I wanted to run away from him—or toward him, I still wasn't sure which—I was going to stay put.

*For Tommy*, I told myself. I didn't let myself think anything other than that.

THE REST OF THE DINNER passed in a blur of cocktails, delicious food, and curious stares from Evie, Cole, and Mr. and Mrs. Preston.

I smiled and ignored the stares. I held hands with James and ignored the battling feelings of desire and impending doom that raged on inside me. He talked to me like I was his girlfriend, and I answered him like he was my boyfriend. I ate the delicious food and pretended to care about the details of the wedding, which were discussed in minute detail by Evie and her cousins, who were her bridesmaids.

Finally, it was over. The party was breaking up, and James pulled me away. "We don't have to say goodbye," he said. "Let's just head out. We'll be seeing them all in twelve hours anyway."

"Great," I said and laughed weakly. His highfalutin family was exhausting. His mother had watched us all through dinner, and had clearly taken notice of the hand-holding.

"I know—I told you they were assholes, right? Let me just go outside and call Kai. He'll be here in two minutes, and then we can go." James squeezed my shoulder, and I stood inside the door, watching him stride outside in his gorgeous suit and tap on his fancy phone.

He was only gone for a second when I felt someone nearby. I turned and jumped a little: Cole Bryson had snuck up on me.

"Hey, Cole," I said. My tone was friendly even though I only felt reluctant at his proximity. He was looking at me the way most men looked at me. But most men weren't my date's best friend.

"Hello, Audrey," he said. He gave me a wide smile. Cole was rich, tall, and muscular. His black, perfectly gelled wavy hair glinted above his forehead and his green eyes. He had a large, square jaw. He was a physically stupendous specimen.

He was smiling at me as though I was his next meal—a juicy piece of meat roasting on the grill—and he just couldn't wait to put a spear in me and make me a Cole-Bryson-dick-shish kebab.

I wished Jenny was here so I could throw her at him. Then she could have her own billionaire, and Cole could just leave me alone with mine.

"James is calling for the car," I said nervously. He was so close but just out of reach, right outside the door.

"I know," Cole said. He lazily leaned up against the wall next to me. "He told me about you, you know."

My heart stopped. But I didn't let my face betray me.

"Really? What did he say?"

"I know why you're here," Cole said. "I know he hired you. He never could stand to be alone with his family. But he also told me things aren't physical between you two. That's why you should come home with *me* tonight. And I'm not saying this to be an asshole—I'm saying it to help."

I felt sick, but I looked up at him with as much indignation as I could manage. "You're not saying it to be an asshole, Cole? Are you sure?"

"I'm sure," he said, smiling at me. "It's a business proposition. You fill my need, I'll fill yours. You come home with me tonight, and I'll pay you your regular fee. And James will still be paying you. You'll make a tidy profit. It's like a twofer."

He leaned over me, looking triumphant—as if he had just solved all our problems. He was ready for his shish kebab. Cole Bryson was a successful, gorgeous man, and he was used to getting what he wanted. I had the feeling "no" wasn't a word he often heard. He smiled down at me, and I winced. The problem was, I didn't know if James *wanted* me to say no to him.

"Don't say no to a tidy profit," he said. "You'll break my venture-capitalist heart."

I felt as though I was going to throw up. "Did James say this was okay?" I asked, my voice small. I held my breath until he answered.

"No," Cole admitted. "I didn't run it by him yet. But James isn't exactly sentimental."

My heart was pounding in my chest, hard, when I heard the door open behind me.

"It's true, I'm not sentimental," James said, coming toward us.

I held my breath a little longer and felt the blood drain from my face. I had a feeling this was about to go very, very badly.

He reached me, and to my complete surprise, he took my hand. I looked at our hands linked together like that. I just stared at them as if they belonged to other people, and then I looked up at his gorgeous face.

He was glaring at Cole. "That was a dick move," he said. "By the way, I heard almost everything you said."

"It's not like I was trying to hide it," Cole said easily.

James looked at my face. "Are you okay?" he asked.

I nodded, biting my lip.

He turned back to Cole. "*You* are on my shit list."

His friend looked at him and snorted, unfazed. "I'm an entrepreneur—you know that," he said. "I see an opportunity and I move for it, fast."

James smiled at him tightly. "You're my best friend," he said, "which is why I haven't punched you in the face. Yet. But for the record, Audrey is a person, not an opportunity. So please do not approach her with any more business propositions in the future."

Cole studied his friend's face and let his glance trail down to our interlocked fingers. "Why James, I didn't know you cared."

I felt James stiffen for a second but only slightly. "I care that you find someone else to put your entrepreneurial hands on tonight. Audrey has agreed to be exclusive with me for the next two weeks. Please don't get her into trouble—not with me, and not with her employer."

A look passed between the two friends, and Cole nodded at James.

"Call me tomorrow," James said. "If I answer, it means I'm speaking to you again."

Cole smiled at the both of us, unabashed, and then he winked at me. "See ya," he said. "It's too bad James can't share—I'm much more fun than he is."

James gave him one final disapproving glare and then hustled me out to the car. I was shaking a little, still biting my lip. I nodded at Kai and got into the car silently. James climbed in after me and sat close by.

"That was unfortunate," he said.

"Is that how all your friends treat you?" I asked.

"Cole is my only friend. And he would never do anything to hurt me," James said carefully. "He must have thought it was okay."

"I wasn't going to say yes, if that's what you think," I said and looked out the window. Cole could have offered me a million dollars, and I wouldn't have taken it. Which meant I was completely fucked up and in deep trouble, as far as I was concerned.

"I can pay you what he offered—so that you don't have a loss," James said quietly.

"I don't consider it a loss," I said. I kept my face turned away. There was a tumble of emotions inside me—I felt betrayed that James had shared our secret with his friend, thrilled that he had stood up for me, and darkly hopeful that he wanted me for himself.

It was the darkly hopeful part that was killing me. That part had to go.

"I'm sorry that I told him about us," James said, and I heard him pour himself another drink. I kept still, my face turned toward the window. "He thought we were an actual couple, in love. He was making such a big deal out of it. So I told him to shut him up. Which was a dick move in and of itself."

I shrugged, looking out at the darkness, but I felt as though my heart was being ripped in two.

*He thought we were an actual couple, in love.*

I'd only met James today. We were not in love. We were playing a game, putting on a show. But I had all sorts of inappropriate feelings for him, bubbling up right underneath the surface. I was not a feelings person—I didn't have the space for them in my already-complicated life. But for whatever reason, or for a whole host of reasons, James had gotten under my skin quickly. He was not just a John to me. That was a huge fucking problem on a long list of huge fucking problems.

I needed solutions, not more problems.

I also needed money. I closed my eyes and willed all my stupid feelings to go away. But they didn't, and I found myself on the verge of tears. I couldn't do this. I couldn't cry in front of him—that was Escorting 101.

"I don't know if I can do this tonight," I said, my voice treacherously thick.

He sighed. "I'm sorry, Audrey. I've hurt your feelings twice tonight. I'm completely fucking this up."

"I think I should go home," I said miserably.

I turned back just in time to see him finish his bourbon, a bleak look on his face.

"I think that would be for the best," he said stiffly.

I HAD THEM DROP me off three blocks from my apartment. I didn't want him to see the crappy building where I lived. Kai pulled over, and James got out with me.

"I'm sorry tonight turned out like this," he said, his jaw clenched.

"It's okay," I said. "I just need to be alone."

"I need your number," James said. I recited it to him and watched him tap it into his fancy phone, wondering when, and if, he was ever going to call me. I wasn't sure what our separation meant. This was supposed to be our first night together, and I was going home to sleep alone. Would I still have him as an assignment? Would he phone Elena and tell her I was too much trouble? Would he decide that I was a pain in the ass, and I'd never see him again?

A lump formed in my throat, but I smiled at him when he was done. "Thanks for the ride," I said. "And the drinks."

"Anytime," he said and unceremoniously got back in the car.

My heart dropped at his curt departure. But I made myself head home with my chin up, taking long, confident strides. As if I knew I was making the right choice by walking away from him.

Plus, I didn't want him to see my hot, confused tears.

MY APARTMENT SEEMED even more disgusting than it had this morning, and that was saying something. I was acutely aware of the contrast to James's multi-million-dollar condominium. *Good thing I'm here alone,* I thought, but it didn't feel good.

I made myself some tea and went and sat on my windowsill. *James Preston.* His big-shouldered, suit-clad image filled my head, crowding out all coherent thought. I would have Googled him, but I had no Internet access, no smartphone. It was better that way. I didn't want to see the society pictures that Elena had mentioned, of him with other women. Real women, real dates.

I decided to worry about Elena instead. If he let me go, she would, too. She would be absolutely furious with me. And then I'd be back to turning tricks on the street, trying to make rent and keep my brother in his residence home. Except that I'd never make enough money.

I thought about getting a legitimate job for approximately

one second. The idea made me laugh—the only other thing I'd ever done was waitress, and I could make more money in an hour turning tricks than I could in a whole shift waiting tables. I had my brother to think about.

My body was just my body. When I was with a John, I could distance myself from what was happening, almost as if it was happening to someone else. I could do at least that for my brother. I was all he had, and he was all I had, and I had to protect him using any means necessary. My body and my pride were a small price to pay for his well-being.

Any dreams or hopes for myself that I'd had were a small sacrifice, too.

I thought about James again, unable to block him out. I thought about how he'd held my hand earlier tonight, and how warm and comforted it made me feel. I couldn't remember the last time someone had held my hand like that—maybe never. I pictured him smiling at me, and my chest got tight. He'd left me on the street just now so easily, it was like I was nothing to him.

*That's because you are nothing to him,* I thought.

I knew that was true, but the tightness in my chest persisted. I realized it was the sensation of common sense strangling the hope that was living there, inside my heart.

It hurt. It really, really hurt.

# JAMES

"I'm sort of surprised you're calling me, James, after your little hissy fit earlier," Cole was saying. I could hear people laughing in the background. Cole was probably still at the party, or at some other party, picking out a woman to go home with.

"I just dropped Audrey off. She was upset," I said.

"Because I asked her to come home with me and I offered to pay her? She *is* a hooker, right? Because I really wasn't trying to offend her," Cole said.

He was an asshole, but he was also my best friend. On top of that, Cole was brutally honest. He wouldn't steal a date from me, not a real date I'd gotten to first. But someone who was for hire, who I wasn't planning on fucking because I wanted to keep my boundaries intact?

He'd do it just so he could tell me everything I was missing.

"I'm not sure why she's upset. Maybe because I told you she was an escort," I mumbled.

"Well, she's right about that," Cole said loftily. "You probably shouldn't have said anything. She was pretending to be your girlfriend and doing a pretty good job of it. You threw her under the bus with that one."

"Thanks a lot," I mumbled.

"So she's gone? Did you fire her? Or did she quit?" Cole asked.

"Neither," I said.

"So why'd she go home? I thought she was with you for the next two weeks?"

I didn't say anything for a moment. "I think she just needed to be alone."

"You mean she quit," he insisted.

I furrowed my brow. "Is that what it means?" I felt like a confused, hormonal teenager. I'd been horrible when I dropped her off, not saying a word about when I would call her. I thought she wanted to be away from me.

On top of that, I was upset for some damn reason. Upset that she was leaving, upset that I was going back to my apartment alone and that I was clearly no longer in control—if I had ever been in control since I'd picked her up this afternoon.

"Sounds like she quit to me," Cole said. He waited a beat. "So if you two are done...can I have her number? There's not a lot of action out here tonight."

My jaw clenched again. "No, you *cannot* have her number," I said hotly. "I'll text you her service's number—there's a girl there you might like. Jenny. She's Audrey's friend. Go get an escort of your own." *Leave mine alone*, I thought.

"I know you like this girl," Cole said. It sounded as though he was yawning. "You can try to hide it, but you suck at it."

"Thanks," I said tersely.

"You might want to call her," he said. "If I want her number, other guys do, too."

"Talk to you later," I said.

"If you're lucky," Cole said and hung up.

I opened up Audrey's contact information and stared at it for a minute. Then I took a deep breath and stared at it for a while longer.

"Mr. Preston?" Kai asked. We were still idling at the curb near her house.

"Just put it in park," I snapped.

ONE HOUR LATER, I dialed.

She answered after the first ring.

"Audrey?"

"James?"

"I'm sorry to bother you. Are you still up?"

"I just answered my phone. What do you think?" she asked.

I sighed. "Would you consider coming back to the apartment with me tonight? My mother just called," I lied. "We have an early breakfast."

"Oh," she said. "Sure." She waited a beat. "Are you sure that's what you want?"

She was going to make me work for this, I could tell. "Of course that's what I want."

"Okay," she said. She sounded cautiously optimistic. "I'll just call a cab. I'll be there in twenty minutes."

"No need," I said smoothly. "I'm still parked on your street."

She was quiet for a second. "Then I'll be right down," she said.

Five minutes later she slid into the car next to me. She was wearing fuzzy boots, pink sweatpants, and a T-shirt.

"I was in my pajamas," she said apologetically.

"It's okay. I want you to be comfortable," I said.

She looked at me with raised eyebrows and said nothing.

We drove to the Stratum in silence. I couldn't tell if it was awkward silence or not, but I felt relieved that she was back with me, which was stupid.

Kai let us out, and we went through the opulent lobby together in silence. She shuffled across the marble floor in her fuzzy boots, not looking at me. I hit the elevator button, and we rode to the top floor. I noticed, against my will, that she looked very cute in her pajamas.

I inwardly groaned. Between the Bambi eyes and the use of the word cute, I needed to slap myself, hard.

I unlocked the door, relieved to be back home. I just wished it was Los Angeles, far away from my past. Audrey went over to the window and looked out at the city spread out and glittering beneath us.

"It's so beautiful from up here," she said, and she sounded very young to me. She *was* young. Too young to be living such a harsh life.

I wished I could explain myself to her. I sighed and sat down on the couch, finally loosening my tie. "Audrey, I'm really sorry about before," I said.

"Which thing?" she asked.

"All of it, actually," I said. "I'm sorry I told Cole about us. He's the one person I'm usually honest with. And I'm sorry I just left you on the sidewalk like that."

She said nothing, still staring out at the lights.

I sighed again. "I'm not good with people," I said. "I'm more of an analysis guy."

"You're fine with people," she said immediately. "You just don't like them very much."

"I'm not *used* to liking people," I corrected her.

She gave me a searching look. "Is that because of your family? Because I know you don't like them."

"I have issues with my parents, like I told you…" I said, my voice trailing off. The headache was coming back. "It's about some stuff that happened a long time ago. Some of that is what makes it difficult for me to trust people."

*I had what I loved taken from me, and I could never let that happen again.*

But I couldn't say that. I could barely stand to think it.

"That and my, uh, present circumstances," I said instead.

"You mean your money," she said.

"That's right. It's hard to tell if people are being genuine with me. It doesn't happen often. So when you turned out to be a nice girl, it was just hard for me to believe it," I said.

Audrey snorted in exasperation. "I'm a fucking escort, James," she said, her hands on her hips. "I'm anything but a nice girl."

"But you are," I said. "You are a nice girl, Audrey."

"Where do we go from here, James?" she asked, her face a businesslike mask. "I need this assignment. I need it to go smoothly. Just tell me what you want me to do, and I'll do it. Even if that means fucking your best friend." She shrugged. "I *am* a hooker, after all. It's not like I have a real right to be offended."

"Yes, you did. Cole was being a complete prick, and so was I. I talked to him again, and I told him to stay the hell away from you." I paused for a beat, willing my hotness to subside. "I also suggested he call Elena and ask for Jenny," I said, almost apologetically. "I hope that's okay."

Audrey's face perked up. "Jenny would love him," she said. "That was actually really nice of you."

I smiled, pleased that I'd done at least one thing right since

I'd met her.

"So…where do we go from here?" I asked, echoing her question. "I want you to stay. I want you to stay with me, and I don't want you to fuck my best friend, and I don't want you to say mean things about yourself, and I don't want to hurt you." The words just tumbled out. Perhaps I'd had one too many bourbons.

To her credit, Audrey said nothing, her face an impenetrable mask.

"Just stay. Let's stick with the agreement." I stood up abruptly, lest I started trying to take her to bed.

"We have a brunch tomorrow and then a bunch of other crap events for the rest of the week. Let's just make it to the wedding. Together."

"Okay," she said. If she was disappointed by something I said, she did not let on.

"It was better tonight with you there," I said, heading off to my room. "It was almost bearable."

"Almost," I heard her say before I closed my door.

# AUDREY

I lay awake all night. Waiting for him. I hoped he would come to me, but he didn't, and I didn't dare go to him.

I wanted to, though. The empty bed next to me was like a physical ache. I could feel him, just down the hall, just out of reach.

The next two weeks were going to be hell.

I DRESSED CAREFULLY the next morning, in linen pants and a pink blouse. I pulled my hair up into a bun. It was all very appropriate, all very unlike me.

I looked out at Newbury Street from my window. The sidewalks were clean. It looked like it had rained lightly late last night, but now the sky was glorious and clear.

I decided that I was going to make the best of this situation. I started forming a plan as I put on my makeup. I applied it carefully, so that I didn't look like the prostitute that I was, and went out to look for the resident Hottest Bachelor.

"You're looking proper," James said as I entered the kitchen.

"It's not my usual style," I admitted. I went and helped myself to coffee.

"I like your sweatpants better," James said.

"Me too."

James was wearing another suit, his hair fixed perfectly. He looked as if he was about to charge through a hundred corporate meetings, not attend his brother's pre-wedding brunch.

"Are you working today?" I asked.

"I have some calls to make," he said. "Other than that, I've had my schedule cleared."

"I'm free, too," I said, joking, "If you want to hang out."

"Hang out?" James asked and laughed.

"Yes," I said. "When was the last time you had nothing to do all day?" *And the last time I had no one to do all day?*

"I don't remember," he said.

"Me either," I said. I sat down and drank my coffee; I had to face his mother and her collarbones soon. I needed to be properly caffeinated. "So let's do it. After brunch we can change. We could go to the park, walk around...we could probably go to a Red Sox game. If you're into that sort of thing."

"You like the Red Sox?" he asked. He was looking at me as if I had three heads, all of which were glorious and gorgeous.

"I was born and raised here, and I have a beating heart," I said and crossed myself. "Of course I like the Red Sox."

He was already on his phone, tapping away, probably ordering tickets. Men were actually a lot easier to manage than they liked to believe. Even the super-rich ones, apparently.

"The game's home—it's at four," he said, looking at me hopefully. "Does that work for you?"

"Your wish is my command," I said. I decided I was going to make the next two weeks fun, whether he ever fucked me or not, whether I had cried alone in my bed last night or not.

*Game face, Audrey, game face,* I chanted to myself.

I DEFINITELY NEEDED it for brunch.

"I hate brunch," James complained as he opened the door for me. We were at another hotel, a stuffy one, and the clientele was beautifully dressed, just like us.

"The concept of brunch? Or brunch itself?" I asked.

"Both. Fucking waste of time," he said and grabbed my hand.

"It's just two hours—and there's booze," I reminded him, trying to be upbeat. That lasted until we got to the table and Celia Preston patted the empty chair next to her and motioned for me to join her.

I didn't even let myself look at James. I just squeezed his hand and went to sit next to the captain of the firing squad.

"Good morning, Mrs. Preston. You look lovely," I said. She was wearing a flowered blouse and diamond studs so large they looked like ice cubes.

"As do you, Audrey," she said. She smiled at me without warmth.

I smiled at James's father, Robert, who was sitting to her right. "Good morning," I said.

"You take good care of my son last night?" he asked in a ribald tone.

They were both watching me.

"Of course, sir," I said and smiled at them without missing a beat. "I took his bourbon away and made him go straight to bed. And look at him. He barely has a hangover."

Mr. Preston snorted and went back to stirring his coffee. When I'd met him last night, all he'd done was stare at my tits. Apparently he couldn't do that with his wife sitting next to him, so I was dismissed as no longer of interest.

*Phew.*

But Celia was still staring at me.

"We didn't have much time to talk last night," she said, "with all the wedding excitement."

"I know," I said. *Thank God,* I thought.

"Tell me about your family. Todd mentioned that you're from New Hampshire."

"I don't have any family," I said. "My parents died several years ago. I don't have any siblings or cousins. Both my parents were only children, and so am I." I briefly wondered what it would be like if that were true, if I had no one left to disgrace me or depend on me.

It would be a mixed bag, I decided.

"How sad," Mrs. Preston said.

"Not really," I said. "But I'm afraid my family wouldn't have been interesting to you anyway—we weren't society. My father owned a shoe store, and my mother was a nurse. Very middle class. Very boring and under the radar, unlike your family."

She smiled briefly at my compliment that was not a compliment.

"I'm sure that James's lifestyle must seem very glamorous to you," she said.

"His house is a lot more glamorous than my dorm," I admitted.

"Is it serious between you and my son? He doesn't tell us anything," she said.

I smiled at her and tried to decide on a course of action. With lying, I'd found it was always safest to tell the version closest to the truth.

"He's out of my league, Mrs. Preston," I said. "I'm sure he'll figure it out sooner rather than later. But right now, I'm still the new and the shiny. We're just having fun."

Some approval actually crept into her smile. "Well, stay new and shiny until we get through this wedding," she said. To my shock, it appeared that she was supporting me. "He hasn't been this easy to get along with in years."

"I THINK YOUR MOTHER doesn't actually hate me," I told James later. We were back at the apartment, and I was digging through the clothes Elena had sent for me while he sat on my bed, watching me.

I was looking for a normal pair of jeans, something that wasn't geared toward high-society functions that I could breathe in. I found nothing of the kind, so I settled for a simple cotton dress that probably cost a thousand dollars.

"In fact, she might even be rooting for me," I said. "And your father didn't look at my tits once. I consider brunch an outright success."

James shook his head at me and laughed. "You asked me what my best outcome was yesterday—this is it," he said. "I had no idea when I hired you that you were going to be able to work magic on my family, but I'm not complaining."

"I think I should charge you extra," I said. "Now go change. We don't have to see anyone in your family for the rest of the day, and you don't have to swindle people out of their land or take their money or whatever it is you usually do. Take off that damn suit."

"I thought I was the boss," he said. He stood up and towered over me, making my heart stop.

I smiled at him anyway. "Will you *please* take off that damn suit? Sir? I would like to go to the park and get a hot pretzel. And then go to Fenway and drink some beer. If that's okay with you."

He traced the outline of my jaw with his finger, and I stopped breathing. My skin lit up on fire underneath his touch. "It's okay with me," he said darkly, and strode out of my room.

*Tease!* I wanted to scream after him as he headed down the hall. Instead I just smiled to myself, enjoying the moment for once, and changed my clothes.

THE COMMONS WERE GLORIOUS. The trees were all in bloom, there were flowers everywhere, and it was warm. Usually in Boston, it was either winter or humid, except for a brief respite during the fall.

But today was the perfect day.

James had changed into jeans and a T-shirt. I finally got a good look at what his upper body looked like, and I almost wished I hadn't. His biceps were enormous. I tried not to imagine what it would feel like to have them holding me down. He grabbed my hand as we walked, and I raised an eyebrow at him.

"We're not on display here," I said. "Unless that's Todd and Evie lurking behind that bush."

"Ha ha." He looked around and nervously scrutinized a nearby bush. "You're kidding, right?"

"Right," I said, laughing at him.

Just to test him, I tried to pull my hand away.

He wouldn't let me.

"We should stay in character. Just in case," he said, pulling me closer to him. His grip was firm, and I was again reminded of those big biceps.

"Would you like a pretzel?" he asked when we came up on a cart.

"Yes, please."

"Would you like to ride the swan boats?" he asked a few minutes later.

"Really?" I asked. He nodded at me. My whole life I'd lived here, I'd never been on them. "I'd love to."

James went and bought tickets and came back, grinning at me. "I'm not usually a swan boat kind of guy, but I've been watching these damn things for years and never had a reason to get on them."

There were lots of noisy children and harried mothers around us; James stood out in the crowd. No, he was not a swan boat sort of guy. I thought that it was sweet of him to offer.

We got into the boat and went back and forth a few times. It was anticlimactic and perfect.

"Did you grow up here?" I asked.

"I did," James said. "Right over on Beacon Hill." He jerked his thumb toward the other side of the park, where the *Cheers* bar stood on the corner.

"But you never came to the swan boats?" I asked.

He shrugged. "Not that I remember. Maybe one of our nannies took us. Could be."

We were quiet for a second. I wanted to ask him all about his nannies, but I didn't want to pry.

"What about you?" he asked. "Where did you grow up?"

"In the lovely city of East Boston," I said. "I couldn't wait to get out of there and move to Southie. I felt like I hit the big time."

"Do you have a family?" he asked. "Aside from your pretend dead one in New Hampshire?"

I felt a lump form in my throat—those were the exact questions I'd wanted to avoid. But he'd shared his family with me, so I had to be fair. I would still leave out the more exciting bits.

"My mother still lives in East Boston," I said, not pausing long enough to give details. "And I have a brother. Tommy. We're very close. He lives in a special-needs group home in Southie. It's really great. They've been taking good care of him, and I get to see him all the time."

"How old is he?" James asked.

"Twenty-four," I said. "Two years older than me."

"Does your mother pay to keep him there?"

I shook my head no. "I do," I said, and I heard a note of pride creep into my voice.

"You're taking care of him?"

"Yeah," I said. "My mom couldn't afford it, but she couldn't keep him at home. It wasn't safe."

"Wasn't safe how?" he asked. He clearly had been curious about me, and unlike me, he wasn't afraid to pry.

"Let's just put it this way—my mother could drink your mother under the table," I said.

"That's saying something," James said.

"I know." I shrugged at him. "Clearly, I don't love my job. But it's given me a way to take care of my brother. I couldn't ever afford his home if I was waiting tables at IHOP."

James gave me a sad smile. "It doesn't seem fair," he said.

"Duh," I said.

He laughed at that. "And your father?"

I shook my head. "Never met him," I said.

James nodded and pulled me to him. He kissed the top of my hair, sending unwelcome shock waves through me. "I'm glad you're here with me," he said, "and the fact that I'm here and glad about anything is a fucking miracle."

I smiled at him, but inside, there was no smile. There was that hope again. And I knew, based on yesterday, that when my common sense got its hands on that hope, it was going to be ugly.

# JAMES

The fact that she wanted to go to a game was almost enough to make me try to buy her outright. But the fact that she was an escort with a heart of gold?

She was fucking killing me.

Normally in a situation like this, I would have been skeptical. I expected the alcoholic mother and the absent father. But the brother in the group home? If she'd been playing me, I'd either say that she was pushing too hard or that she was predictable.

But Audrey was telling me the truth. How did I know? Because she offered nothing, and because she clearly didn't want my sympathy. She wanted to hide it from me.

I understood her perfectly.

I called Kai, and we went to the game straight from the Commons. We had box seats, bought from an old friend for an exorbitant fee earlier this morning. "These are great seats, James," Audrey said, nodding in approval. "Killer."

"I'm glad you like them," I said.

"You know what else I'd like?" she asked me, grinning.

I would have given her anything she asked for right then.

"A beer, James. A big one."

We ordered enormous beers and later, hot dogs. To my delight, Audrey completely ignored me during the game. She stuffed her hot dog into her mouth unselfconsciously and watched every play.

She even recognized Johnny Pesky when he came out for an awards presentation at halftime. "That's Johnny Pesky!" she exclaimed, practically spitting out her beer. "This is so fucking awesome!"

After she calmed down enough to watch the last couple innings, I let myself have the extreme and very dangerous pleasure of putting my arm around her. And just like that, she settled in next to me, as if she belonged there.

BACK AT MY HOUSE, we had a glass of wine.

"What's on the docket for tomorrow?" Audrey asked, yawning.

"I have to be fitted for my tuxedo. And then there's some sort of ladies' tea, followed by another dinner."

"Do I have to go to the tea?" she asked. She looked wary.

I sighed and looked at her. "Evie asked my mother to include you," I said. "But I'd be happy to say no if that's what you'd prefer."

She put her chin up. "I can handle them," she said bravely. "I think."

"I don't care if you go," I said, but I knew that my mother and Evie would be all over me about it if she didn't. I think they wanted to inspect her more closely. Fortunately, Audrey had proven herself up to the challenge.

"It's only for a few hours. They'll just be talking about dresses. Or whatever it is Evie and her douchebag cousins talk about right before one of them gets married."

"I think I can handle that. If not, I'll just text you and make you come rescue me." She laughed, and I poured her some more wine.

"Is there anything you need to do tomorrow?" I asked.

"I'd love to go see my brother in the morning," she said, "if that doesn't interfere with anything."

"Of course. I'll have Kai drive you. We're going to Copley Plaza for the fitting, so I can walk."

"Thank you. That's really nice, James," she said, suddenly sounding formal. She hopped down off her barstool. "I should probably get going to bed. Thank you for today, though. It was great. Those were amazing seats."

She smiled at me and started heading toward her room, her sandals clicking awkwardly on the hardwood floors. Aside from that noise, the silence boomed around us.

"Audrey."

She turned around and looked at me, biting her lip.

"Can you sleep with me tonight? No sex," I said, holding up my hands. "I promised you—and even if I hadn't, I wouldn't ask you like that. I just want you to stay with me."

"Like a sleepover?" she asked, a little skeptically, but she looked pleased.

"Yes, like a sleepover. Just don't try to put a mud mask on me or put warm water on my hand. That would piss me off," I said.

"Let me change. Your room or mine?"

"Mine," I said. "I have the best bed."

"Of course you do," she said.

SHE CAME IN A FEW MINUTES later in those pink sweatpants again, her face scrubbed clean of makeup. She looked so beautiful and innocent it made my heart actually hurt, and I wasn't technically sure that I even had a heart.

"Hey," she said and sat on the edge of my bed. "You're still in your clothes."

"I wasn't sure what you were going to wear," I admitted. "I wanted to show you some solidarity and dress similarly." I got up and pulled out an old Wharton T-shirt and a pair of flannel pajama bottoms. "Is this okay?" I asked.

"It's fine, James. I approve of the flannel." She scooted up on the bed and grabbed the remote off the side table. She turned the flatscreen on and switched the channel to NESN, the New England Sports Network.

I was pretty sure that I still had a heart because it felt right then like I loved her, at least a little.

LATER, AFTER AN HOUR of sports news, we turned out the lights.

"No sex?" she asked.

"That's right," I said. I paused. "Why are you asking?"

"I just don't want this to be awkward. If we're not doing it, let's go to sleep." She rolled over onto her side, toward me.

I rolled over toward her, too.

Eight hours later, I woke up holding her hand.

# AUDREY

James was gone when I woke up the next morning. Sleeping next to him had been nice and horrible all at the same time. I loved being with him, but I'd wanted to be closer. In other words, I'd wanted him on top of me and inside me and behind me and all sorts of other places. I'd had to push those images, appealing as they were, and the heat I'd felt between us away last night. Just so I could get some sleep.

Still, we were making progress. I had no idea what that meant except that it thrilled me. It thrilled me, and I was fucked. Our contract was up at the end of two weeks, and I would be left with only the memory of him. The memory of him putting his arm around my shoulder at Fenway Park, which was now in my top-five favorite guy memories of all time.

I didn't have the other four. Not yet.

I could still feel his touch on me now, and I imagined that I would feel it forever, even after he was long gone. The ghost of him, the memory, would be a blessing and a curse, I knew.

I waited for my common sense to wake back up and start choking my dreams again, but it still hadn't happened, even after I had my coffee. So I let myself be in a good mood, a state which was very foreign to me, and got dressed to go see my brother.

Kai drove me. I signed in at the front desk and gave a check to the clerk to pay for the next two months. After some begging, Elena had given me an advance against my latest assignment. I wanted to make sure all of it went toward my brother's expenses.

I found Tommy sitting in the common room, wearing an *Angry Birds* T-shirt and eating crackers, working intently on a 3-D puzzle. His brown hair was its usual spiky mess.

"Hi," I said as I went up to him, and his face opened up into such a wide grin that it warmed my heart. It had only been a couple of days, but I'd missed him so much. I wrapped my arms around him and held him close. Even though he was my older brother, I'd always taken care of him. I had a protective feeling for him and loved him fiercely, like I imagined a mother loved her child.

A normal mother. Not my mother.

"You haven't been to see me in three days," he complained.

"I've been working," I said, sitting down next to him. "But it's been good. I'm going to make a lot of money over the next two weeks. Then we're going to be in good shape, okay?" I squeezed his arm. "Has Mom been here?" I asked.

"No," Tommy said. "It's been longer than you."

"Well, she'll show up eventually. She always does. And when she's here, just make sure you don't mention anything about the money," I said.

Tommy nodded at me solemnly. We'd both learned the hard way.

JAMES WAS STILL GONE when I got back to the apartment, and I rattled around for a minute, missing him. Then I went to my bedroom, nervously scouring through my clothes for something to wear to the ladies' tea. There was something about the event that scared the bejeezus out of me. First of all, I'd never been to a tea. I didn't think people in the United States even did that.

Second, I knew the difference between a salad fork and a dinner fork, but that was about it. If there were etiquette rules to observe at high tea, I was not aware of them. I hoped that Evie and Mrs. Preston would overlook that, but they probably wouldn't.

Third, James wouldn't be there.

Fourth, he wasn't here right now, and that was a problem, too.

I sighed, wishing that I could see inside his head. If he felt what I was feeling between us, why hadn't he tried to claim me last night?

At the same time, I was relieved that we hadn't done it. If sex was added into the mix of whatever it was that was going on between us, it would get complicated, fast. Or maybe the opposite would be true, and he would suddenly seem like every other John. Honestly, I didn't know which one I was more afraid of.

I couldn't decide what to wear, so I started looking at the tags on the clothes. I would wear whatever was most appropriate *and* most expensive. That sounded about right for high tea.

JAMES STILL HADN'T COME back by the time I was ready to go. I checked my phone for what was probably the hundredth time, but there were no messages.

I turned and looked at myself in the mirror. I was wearing a short, full floral skirt and two white shirts layered together. I'd put on several delicate gold necklaces that Elena had insisted were very stylish right now. I wore nude lace-up wedge sandals that probably cost more than my grocery bill for five months. I grabbed an enormous designer bucket bag and some aviator sunglasses to complete my look.

*Damn,* I thought when I looked in the mirror, *no wonder rich people always looked good.* It was pretty easy when your outfit cost as much as a large mortgage payment.

My phone beeped and I lunged for it, glad that I was alone so I didn't have to be ashamed by my eagerness.

*Go get 'em Audrey,* it read.

*I'll pick you up at four. Text me if you need a rescue.*

I held the phone close to my heart for a second. It was as though I could hear his voice, and feel him through his words.

*Ok,* I texted back, as if I was a normal, calm person.

Then I held the phone against my heart again because right now, I was anything but.

THE LOBBY OF IMPERIAL HOTEL was even more impressive than the Stratum's, and it was eminently more stuffy. Oriental rugs, oil paintings, and crystal chandeliers emphasized the exclusive luxury of the place. I did not fit in here. I felt a cold trickle of sweat run down my back as I headed in toward the restaurant.

The firing squad was waiting for me, dressed in their finest.

"Audrey!" Evie said, coming up to me instantly. She was wearing a hot-pink sheath that hugged her body. It was obvious that Evie had been on an all-lettuce and Pilates diet leading up to the wedding: she was rail thin, her collarbones jutting out almost painfully. She was all sharp edges and blinding-white teeth.

I smiled at her, awkward and wary. "Are you getting excited?" I asked. "It's only a few days, now."

She gripped my arm. "I am *so* excited. Todd is the love of my life." She searched my face with a laser-like glare.

"I know he is," I lied. *Except you tried to swap him out for his wealthier brother.* "You two are perfect together." *I hope he comes to his senses and divorces you, then marries someone who's eaten something in the last six months.*

I decided to keep my thoughts to myself and pretend to be excited for her. "So, is everything all set for the ceremony?" I asked. "Is there anything I can do to help?"

To my relief, Evie started talking about the flowers and the photographer and the weather forecast. Like so many brides before her, she couldn't see past the ceremony. She had wedding myopia, which was fine with me. I followed her to some nearby couches where her cousins and Mrs. Preston were seated.

Her cousins were Meghan, Michelle, and Sarah; if I'd understood James correctly, they all lived outside the city in Wellesley, a wealthy suburb. All three cousins were former investment bankers, married to investment bankers. All three of them had children, but you'd never know it by looking at them: their bodies were rock hard, sinewy with muscle, contrasting sharply with the soft, summery fabrics they wore. They scared the bejeezus out of me, too.

There were platters of delicious-looking appetizers, finger sandwiches, and cookies laid out before us, but no one had touched a thing. My stomach growled, and I self-consciously grabbed a sandwich. But Mrs. Preston smiled at me while I ate. "Hello, dear," she said, turning her attention to me. I startled. Her face looked different today, oddly puffy.

"Oh, I've just had my facial filler today, don't be alarmed," she said. Her cheeks were big and round, like a chubby toddler's.

"You have to get it done a few days before a big event so the swelling has a chance to go down," explained Evie.

"Oh," I said. "Well, I'm sure you'll look perfect, Mrs. Preston. But I already thought you did." I reached for another sandwich and stuffed it into my mouth before I had to talk some more. I forgot all about being self-conscious—if Mrs. Preston could talk about filling her face up with pharmaceuticals, I could fill mine with food.

Besides, I could not handle these bitches on an empty stomach. They were being friendly, and it set off all my internal alarms.

"Isn't she sweet?" Evie said and patted my hand. My back immediately stiffened. I took another sandwich and stuffed it into my mouth. I had the sinking feeling this was a set-up.

"You're starving," Mrs. Preston clucked. It looked as if she was trying to smile, but her face was too puffy to move. "Any chance you're eating for two?"

I shook my head no, horrified. "Not a chance," I croaked out, past my sandwich.

"But wouldn't that be nice?" Evie said, still fake-smiling at me. I should have just told her to stop, she sucked at it so hard.

I swallowed my food. "Not for me," I said. "But *you're* another matter." Now I showed her what a genuine fake smile looked like and turned the tables, making the conversation all about Evie. "You could get pregnant on the honeymoon...wouldn't that be exciting? Another little Preston?"

"It would be wonderful," Evie said reverently. It sounded as though the idea made her salivate. But Evie didn't strike me as all that maternal. I wondered just how much of a trust fund little Baby Preston would have.

"I expect a grandchild," Mrs. Preston said to Evie. It looked as if she was trying to arch an eyebrow for emphasis, but nothing was really moving.

She turned to me. "But not from you," she said.

I held up my hands, as if to surrender. "Don't worry about it," I said, "'cause it's not happening."

She and Evie looked at each other for a beat and then refocused on me. I grabbed yet another sandwich and looked around desperately for a waiter so I could order some wine.

"What exactly is going on with you and my son?" Mrs. Preston asked.

I sighed. "Mrs. Preston, we just talked about this yesterday. We're dating and having fun. That's it," I said. "It's not serious. You and I both know he's out of my league."

I looked at Evie. "You know it, too."

She shrugged and nodded in agreement. "You're right. He's totally too good for you."

"Thanks," I said flatly.

"But Audrey—even though you said it isn't serious, James told Todd that you went to the Red Sox yesterday. And that you had a great time," Evie said.

"So?"

"And he told him you went on the swan boats," she said accusatorially. It was as if she was presenting a particularly damning piece of evidence against me. Mrs. Preston leaned forward, waiting to hear my response.

I rolled my eyes at both of them. "That was my idea," I said, even though it totally wasn't. "Ladies, James is a great guy, and I like him a lot, but I can't imagine he'd ever be serious about me."

"Are you serious about him?" Mrs. Preston asked, not skipping a beat.

"Only as serious as you can be about something with an expiration date," I said. I grabbed another finger sandwich and cursed the existence of finger sandwiches—why couldn't they just make full-size ones? Then I wouldn't have to keep grabbing them and feeling like a cow stuck in a herd of flamingoes.

I looked up to find Mrs. Preston studying my face.

Evie nudged me. "You two seem like you're having a good time, though, which makes my life a lot easier." She sounded as if she was apologizing to me. "If James was being an asshole like usual, these two weeks would be a total cluster fuck."

"I agree," Mrs. Preston said. A waiter approached, and she ordered a vodka gimlet.

I raised my hand. "May I please have a glass of wine?" I asked.

"Bring the bottle," Mrs. Preston commanded, and I settled in for what I knew was going to be a very long afternoon.

JAMES CAME THROUGH the door at exactly four o'clock, resplendent in another steel-colored suit. I practically sprinted to him.

"I'm pretty sure your mother was trying to get me drunk so she could interrogate me," I told him once we were safely in the car.

"Are you drunk?" James asked. He almost sounded hopeful.

"No," I scoffed. "Your mother had four gimlets and I had a bottle of wine. It was junior-varsity time."

James shoulders shook in silent laughter next to me. "I can't believe you can out day-drink my mother. You really are the perfect woman."

His words sent shivers through my body, which I ignored. "She didn't get anything out of me. I told her that we were happily dating, but that you and your gazillions of dollars were totally out of my league."

James snorted at me and grabbed my hand. "The opposite is true—you're out of *my* league," he said. "Gorgeous, kind, and young like you are."

"Ha," I said, but I felt myself blushing from the compliment. "You're all of those things, too."

"Except for the kind and young parts, yeah—I guess I am," he said, still laughing.

I shook my head at him. He was in a playful mood, which was a first. Maybe he should take more days off and eat ballpark hot dogs more often. If I had all of his money, I certainly would.

"Your mother even asked me if I was pregnant, or trying to get pregnant," I said, snorting. "I wanted to explain to her that I was a working girl, not some sort of *gold-digger*."

"She asked you that?" His voice was like ice.

I shrugged, trying to hold onto the happy mood we'd shared just a second ago. "It's not like it surprised me. She's been pretty direct with me from the start."

All the amusement had drained from James's face. He let go of my hand and turned toward the window.

"I fucking hate her," he said. The violence in his voice stunned me.

"I'm sorry," I said, desperately wishing I could back-pedal. "Should I not have told you that?"

He sighed and shook his head. "It's not like it surprises me. She's always been ruthless about it."

"About what? What do you mean?" I asked.

"All she cares about is the family name and the family money," he said.

He turned back to me. "My children and Todd's children are set to inherit an enormous amount of money from my mother's side of the family. It's in a generation-skipping trust. My mother is very protective of its future."

I sat there, not understanding.

"Audrey—any children I have are going to inherit so much money that it's going to make my fortune look like an allowance. My mother's family owned coal mines. They were loaded up to their eyeballs. My mother and her siblings got some of that money, and so did Todd and me and our cousins. But the way the trust is set up, it's the next generation that will inherit the corpus of the trust."

"The what?" I asked.

"The corpus—that means the bulk of the trust."

"So she thinks I knew about that?" I asked. "She thinks that's why I'm dating you? So I can get knocked up and have a super-gazillionaire baby?" I was starting to get pretty pissed at Mrs. Preston and her puffy, chemically-refreshed face.

"I don't know what she thinks," James said. "But she's been very clear, since I was a boy, that I need to have kids with the 'right' person. One who has the right background. Not some graphic design student from New Hampshire, whose father owned a main-street shoe store."

*Or a real-life bastard escort,* I thought, but said nothing.

"She wants my children to have a pedigree," he said. "So you're fine for the wedding, but you're not good enough to be the mother of her grandchildren. And she just wanted to know if that was your long-term goal."

"What would she have done if I said that it was?" I asked.

"Something, I'm sure," he said darkly.

"What about Evie?" I asked, a curious mixture of envy and sadness running through me. "Is she approved?"

"Evie is unfortunately approved," James said. "Her family's wealthy and from Wellesley. From a long line of wealthy people from Wellesley."

"And her cousins are all investment bankers married to investment bankers," I said.

"Something like that," he said. He went back to staring out the window.

This was more of a story than I'd bargained for. Now that I knew the truth, it was surprising how swiftly that hope I'd been clinging to just drained away. Not only was I not good enough for James, I was *really* not good enough. In a way that could never be fixed, could never be overlooked or hidden.

I took his face gently in my hands and turned it back toward me. "I hope you meet the right girl someday," I said to him, and I meant it. I would shed tears over this later, about the fact that I would never be that person. Still, I meant every word.

"The kind of girl that would be a good mom and a good wife. The kind of girl your mother would approve of, to make your life easier—'cause your mom's scary. She could do with a nice bitch slap."

James smiled at me, but there was a sadness behind the smile.

"I might bitch slap my mother someday, but the rest of that's never going to happen for me," he said.

"How do you know?" I asked, and dropped my hands from his face.

"I just do," James said darkly, and turned away again.

# JAMES

We got back to the apartment, and Audrey went to go change. I poured myself a drink and stormed around the living room, watching the city below, wondering what the hell I'd gotten myself into.

After I'd woken up holding her hand, I'd panicked. I'd dressed quickly and headed out of the apartment before she woke up. I needed to be alone. I'd grabbed a large, black coffee and decided to go for a walk.

I found myself back in the Commons where we'd been yesterday. The sun was just coming up. I was marching through the park as if I had a meeting to rush to—because I usually always had a meeting to rush to. I finally gave up and sat down on a bench, staring at the abandoned swan boats, docked and covered with morning dew.

I needed to think, but all I could think about was her. Nestled against me at that game last night. Laughing and drinking her beer. Sound asleep in her T-shirt, right next to me but still out of reach.

I was so, so fucked.

*I should have just fucked her when I had the chance*, I thought now. So that maybe she never would have talked to me, never would have gotten under my skin. Then she would just be another faceless lay, someone else I'd fucked and could forget about.

But oh, no. I had tried to keep control, and now the whole thing had gone to hell.

*I had feelings for my escort. Real. Feelings.*

I wanted to bitch slap myself, but I wasn't sure what a bitch slap actually entailed.

I'd gone through the fitting and the rest of the day on auto-pilot, trying to at least be semi-pleasant and not ruin Todd's stupid almost-wedding. I'd told him about the swan boats and the Red Sox, trying to play up my relationship with Audrey so he'd believe in it. But I didn't need to play it up. It was real, and he already believed in it. He nodded and smiled when I told him about my day.

"She's a really nice girl," Todd said.

She *was* a really nice girl. She just also happened to be my escort.

What she'd told me about my mother had set off a rage-spiral in me, and I had to control it. For Audrey's sake.

I also had to keep my feelings for her to myself. Also for her sake.

I just had to get through dinner tonight and the next couple of events, I told myself. Then we had the rehearsal dinner and the wedding this weekend. The trip was after that, but I didn't have to think that far ahead. Not yet. I was going to take it one step at a time and try not to fuck everything up further.

"Where are we going tonight?" she asked me, jarring me out of my self-admonishing reverie. I hadn't heard her come back out.

"A restaurant called Ministry, in the Back Bay—it's very trendy. And very overpriced," I said.

"Perfect," she said. "What does one wear to a very trendy and very overpriced Back Bay restaurant these days? When one is pretending to be a real-life person, I mean?"

I looked at her, and I couldn't help myself: I smiled. I wanted to be a glacier, and here she was like the sun, melting my angry resolve.

"Something sexy and black," I said, instantly regretting it.

She nodded, looking game. "I've got that, boss."

"Would you like some wine before you get ready?" I asked. "We've got an hour."

She marched to the kitchen and parked herself on a barstool. I noticed that she'd changed out of her earlier outfit to a pair of leggings and the T-shirt she'd slept in.

"I never say no to wine. Especially not your wine, James—it's good," she said approvingly. "Mine usually comes from one of those big bottles. Or a box."

I shuddered. "Promise me you'll never go back to drinking that," I said, and she furrowed her brow at me.

Of course she was going to go back to drinking that.

"You promise me something," she said.

"What," I said, looking at her suspiciously and pouring us both hefty glasses of wine.

"Let's try to have fun for the rest of the time we're together," she said quickly, in an earnest rush. "I was just thinking about it—I had *fun* yesterday. I can't remember the last time I had fun. I didn't think I was capable of it, to be honest."

"I don't know if I can commit to that," I said. "Being around my family is usually the opposite of fun."

"You've been handling them pretty well," she said, shrugging. "Just thought I'd point that out."

"Because you're the pointer-outer of things," I said.

"That's right."

I laughed in spite of myself. I wasn't sure how I'd gone from berating myself about her to suddenly asking her to wear something sexy and pouring her wine, but it was like I could suddenly hear the clock ticking. She was only mine through next Friday. This was all I was going to get.

"I'm sorry about before," I said, "after I picked you up. I can get a little moody sometimes."

She shrugged, forgiving me easily. "Well, I'm sorry I said your mother needed a bitch slap," she said.

"She does need a bitch slap," I said. "You might have to show me how to give her one."

"It'd be my pleasure."

I PUT ON MY NICEST dark suit, which was saying something. Audrey put on a cocktail dress with a plunging neckline. It was black, and it was very sexy.

I sucked in my breath, hard, when I saw her.

She was wearing black high heels, and her hair was loose and glossy around her shoulders. Her breasts looked fantastic—perfectly round and alert, like only a twenty-two-year-old's can. Or Jennifer Lopez's.

"Is this approved?" she asked.

"Yes," I said, completely monosyllabic.

My cock twitched just looking at her.

"You look dashing, as usual," she said and linked her arm through mine.

Kai averted his eyes when we came outside so I knew that it wasn't just me—Audrey really was stunning. I felt stupidly proud then that she was with me, that no one else could have her.

I didn't let myself examine the irony of that particular train of thought.

# AUDREY

Ministry was insanely beautiful. There were lush flowers and candles everywhere. We sat on reclaimed church pews at the table. Evie's cousins and their besuited husbands sat on my left; James sat on my right, protecting me from his parents. He'd said hello to them but otherwise wasn't speaking, concentrating instead on his food and on me.

To my simultaneous delight and horror, I'd caught him looking down my dress several times.

Todd was across the table from me. "Are you getting excited?" I asked.

He beamed at me. "You have no idea. It's the best feeling in the world."

He *was* earnest, as James had said; he was also open and kind, very unlike James.

"Evie told me about the flowers. Everything is going to be so beautiful," I gushed. I couldn't help myself. I liked Todd, and even if Evie *was* a total c-word, he was excited to marry her.

"She and my mom have taken care of every detail," Todd said. "It's easy for me. All I have to do is show up."

James snorted. "And be married to her," he said. I noticed that he was on his third bourbon, and I frowned at him.

"What," he said, not bothering to make it a question.

"I am pointing it out to you that this is your brother's special time, and you shouldn't be a prick," I said to him quietly, so nobody else could hear. "If you behave, we can watch *Sports Center* when we get home. And you can keep looking at my boobs." I put my hand on his thigh and I felt him tense up, but it wasn't a bad tense.

He was tensed as though he was ready to spring. At me.

"Do you promise?" he asked darkly, and it was as if someone

lit a match between us. My hand was on fire where I touched him.

"Yes," I whispered. I kept my hand on his thigh, inching it up a little, and turned back to Todd. "Now, tell me about the honeymoon. I want to know everything."

Under the table, James put his hand over mine and moved it up toward his cock. He was rock hard. I ran my hands over it reverently, trying not to either moan or climb on top of him right there, while Todd was gushing about the villas we were going to stay at.

Then James took my hand and removed it from his lap. And put his hand on *my* thigh. My bare thigh.

It was as if my skin was scalded, branded from his touch, the feel of his skin on my skin. He moved his hand up higher, dangerously higher, and under my dress. I jerked at the tablecloth, making sure my lap was covered. I looked nervously to my left; the investment banker sitting there was fully engrossed with his steak. I could feel my heartbeat thrumming through me as James's hand crept up to my underwear. He fingered the lace and quickly slid his hand underneath before I had time to prepare myself.

Still, I didn't cry out. I nodded at Todd, pretending to listen about the best snorkeling reefs in Eleuthera as James began to run his fingers along my slit.

I was wet already. Hell, I'd been wet since I met him. He used the slickness against me, rubbing me until I was almost panting. He found my clit and swirled it, lazily, and then pinched it in between his two fingers.

That was all I could take; I almost came right there. I grabbed his arm as calmly as I could and moved him off me. I took the napkin off my lap and gently wiped his hand with it.

And then I took his hand and held it, counting the seconds until dinner was over.

WE SAT PRACTICALLY on top of each other in the back of the car. There was no divider, so we behaved, better than at dinner, anyway.

James had his arms around me and was crushing me to him. I could feel his cock, large and hard, against me. I shifted, uncomfortable with desire, and he moved his hand down to my ass. He rubbed it, drawing small, hot circles with his palm, mesmerizing me, until I almost didn't care that there was no divider.

James didn't even wait for Kai to open the door. He jumped out and dragged me with him. We practically ran through the lobby.

There was an elderly couple waiting for the elevator. I smiled at them while James cursed under his breath. We rode upstairs in silence, while I privately prayed that James and I didn't smell like almost-sex.

"Finally," he said when the door opened at his apartment. He punched in the code and then turned and swooped me into his arms.

I laughed as he hustled me down the hallway.

"I have to get that fucking dress off of you. Now," he growled.

"How romantic," I said.

He placed me gently on my feet, just inside his bedroom. I looked up at him and threw my arms around his neck, drinking him in. His gorgeous steel-colored hair, his square jaw, his blue-gray eyes.

"Tell me that you want to do this," he said. He ran his hands down my back.

"I want to do this," I said immediately. "I want to do this *now*."

I leaned up and kissed him, hard. He crushed his lips to mine and our tongues found each other, causing electricity to shoot through me. He pressed the small of my back and moved me against him, so that I could feel his rock-hard length pressing into my belly.

I unzipped his pants and freed his cock. It sprang out, enormous and thick, ready for me.

*Oh thank God,* I thought, relieved. If he'd been small after all this buildup, I might have run from the building, screaming.

He unzipped and removed my dress in what seemed like one motion. I took off his jacket, unbuttoned his shirt, and undid his pants so they dropped. Then I stopped, running my hands down his gorgeous, chiseled chest reverently. I wanted to enjoy this moment.

I kissed him, tracing his pectoral muscles with my tongue, and he moaned. It made me feel triumphant. He reached down and undid my bra, gently taking my breasts in his hands. He rubbed my nipples in circles with his thumbs, and I leaned into him, moaning with ecstasy and relief. *His hands were finally on me,* I thought.

It felt like they belonged there.

James ran his hands over my body and cupped my ass, pulling me to him. He grabbed the side of my black lace underwear and pulled them down gently. His tongue searched my mouth and I gave myself to him, surrendering to the urgency and surprising sweetness of his touch.

He laid me down on the bed, and his naked body loomed gloriously over me. He pushed the hair off my face and just watched me for a moment. Then he leaned in and kissed me again, deep and probing.

There was something else going on here, something besides sex, but I didn't recognize the feeling. All I knew was that I wanted him inside me, right now, and that I wanted to cry.

I spread my legs a little, offering myself to him. He took a finger and ran it along my slit, making sure that I was wet enough. He slid it inside of me, testing me, and I moaned. I grabbed his muscled ass and pulled him to me, running the head of his cock over my sex, getting it slick and wet.

"Are you ready for me?" he asked, and I nodded.

He entered me then, all at once, and I cried out. He buried himself into me, and my body stretched to accommodate his. He was gentle at first. But I was impatient, and I grabbed his ass and pushed him deep into me, wanting to feel all of him, wanting him to overtake me. His body listened to mine, his long, deep strokes pushing me to the edge almost immediately.

He leaned up, and I greedily drank in the sight of his taut, muscled body.

And then he continued to fuck me, hard.

"Come in me," I begged. I was on the edge, and I wanted him there, with me.

His strokes got deeper, more urgent, and then he did come,

hard, filling me as my body clenched around him.

Our orgasm shook the bed.

"Audrey," he cried out, shuddering on top of me.

AFTERWARD, HE LAY NEXT to me and I stared at his gorgeous face, pushing the hair back from his forehead.

He opened his eyes and watched me watching him.

"That was incredible," I said, too undone to be anything but honest.

"It was," he said. He kissed me slowly, deeply. "Let's do it again."

So we did it again. And again. With me on top, with him behind me. He took me in his mouth and then I took him in mine. By the time the morning came, we'd done it just about every way you could think of, and I was pretty sure I wouldn't be able to walk straight ever again.

Which was fine with me. It was absofuckinglutely worth it.

I woke up, and now it was my turn to find James watching me, pushing the hair back from my forehead.

"What," I said. I stared back at his gorgeous face.

"Audrey," he said, stroking my hair. "You're fired."

# JAMES

I looked out the window as the sun came up. The roads outside were empty, just like my apartment.

I'd just had the best night of my life, and true to form, I'd managed to ruin everything.

Audrey was gone. She'd gotten up as soon as I'd said those horrible words. She left in her sweatpants and a tank top, leaving the wardrobe that Elena had packed for her behind. I'd followed her out of the bedroom and silently watched as she'd thrown on a pair of aviator sunglasses and grabbed her pocketbook.

"Do you want to take the car?" I asked just as she was almost out the door.

She turned, pushing her sunglasses down on her nose to look at me. "James." She looked as if my name tasted like poison in her mouth. "Go fuck yourself."

Then she slammed the door behind her.

I didn't blame her. And even though I had forced her to leave, I hated that she was gone.

I hated myself even more.

I got dressed for the gym. I was going to punish myself, starting right now.

# AUDREY

I was sitting in the common room at New Horizons, watching dust motes fly through the early morning light. Tommy was drinking orange juice and reading a graphic novel. He'd been happy to see me, and now we were just sitting together, both comfortably lost in the silence—me in my thoughts, him in his novel.

James had broken my heart. I had given myself to him last night. For the first time in quite possibly forever, I hadn't held anything back. I was with him because I'd wanted him. And when he took me, every single cell in my body told me it was right. That I belonged to him.

I was his escort. His hired plaything. But there was something else going on between us. Something real that you couldn't pay for or pretend.

I'd thought he felt it, too.

*So. Fucking. Stupid.*

Tommy reached over and patted my shoulder. "What's the matter?" he asked.

"Nothing," I lied. He watched me for a second and then went back to his book. I went back to my study of the dust motes. I loved Tommy. He was the one person who loved me and now I was sure, the one person in the world I could trust.

And now I didn't know how I was going to be able to keep him safe.

"ELENA, I'M SORRY," I said, fighting back tears. I paced back and forth inside my apartment. "I told you, I don't know why he did it."

"He must have had a reason to fire you two days before the wedding," she wailed. I held the phone back from my ear and winced.

*I fucked his brains out, and then he told me I was fired,* I wanted to say. That was the truth.

I was his escort, and he hadn't wanted to fuck me.

Then he finally did.

Then he fired me.

It. Made. No. Sense.

"I'm sure you can keep the deposit," I said, trying to be upbeat. James had paid her one hundred thousand dollars, cash, up front. "That's decent payment for one week's worth of work."

"I was pretty interested in the other half, too," she said.

"Maybe you could offer him one of the other girls," I said over a large lump forming in my throat. "Someone more to his liking."

"I *thought* he liked you," she said.

"I thought he did, too," I said, and I could feel the tears about to come. I bit the inside of my cheek to stop them.

Elena sighed again. "I'll call him now."

"Elena—one more thing," I said. My stomach flipped nervously; I didn't want her to be any angrier with me than she already was.

"What?" she asked.

"I left all the clothes and the jewelry over there," I said, the words tumbling out on top of each other. "I had to leave quickly and I just... did. I left. Without taking them." It was thousands of dollars' worth of clothes, shoes, bags, and jewelry. A lot of it was on loan from a luxury goods company. Elena was going to kill me.

I took a deep breath. "And I sort of told him to go fuck himself. So he might be a little angry."

The silence on the other end of the line was deafening.

"Dre," she said finally. Her voice was flat.

"What?" I asked, bracing for it.

"You're fired."

*FIRED TWICE IN ONE DAY, just when I thought things were finally turning around.*

I should have known better. In my twenty-two years, things

had never turned around for me. I curled myself up into a ball on my futon, watching as the sun came up over the sky. *I hate the sun,* I thought, and I did. I hated the sun, the sky, my futon, and James Preston. Not necessarily in that order.

I had no idea what I was going to do now. Without Elena's assignments, it would be back to trolling for dates online. Or parking my ass on a street corner, trying to flag down Johns. Or waitressing.

Probably, it was going to be a combination of all of these. But none of it would be enough to keep up with Tommy's rent. I couldn't even bear the thought. Before he'd moved in there, he'd lived with my mother. It was a bad situation. My mother was, at best, a drunk. At her worst, she was an irresponsible, abusive user. She'd almost set their apartment on fire three times over the last couple of years by passing out with a lit cigarette in her hand. It wasn't safe for Tommy there. She never bought him the food he liked or took him to the library. And then there was the string of dirty men she brought home.

I'd tried to move him in with me but I couldn't do it and work. He needed someone to watch him, to take care of him. Once he'd wandered off and once he'd burned himself trying to make a grilled cheese. New Horizons was the right place for him; it was the happiest he'd ever been.

I needed to help him, and now I couldn't help him.

I let the tears come then, hot and ugly. And then just as quickly as they'd come, they stopped. *Winners never quit and quitters never win*, I told myself, wiping my eyes roughly. I'd read that quote somewhere, and I often repeated it to myself, even though my definition of "winning" was probably wildly different from most people's.

I made myself sit up—I wasn't any good to anyone if I was just sitting here and wallowing. I'd found a way to keep Tommy safe this long, I reasoned. I could still do it.

I could do it because I had to do it.

I got up and washed my face. I had the idea of going to the library; they had computers and Internet access. I could look for a job online. Part of me wondered whether I'd be able to google "escort services" or "exotic dancer positions" at the public library, but it was better than sitting here, cursing James Preston for firing me and sniffling into my T-shirt.

The phone rang as I was getting dressed. It was Elena. I took a deep breath before I answered it, preparing for the worst. Maybe James had taken my clothes and thrown them all out. Maybe he'd told her that I'd stolen from her, and that he was going to press charges. *He wouldn't do that,* part of me wailed, but that was the same part that had believed he'd cared for me.

The common sense part of me bitch-slapped that part, hard, so she'd be quiet.

"Dre," she said.

"Yes?" I asked, willing myself not to start crying all over again.

"You're back in my good graces, young lady. I just got off the phone with James Preston—he says he wants you back. He made it clear that he *only* wants you. He also very generously offered to triple the fee for our trouble. Half is now coming directly to you, per his very specific instructions."

I couldn't breathe. I stood there, reeling for a bunch of different reasons. I wasn't good at math, but this was pretty easy to figure out—three hundred thousand dollars. *Holy fucking shit.*

"It appears you have nine lives, Dre. But only seven left."

"What?" I spluttered, finally finding enough breath to talk. "What did he say, exactly?"

"Just what I told you. Oh—and one more thing," Elena said.

She waited a beat.

"He said that this time, he wants to fuck you."

# JAMES

In the Stratum's gym, I made myself run hard. Then I lifted weights. I did squats. Lunges. Pull-ups. An attractive young blonde nearby kept looking at me, smiling. She started following me on the weight circuit, that stupid friendly smile plastered on her face.

Finally, I just turned and glared at her. "I'm not interested," I said before she even had the chance to say hello. She just raised her eyebrows and, scowling, backed away.

Smart girl.

My phone rang, and for a second, my heart stopped. *Audrey.* But of course, I'd driven her away so cruelly that it wasn't her. It wasn't ever going to be her.

Instead, it was Elena.

"*What?*" I snapped.

"Mr. Preston," she said in an apologetic tone, "I just got off the phone with Dre. I am so sorry."

"What did she tell you?" I asked.

"That you fired her. She wasn't forthcoming with a reason, but I can only imagine," she said. "The wedding is this weekend—please, let me make it up to you. Let me send another girl. You can tell your family that you've been dating her on the side, and that at the last moment, you decided to bring her as your guest instead."

"Elena," I said, wiping my face roughly with a towel, "that's a stupid fucking idea."

I heard her sigh. "What do you want me to say? We have to figure something out. I don't want to leave you like this."

"You mean you don't want to lose my business, and you don't want me saying bad things about your service."

"That's certainly true," she said, "but I also don't want to leave you stranded right before these big events. Please tell me what I can do to make this better."

I watched the blonde I'd scared off eyeing me warily from her spot on the treadmill. I thought of my perfect apartment upstairs, immaculate and barren.

"Please tell Audrey I'd like her to come back. I'll triple the fee for her troubles. You need to ensure me that half of that money will go directly to her. She's the one earning it."

"Of course, Mr. Preston," she said, and I heard barely concealed glee in her voice.

I watched the blonde begin to run, her tits bouncing up and down. But I only thought of Audrey. How she'd arched beneath me last night, moaning. How she'd slept in my arms.

"And Elena, please tell her that this time, I would like to enjoy the full range of her services."

I HAD KAI TAKE ME to her right after I took a shower. I was worried that if I let more time pass, she would run away and hide.

I called Elena again from the car. "I need her street number, please," I said.

"Mr. Preston, I don't usually—"

"I'm in her neighborhood right now. Give it to me," I snapped.

I repeated it to Kai, and he turned down the street into a sad-looking neighborhood. The yuppies had clearly not gotten to this part of town yet. The row houses were all triplexes, in various stages of sagging. Audrey's was painted a bright turquoise; the paint was peeling in large, insidious-looking curls.

I went up and rang her buzzer.

"What," she said flatly.

"It's me," I said. "James. I'm here to pick you up."

There was nothing but dead silence for a moment, and I held my breath. I wasn't sure what she was going to do. I buzzed again.

"Audrey."

"What," she said again.

"Let me up."

"Yes, sir," she said and buzzed me in.

I went up the ramshackle, worn stairs to her apartment, located on the second floor. The building smelled foul, of odd spices and indoor cats. I knocked, and she opened the door, a neutral look plastered across her face.

"I could have just come to you, you know," she said, stepping aside so I could enter. "You don't need to see this—it's not exactly the penthouse condo at The Stratum."

I went past her into the apartment. It was neat and clean but otherwise in very sad shape. The sagging hardwood floors were worn thin. It was a studio, so the so-called kitchen opened onto the main living space. Her oven looked as if it were built for a doll. There was a forlorn purple futon in the middle of the room. Other than a boxy television set and a stunted-looking spider plant, that was pretty much it.

"I thought you made decent money with Elena," I said, looking around.

"I do," she said. "But I have other people to take care of."

"Your brother."

She nodded, her face impassive. I was pretty sure her brother was the only reason she'd agreed to come back to me.

I stood there, clenching and unclenching my fists. Audrey said nothing. Her face looked puffy and red, as if she'd been crying.

"Are you ready to go?" I asked.

"Of course," she said formally.

I wasn't sure how to handle her right now, or what to say. I just wanted her back. The dark mix of emotions behind that want, the pressing need I had to be with her—all of that got shoved to the back of my mind, where I could ignore it at my leisure.

"Audrey..." I grabbed her arm and pulled her to me, but she was as stiff as a board against my embrace. I immediately let her go. I couldn't stand to feel her like that, indifferent and limp against me. I remembered her face last night. She'd smiled at me at one point, when I was on top of her. And I'd known then what I knew right now.

But I didn't let myself think about it. Instead, I led my highly compensated prisoner out the door and pondered my next move.

# AUDREY

James had now seen my flea-trap apartment. He knew about my brother. He'd been inside me every which way, and he knew what I tasted like. He knew what I sounded like when I came…

What I sounded like screaming his name.

He had all of my ugly pieces laid before him, exposed.

I didn't want to be in this position—getting back into his car, Kai studiously not looking at me.

I knew my face was puffy, and I knew James knew why.

I hated him.

But I needed him.

*Not him*, I reminded myself—I needed his money. I had to keep Tommy at the home. If I could finish this job, I would make enough money to pay for his expenses for a long time. And I could try to earn as much as possible in the meantime, to finally get ahead for once in my life. Maybe I could even stop turning tricks. Go back to school. Get a day job.

This could be a dream come true. It would be like a winning lottery ticket.

But to get to that place, I had to be with James again.

And all I wanted to do was run.

I sighed, resigned, and slid into the seat. James closed the door behind us and stared out the window. He didn't bother trying to touch me again after our awkward embrace upstairs. And yet, he'd told Elena that he now wanted me for sex.

He was buying. I would give him what he wanted. Even though I wanted to run, I would make myself stay. I would go to the remaining events and the wedding, and then I would spend the following week on the beach with his family. I would pretend to be his adoring girlfriend. I would bend over backward for him, come when he called, and suck his cock so hard he would have an atomic orgasm. If that's what he wanted.

We drove over the bridge and back into the city. The early-morning traffic was just picking up. I looked up at the buildings in the Financial District, and I remembered how he'd wrapped his arms around me last night, the way he'd looked at me. I thought I'd seen something in his eyes, something that mirrored what I'd been feeling. My heart twisted. It was all a lie, and it was no one's fault but my own. I'd lied to myself, and I could no longer pretend that there was something between us.

*Don't think about it,* I warned myself.

If I'd ever felt like a whore, it was now.

JAMES IGNORED ME the rest of the way to the Stratum. He ignored me in the lobby and in the elevator, opting instead to send out texts furiously on his phone.

That was fine by me.

I'd only been gone from the apartment for a little while, but it didn't seem the same when I came back. It seemed colder, less inviting. Exactly like James.

"Where's the dinner tonight?" I asked, willing my voice to stay neutral.

"This afternoon is actually the photo shoot, followed by a cocktail hour," he said. "Evie somehow wrangled *New England Brides Magazine* into featuring the wedding in an upcoming issue. They want to get pictures of the families and the wedding party ahead of time. Then we're going for drinks somewhere in the Leather District. I'd like you to come, of course," he said.

"Of course," I said. Anything he asked of me, I was going to do. I was here to perform.

He put down his phone and looked at me. "You seem like you're being… accommodating," he said. There was an undercurrent to his voice that tugged at me.

I shrugged. "I'm here to do whatever you want, James. I'm yours for the next nine nights."

"Is that all I have left?"

"If I'm doing the math right," I said.

He walked over to me slowly. I noticed for the first time that he was wearing jeans and a T-shirt, not his customary suit, and that he hadn't shaved. He looked a little rough around the edges. It was only a few hours ago that he'd held me in his arms, his skin on my skin. Heat pooled in my belly as he approached me, but an icy fear circled my heart. I didn't want to want him. I didn't want to look at his big stupid biceps and the shadow of a sexy beard forming on his face.

He came close to me and then stopped. I froze in fear, worried he was going to touch me, worried that I was going to have to perform already, when I couldn't even bear to be near him like this. "We have all day before the shoot. I have to make a few more calls, but then I'm free," he said. "What would you like to do?"

I looked at him and shivered. Was it really only a few days ago that we went to the Red Sox game, laughing and drinking beer? Was it really only last night that he'd made love to me and run his hands down my body reverently? Things between us had changed so quickly that I had emotional whiplash.

"Whatever you'd like, James," I said, hoping I sounded obedient.

"I'll see you in my bedroom in fifteen minutes, then," he said. His face was impassive, and his voice gave nothing away.

I wanted to run from the apartment, screaming. I didn't want this. "Of course," I said, squashing my feelings. I didn't want this, but I needed it. Knowing the difference was what being an adult was all about.

That's why being an adult sucked so hard.

I left and went to my room so that I could change. I chose some expensive lingerie that Elena had packed for me. I took a deep breath and calmed myself down. If a whore was what he wanted, a whore was what he was going to get.

THE ONE TRICK That Jenny had taught me was to think of it like a movie. If it was bad, she'd said, pretend you were watching it and that it was happening to someone else. If the movie took a turn for the worst and got really scary, just close your eyes, she said. Then it would be as if it never happened.

I started pretending this was a movie right now. I needed this to be an out-of-body experience in the most desperate way. I put on a black lace thong, a garter, sheer black stockings, and a very sexy push-up bra. The outfit was over-the-top escort. I shook my hair out in loose waves around my shoulders. I picked out black spiked heels, and then I sprayed my mouth with breath spray about a thousand times. My heart was beating rapidly in my chest, but I ignored it, trying to get myself under control. I even tried yoga breathing, taking a breath in through one nostril and breathing it out through the other.

It just made me have a coughing fit.

Finally, I calmed down. James was not my first John, nor was he my first disappointment. I went down the hall to his bedroom, my heels clicking loudly. *This is the part where the heroine shows the hero what she's made of,* I thought. But that was only in a regular movie. In a porno, this was where the heroine was about to get fucked six ways from Sunday.

I hated myself for it, but I got a little wet at the thought.

James was waiting for me in his room. He was sitting on the bed, still tapping things into his damn phone. He didn't even look at me as I clicked past him to the other side and stood there, trying to feign confidence and indifference.

Finally he looked up, and I thought I saw a flicker of surprise cross his face. He quashed it immediately. "Don't move," he commanded. "I just want to look at you." It was a good thing I was twenty-two and had a smoking-hot body, because this was happening in the harsh light of day. I took a deep breath as James came toward me, his eyes drinking me in greedily. I felt so exposed right now, so different from how I'd felt last night.

"Well, you look *awfully* nice for what I have planned," he said darkly.

"Will I do?" I asked, playing his game.

"Oh, yeah. You'll do nicely."

He went back and sat down on the bed. He leaned back against the headboard and put his arms behind his head, just relaxing and enjoying the view while I stood on display. I could see his stupid bulging biceps. I hated myself for it, but the way he was inspecting me, coupled with those stupid bulging biceps, was getting me a little more wet. I didn't know what he had planned. My heart was beating fast.

"Please," he said. "Sit." He patted the bed beside him, and I tried to sit seductively. Unfortunately, the thong was giving me a major wedgie.

My face betrayed nothing.

"Can you pass me that?" James asked.

"What?" I started looking around for a tube of lubricant, a whip, or some handcuffs.

"The remote," he said matter-of-factly.

I handed it to him. So I guessed we were going to watch some porn.

James turned on *New England Sports News* and sighed happily. "They're on the road. Tampa Bay. The game's on in half an hour," James said.

"Huh?" I asked, thoroughly confused.

He turned to me with a shit-eating grin on his face. "I said the Red Sox game's on in half an hour."

"You want to watch the game?"

"Don't you?" He asked innocently.

*Well,* I thought, *two can play this game.* "Absofuckinglutely," I said, turning back to the television. I decided to ignore both him and my wedgie.

# JAMES

The Red Sox weren't playing well, but for once, I didn't care. Audrey was back, and she was next to me. She was also wearing some very hot black lingerie, but I wasn't going to address that. Not yet. There were hours before the photo shoot, hours I had to spend with just her.

I wasn't good at apologies—I had no experience making them. But I did want to make this morning up to her, so I was doing it the only way I knew how. I was going to give her what she liked: baseball and food.

"You want something to eat?" I asked.

She looked at me suspiciously. She probably thought I meant my cock. "What's on the menu?"

I grabbed my tablet and pulled up the menu from the Stratum's restaurant. "Burgers, Caesar salads, steak tips..."

"I'll have a burger," she said and shrugged, trying to sound casual. "And a Caesar salad. And a beer." She looked at me quickly. "If you're having one."

I picked up my cell phone and ordered two burgers, two Caesar salads, and extra onion rings. "They're good," I mouthed to Audrey while I was on the phone.

"What about the beer?"

"I have some."

She got up in that outfit and went out the kitchen. I got to see her glorious ass, round and muscular, in a thong. She made her way out the door slowly, making sure I got a good, long look. *Holy shit.* My dick got instantly hard. One minute later, she clicked back in, carrying two IPAs. She placed one gently on my nightstand, leaning down so her tits were practically in my face. She looked over and saw the obvious bulge in my pants. Then she stood up and smiled, as if she'd won something. She strutted back to her side of the bed and showed me that ass one more time. Then she sat down, drinking her beer and ignoring me until my erection gave up and finally withered, dejected and alone.

The door buzzed, and Audrey looked down at herself. "I think you better get it," she said. She eyed my pants. "You okay to do that?"

"I'm fine," I said, grinning. "I've just seen your ass in a thong. I'm gonna die a happy man."

WE STARTED TO EAT on my bed. I got up and threw Audrey one of my old Wharton T-shirts.

"What's that for?" she asked.

"You need to be comfortable while you eat. I hate to ruin the view, though." She went into the bathroom for a second and came back out wearing the T-shirt and only the T-shirt, which made my cock stir again.

I knew what was under that shirt and I wanted it, bad.

She padded out barefoot to the kitchen and came back with two more beers. It was almost as if this morning had never happened, that I'd never fired her and she'd never left. We ate in silence, watching the game, sharing the onion rings.

I picked up the dishes when we'd finished. Audrey looked up at me, the bravado gone from her face just like the lingerie was gone from her body. "Thank you," she said, and it was a loaded thanks, not just for clearing the dishes.

"I should be saying that to you. You were brave to come back here."

I went out to the kitchen and threw everything in the sink. She was brave, and I was a coward. When she'd put her hand on me last night at the restaurant, I'd lost my mind. I'd lost all control. Her touch had scorched me, and without thinking, I'd let my instincts take over. My instincts wanted to fuck her, hard.

But that's not all they wanted, and that was the larger part of the problem.

I went back to my room and sat down next to her, closer this time. I stroked her arm lightly and I felt her stiffen, as if she was bracing for the worst. I couldn't blame her, not after the way I'd betrayed her this morning.

"Do you remember everything that we did last night?" I asked her, my fingers trailing up her arm.

She bit her lip and looked at me. I could see the traces of puffiness around her eyes still, the vulnerability in her face. "I wish I could forget it," she said.

I continued to stroke her arm. "I have…issues, Audrey. I sort of told you about them. I have a hard time getting close to people."

She was watching my face.

"Last night was pretty intense," I said. "I didn't know how to handle it in the morning. I was confused and feeling…" My voice trailed off as I struggled to articulate my thoughts.

"Feeling what?"

"Just *feeling*." I watched my finger move up and down her arm. I didn't look her in the face. "It made me uncomfortable. That's why I fired you."

"So why'd you hire me back? And also say you wanted sex, if it was the sex that caused the problem?"

One of the things I liked about her was that she was direct. But that could also be a challenge—especially when you were trying to obfuscate the truth from yourself. I sighed and rolled onto my back. "We don't have to have sex if you don't want to, Audrey."

"I didn't say that." Her voice was defensive, but it also sounded hurt.

"I hired you back because you're a nice girl, and we had a deal. I told Elena that I wanted sex to be included in our arrangement now because I enjoyed last night. If you came back, I wanted that to be out in the open. Part of our agreement." I paused for a second. "Services requested and services rendered."

It didn't feel good coming out of my mouth, but I made myself say it anyway. Going forward, sex was going to be part of our contract. Last night had just been us, and it had been dangerous. I'd come so many times I'd barely been able to see straight, and the depth of my orgasms had shocked me. I knew Audrey had orgasmed, again and again, because I'd felt her body clench around mine.

I'd also heard her screaming my name.

"I'm fine with sex being part of the arrangement. I like things to be straightforward. It makes them easier to deal with," she said.

"That's exactly what I mean," I said, relieved that we seemed to be on the same page. "So... will that be okay? You're back, and we have the same arrangement as before. Except now sex is part of the deal."

"Works for me," Audrey said, business-like.

I smiled at her. "Let's just enjoy each other. We have a whole week left."

"Deal," Audrey said. She sounded relieved, too.

She leaned back on the pillow and went back to watching the game. I lay beside her, stroking her arm again. She was so beautiful, even with no makeup and my old shirt on. *Especially* with no makeup and my old shirt on. After a while she turned to me, running her fingers along my face. I leaned over and kissed her then, tasting her sweet mouth, crushing my lips against hers.

I was going to have to fuck her. The need rose up in me, large and insatiable. There was no going back after last night. But I could relax this time. It was safer—she was mine for now. We had an agreement with parameters, a mutually beneficial one.

I eased my hand under her T-shirt and stroked her flat belly, my hand rising up to her luscious breasts. She sat up and took the shirt off, and I laid against her hot skin, playing with her nipples, alternately sucking and blowing on them. She arched her back, her nipples hardening and elongating beneath my touch. Then I slid my hand down and swirled my fingers against her clitoris, pinching and rolling it between my fingers until she was moaning and slick with wetness.

By that time, my cock was enormous and heavy against her. I was about to burst.

She turned to look at me, and for a moment, her eyes looked sad. I was going to fuck that sadness out of her, make her forget it—especially if I was the one who'd caused it. She pulled down my pants, and I eased out of my shirt. Then I swung my knee over her and put my cock against her slit. I rubbed myself against her slowly, lazily getting myself lubricated. She grabbed me and rubbed me against her, getting my hard length slick.

"Tell me you want me," I said, my voice thick.

"I want you. I fucking want you, James," she said.

I couldn't wait any more. I entered her swiftly and without preamble. She was more than ready for me, slick with wetness. I slid all the way in, to the base of my shaft, and we both moaned as her body opened up to accommodate me. I fit tightly within her. "Fuck, oh fuck Audrey—that's good."

I drove long, hard thrusts into her. It felt so good. She dug her nails into my ass, driving me in even further. I could feel her clench, trying to squeeze everything out of me. Being inside her again was making me crazy. It was as if her sweet, tight body was made for mine.

I wrapped my arms around her and covered her body with mine, claiming her with each thrust. I wanted to own her and possess her.

"Tell me you want me. And only me," I said, out of my mind.

I could tell she was close. Her body clenched around me, shaking. "I only want you. I only ever want you." The way she said it, I believed her. That made me feverish, and I continued to drive into her ruthlessly, taking us both right to the edge. "James," she cried. "James—"

My name on her lips was all I needed to hear. I felt so out of control. I came in her, hard, my hips still thrusting as she cried out and shook beneath me. I pumped into her over and over, until my orgasm had subsided and I was spent.

She'd come back.

She'd come back because I was paying her.

But still, she'd come back.

I crushed her to me, willing myself to stop thinking, not ever wanting to let her go.

# AUDREY

We stayed in bed for the rest of the day. The Red Sox managed to win. I now knew where I stood with James. Even though I'd felt as if he'd broken my heart this morning, his clumsy explanation about his feelings put it back together again. And then subsequently melted it.

He was a John, but he was the best John ever. He'd fucked me like I'd never been fucked before, and I was going to make enough money to keep Tommy in New Horizons for the near future and then some. I had the next nine days to look forward to with James, nine days of luxury and pleasure.

In theory, I should be sitting back and relaxing, counting all my money and all my orgasms. In practice, I felt as if my heart was about to break all over again. And this time, all James's money and all James's sexual dexterity wouldn't be able to put it back together again.

I was in love with him. The realization spread over me with sick dread as I was getting dressed for the evening and James was taking a shower. He was an assignment that was only going to last one more week, and I was in love with him. I looked at myself in the mirror and laughed. *I sure know how to pick 'em,* I thought. It just figured. I finally fell in love and it was never going to happen. That was typical Audrey Reynolds luck.

Not only that, but I was finally going to have enough money to make things okay, all the things I'd been wishing for. And now I wouldn't even be able to enjoy it. Because I was in love with James Preston, and he was going to leave my world next week, and my life was going to be ruined forever.

*Way to go, Audrey.*

My phone beeped, and I got up to look at it. It was a text from my mom. *Shit.* It was never good when my mom came looking for me. She either wanted money, or she was in trouble, or she wanted money because she was in trouble. But I wanted to make sure there wasn't anything wrong with Tommy, so I called her back.

"Audrey," she said immediately.

"Everything okay?" I asked, not bothering to say hello either.

"No, it is not," she said. "I got into a car accident earlier, and the Sentra's totaled."

"Was everyone all right?" I asked. I meant, *were you high, and did you kill anybody?*

"I'm fine," she said. "I just ran off the road and hit some construction stuff that the stupid city workers left there. Can you imagine that? Just leaving concrete tubes and jackhammers and shit everywhere? It totaled my car!"

"It was on the side of the road, Ma. Not *in* the road." I sighed. My mother always had a problem, and someone else had always caused it. I don't think I'd ever heard her say she was responsible for one thing that had gone wrong in her life, not ever.

"So where's the car?" I asked.

"I left it there."

"Where are you?"

"I'm at a bar," she said. Of course she was. I knew my mother. She was going to have a few drinks and tell the cops she'd been at a bar, drinking—*after* she'd totaled her car. They'd never be able to prove that she'd been drinking before, too, although they would expect as much. The cops knew my mom, and my mom knew the cops.

"Did you call anybody?" I asked.

"No. That wouldn't have been a great idea," she said. That was as close as she would come to admitting she'd been drunk earlier. "So I'm just in here for an hour. I'm gonna have a couple of drinks and then I'll call them."

"They might find you before that, Ma."

"Whatever," she said. She was muffled for a bit, and I heard her lighting a cigarette. "Hey, I talked to the clerk at Tommy's center. She said you'd paid ahead through August. Business must be pretty good, huh?"

"It was a one-off. There's no more money," I said, bristling. I was disgusted that my mother was happy I was making money as a prostitute. I was even more disgusted by her tone—the one that told me she was going to be asking me for some of that money soon. "I gotta run. Be safe."

"Have fun," she said, and it made my skin crawl.

James came in then, a towel wrapped around his waist. "Who was that?"

"No one," I said, and I meant it.

JAMES HAD ON ANOTHER dazzling suit, this time with a lavender tie. "What should *I* wear?" I asked, going through the racks of designer clothes in my closet. I wasn't used to this many choices.

"That dress you had on last night worked for me," he said, grinning.

"I'm pretty sure that's dirty," I said and smiled back at him. "Plus, I don't want to wear anything that's going to have us going at it under the table again. I don't think your mother would approve." I pulled out a conservative grey sheath and showed it to him. "What about this?"

"It's fine," he said. "But we'll still probably go at it. It doesn't matter what you wear. I know what you look like underneath—and I *like* it." I went to him and kissed him on the lips, dropping the dress onto the bed. He wrapped his arms around me and kissed me back, hard, and that wasn't the only thing that was hard.

I ran my hands over him, relishing the feel of his enormous, sculpted chest, but then I stepped back. "Too bad we don't have time for that right now," I said innocently. "You have to be photographed for your *New England Brides Magazine* spread."

He sighed raggedly. "This fucking wedding."

I started to put the grey dress on. "I don't know—I'm enjoying it so far," I said, and I meant it.

He came and zipped up the back for me. "I am, too. And that was the last thing I expected." He ran his hand gently down my back, sending shivers through me.

His phone buzzed, and he grabbed it, reading the screen intently. "I have to deal with this. Sorry," he said, and started quickly tapping out messages on his phone. "But we have to get going, too."

I put on some metallic sandals, lipstick, and a bunch of bangles. Then I grabbed his hand, leading him to the elevator and out to the car while he dealt with his business. It was beautiful outside, and Kai was waiting with a friendly smile. James was holding my hand while he barked into his phone. It all seemed so normal, so natural. For one moment, I imagined that this was my real life, and I was his real girlfriend.

It was perfect. It was absofuckinglutely perfect.

He was on his call during the drive to the Isabella Stewart Gardner Museum, where the photo shoot was taking place. I took the time to look at my phone, worried that my mother had managed to end up in jail.

To my surprise, I had three voicemails. The first was from my mother. "Audrey, they towed the car, and I can't afford to get it. Call me. Please."

The second was from Elena. "Dre, call me as soon as you get this. On my cell."

I looked over at James, and he was still on his phone, listening intently to something. Blowing out a shaky breath, I called her back immediately. "Dre," she said after it had barely started to ring.

"Hi, Elena," I said nervously. She rarely, if ever, called us while we were on a job. "What's up?"

"Your *mother* is what's up," she said. "She came by the office this afternoon. She said she knew you'd made big money recently and that she needed some of it."

All the blood drained from my face. "Elena, I'm so sorry," I said.

"It gets better. I told her that she was not welcome in our office. She smelled, Dre. She was butt-ass drunk in broad daylight, and she was belligerent. I proceeded to tell her that you were making your regular salary and that I didn't know anything else, and then I asked her to leave."

"What happened then?" I asked.

"She went into the bathroom and stole a bunch of those mini hand soaps," Elena said, sighing. "Then she left. But I have a bad feeling she'll be back again tomorrow. Dre, I can't have this sort of drama associated with my business. I run a *luxury* company. I can't have your alcoholic, bag-lady-looking mother coming in and yelling at me in front of clients."

"I know," I said. I could feel myself turning crimson red. My mother had been ruining things for me since I was a child. I was so ashamed of her. For years, I'd felt bad because of that shame. I'd always felt as if I should be spending my time trying to help her more, not being embarrassed by her.

But now I was a grown woman, and I'd been taking care of myself for a long time. And I'd also taken care of Tommy because she couldn't—and she never had. I'd seen her ruin everything that she touched, take advantage of everyone who came into contact with her. And now she was threatening my livelihood, the livelihood that was keeping her son healthy and safe.

I didn't feel bad anymore that I was ashamed of her. She was worthy of my shame.

"I'll talk to her," I said. "She won't be coming back."

"I need you to take care of this and still take care of our most prestigious client. Don't let your personal problems get in the way, Dre."

"I won't," I mumbled. "I promise."

I hung up and nervously checked my third voicemail. It was from Reina, one of the clerks at New Horizons. "Hey Dre, just wanted to let you know that your mom stopped by this afternoon. I need to talk to you about your account. Give me a quick call when you have a second."

We pulled up in front of the museum. James was still on the phone, talking lowly. I hopped out of the car and called her back immediately, a pit of dread forming in my stomach. "Hey, Reina. It's Audrey Reynolds. Is something wrong?"

"You need to change Tommy's account here, hon," she said. "Your mother is listed as a responsible party for him, in addition to you. She came in today and demanded that we refund some of the money you prepaid on his account. I couldn't do it, because the manager had already gone, but I wanted to give you a heads up."

"She didn't. Please tell me she didn't do that," I said, my stomach sinking. But it was true, and I knew it: that was just like my mother. She would take Tommy's rent money for herself. She really was that low.

"Sorry, hon," Reina said. "I just thought you'd want to know."

I thanked her and hung up, my hands shaking.

And then I turned to find James, standing on the sidewalk next to me, a worried look on his face.

# JAMES

"*What's* wrong?" I could tell that the phone call had made her upset.

"Nothing," she said and shrugged. "Work stuff."

I just looked at her for a beat. "I can tell you're upset," I said. "You can talk to me about it, you know."

She nodded at me. "I know. Maybe after this." She waved toward the museum entrance.

"Okay. If you're sure." I didn't want to push her. She would tell me when she was ready, I hoped. I grabbed her hand and led her inside.

The Gardner Museum was gorgeous. It had an inner courtyard that looked like an English garden. I'd always loved it. As children, the Guatemalan nannies had been under strict orders to bring Todd and me here on a regular basis. We used to go back and forth between the Gardner and the Museum of Fine Arts, located a few blocks away. My mother thought it was important that we were cultured. So she left the instructions and went to lunch with her lady friends, and one nanny after another cultured us.

We went out to the middle of the courtyard, the ceiling soaring high above us. I saw Evie and her cousins all in fancy beaded dresses, sitting in an arrangement and having their hair and makeup fussed with. My family also was nearby, as was the camera crew and all their equipment.

I ignored everyone but Audrey. I watched her take in the glory of the space. "Oh. Wow," she said, looking dazzled. "I've never been here before."

"It's perfect," I said, and I didn't mean the garden. I squeezed her hands and drank her in. She was so beautiful, it was as if it cut me.

"I love it here," she said, still looking around, dazzled. "I've never seen anything like this."

"We should come back here sometime," I said. I drew her to me and kissed the top of her head. She didn't say anything, but she hugged me, hard.

Todd came over, a hesitant smile on his face. "Hey, guys. I hate to interrupt."

"So don't," I said, not letting go of Audrey.

Todd's eyes widened a little, but he knew better than to say anything. He looked at me for a beat, studying my face, the way I was holding her.

I pulled back from her and gave him a wary smile. I needed to deflect attention from us. "Are they ready for me?" I asked, motioning to the camera crew.

"For both of you," Todd said. He rubbed Audrey's arm in greeting and beamed at her. "We want you both in the pictures."

Audrey smoothed her dress and looked at me nervously. "I don't need to be included, Todd. That's really nice of you, though."

"Nonsense. I insist. I want to remember everything about this time in my life, including you," he said, holding out his arm for her.

"Okay," Audrey said hesitantly. She smiled at him. Clearly, Todd had gotten the lion's share of our family's limited charm genes.

Pleased, I squeezed her hand in reassurance. We went over to my parents. Celia was watching us as closely as ever.

"Hello, Mother," I said.

"Hello, James," she said formally, mocking me. She turned to Audrey, inspecting her from head to toe. "And how are you this evening, dear? You're looking very… satisfied."

My mother was an astute observer. Plus, she'd been next to us at dinner last night. Looking at Audrey right now, I could see what my mother must have seen: Audrey's skin was positively glowing, as if her every cell was lit up.

Audrey smiled at her without missing a beat. "I *am* very satisfied," she said kindly and without irony. "Your son has been showing me a wonderful time."

"I'm so sure," Celia said, and she did not look pleased.

"Okay everyone, it's time," Todd called, breaking up the conversation and saving us. "We're going to start with our family on one side of the fountain, Evie's family on the other." He grabbed Audrey's arm and steered her toward the photographers, chatting happily.

My mother watched him, the look on her face shifting quickly from surprise to utter indignation. "These are family photographs. Where is *she* going?"

I gave her a savage smile and grabbed her arm, following after them.

"With the rest of us, mother," I said loud enough for Audrey to hear. "My girlfriend is going to be in these pictures." I unceremoniously dropped my mother in front. Todd winked at me as I went toward the back and grabbed a stunned Audrey's hand.

I held it for every photograph they took.

"WELL, THAT WAS... INTERESTING," Audrey said when we were back in the car. "I thought your mother was rooting for me for at least the rest of the wedding celebration, but now I'm pretty sure I'm on her radar. Her *bad* radar."

"Oh, well." I shrugged, not giving a fuck about my mother or her radar for the moment.

"And you didn't have to say I was your girlfriend," she said. I watched as a hot blush crept up her neck.

I played with her hair, brushing it off her face. "Yes, I did."

"No, you didn't."

"Audrey." I waited until she turned to look at me. "Not only am I paying you to act like my girlfriend, I wanted to say it. So let's leave it at that, okay?"

"Okay," she mumbled and looked out the window.

"Are you going to tell me about before? What that phone call was about?"

She sighed. "Honestly, you don't want to know."

"I can't help you if I don't know what the problem is."

"That's okay—it's not your problem. It's mine, and I'll deal with it." She took out her phone and looked at it. "I have a voicemail," she said miserably. "I have to listen to it." She was quiet for a minute, her brow furrowed. When she hung up the phone, she looked pale.

"What is it?" I asked.

"Do you think Kai can take me somewhere after this? I have to deal with something," she said in a small voice.

"Of course," I said. "I'm coming, too."

She looked at me, her face reddening some more. "No, James. Please. You've seen enough. Let me handle this by myself."

"Is it a guy?" I asked. I was suddenly, unmercifully angry.

"No," she said, shaking her head. "I wish."

"Then what?" I was surprised by the frustration in my own voice. I wanted her to stop being so stubborn, to stop holding back from me.

Audrey sighed. "It's my mother, James. She's just causing trouble. I need to go see her tonight."

I was relieved it wasn't a guy, some boyfriend I didn't know about. I was also relieved that she'd told me. My anger eased back a bit. "Fine," I said. "But I'm coming, too."

FOR SOME INEXPLICABLE REASON, Cole was at the bar waiting for us, looking like the cat who'd just swallowed the canary. "I didn't invite you here," I said, clapping him on the back. "But it's nice to see you anyway."

"Todd texted me," Cole said. "He wants me to come to everything I can. He said he wants to make you happy."

"Aw, that's sweet," I said. I inspected him further. "You're looking smugger than usual," I said, making sure that Audrey was tucked safely behind me. "Why's that?"

Cole beamed at me. "That's why." Cole pointed to a woman hustling into the room. She was walking fast and applying lip gloss, her curls bouncing and her voluptuous chest jiggling as she went.

It was Jenny.

"Ho my frickin' God!" Jenny shouted when she saw Audrey. She practically bowled me out of the way to get to her.

"Yay!" she yelled, grabbing Audrey into a hug and jumping up and down. "You got me my own billionaire! I'm so freaking excited!"

"Oh, Jesus." I said to Cole. "You didn't."

"Yes, I did. Ho my frickin' God, I did," he said. He looked very pleased with himself. "I'm gonna marry this girl. She's got a mouth like a—"

"Cole," I said, cutting him off. "My mother is ten feet away from us. Please."

"I don't have to finish the sentence, anyway," Cole said. He was watching Jenny. "You know what I mean."

I sighed. "I can guess." We stood and watched the girls talking excitedly to each other.

"You're the one who told me to call her," Cole reminded me.

"I didn't mean for you to bring an escort to my brother's wedding functions," I said.

He raised an eyebrow at me. "You should talk, bro."

I glared at him, but I didn't mean it. "Buy me a free drink. I need one." He motioned for the bartender. "I'm happy you're here and that Jenny's working out for you. But I need to protect Audrey. No one but you knows the truth. It has to stay that way." Cole slid a martini in front of me, and I ordered some wine for Audrey.

"Of course. I promise I won't say anything about either of them," he said. "I wouldn't do that to you—you know that. But I have to say, for the hired help, you're being very protective of her."

"She needs my protection," I said darkly. I took a sip of my drink, and the vodka warmed me instantly. "She's a sweet girl. I know that sounds ridiculous, but it's true."

"It doesn't sound ridiculous. But what are you going to do after this is all over?"

I shrugged. "Probably nothing."

"*That* sounds ridiculous," Cole said. "And I'm only saying that because you're my best friend."

"Sometimes I think I need to protect her from myself," I said lowly.

Cole looked as if he was going to say something admonishing, but Jenny and Audrey came to the bar then, still happily chatting. I put my arm around Audrey and pulled her to me, kissing the top of her head. The two minutes we'd been apart were too long. Cole looked at me, reading me like a book, and just shook his head in mock disgust.

"I didn't know you owned part of the Rhode Island Thunder, Cole. Jenny just told me. That's so cool," Audrey said.

The Thunder was the NHL farm team that Cole was currently obsessed with. "We have box seats tonight," Jenny squealed. Cole put his arm around her and squeezed her against him.

"We can have box seats whenever you want, Princess," he said and kissed her on the nose. Jenny smiled at Cole happily, and he beamed down at her. I didn't know how sophisticated Jenny was, or how well she could read people. But I hoped she knew that Cole was a player, through and through. He would be happy to play with her and spoil her for a while, but he was not a one-woman man. Never had been.

Jenny snuggled up against Cole, and Audrey watched her friend carefully. "Jenny, come to the bathroom with me," she said after a while, grabbing her by the hand. She flashed a dimpled smile at us. "We'll be back in a few, guys."

"What's that all about?" Cole asked, watching Audrey drag Jenny away from him.

"I think Jenny's going to get a talking to," I said.

"About what?"

"Not getting her hopes up about the billionaire with the box seats," I said.

"Huh," Cole said, watching them retreat.

# AUDREY

I steered Jenny past the ladies' room, down the hall to the empty coat check. I looked around carefully, making sure that no one from James's family was nearby or could see us. "Jenny," I said gently. "Cole hired you through AccommoDating, right?"

"Of course," she said.

"He seems like a nice guy."

"He's *awesome*, Dre. We've been having so much fun." She beamed at me and grabbed my hands. "Thank you for doing this for me. Elena's so happy that James sent her a referral. I told her I was going to rock Cole's world and make him a regular."

"Okay," I said. "I just want to make sure, though..."

"What?"

"That you don't think he's gonna buy you, or anything," I said miserably. "The way you were looking at him out there—"

"Aw, Dre, c'mon!" She said. She was laughing at me. "This isn't my first date. You don't think I have an actual *crush* on Cole Bryson, do you?"

"Don't you?" I asked, dumbfounded.

Jenny shrugged. She looked exasperated. "I like his wallet. I like his thick cock. I like his box seats. I like batting him around like a cat toy."

"You don't like *him*?"

"Oh yeah—I like him, all right. Who the fuck wouldn't? He's wicked hot, and he's a billionaire! But he's a *John*, Dre. He's paying for me to do whatever he wants. And he wants to do lots of things, let me tell you. He's nasty, and I like it." She paused to fluff her hair.

"But just because I'm enjoying myself doesn't make it any less of a job. Or any more than a job. I mean—oh, you know what I mean."

My heart sank, and I nodded at her. "I know exactly what you mean."

"Enough about me. I can take care of myself." She looked at me with her big, blue eyes. "How's it going with Mr. Sex in a Suit?"

"Great," I said noncommittally.

"He *did* fuck, you, right? I saw you two out there."

"He fucked me," I said. "We fucked."

"Was it that bad?" Jenny was looking at me as if I had three heads. "Dre, are you going to cry or something?"

"No," I said, but my eyes were totally filling with tears. I blotted them carefully. "Jenny, I can't cry. His whole family is out there. And they can't know how we know each other, either."

"Okay," she said. "We can handle that. I've had to lie to so many wives and girlfriends that the lies just spring out, Dre. And they're usually pretty good. Don't worry about that part. But we *do* need to worry about those tears. Tell me what's going on."

I shook my head almost violently. "I can't. I can't talk about it."

"He hit you or something? Is he some kind of freak?"

"Nope," I said.

She played gently with my hair. "You cross some kind of line with yourself?" she asked.

I probably never gave Jenny enough credit for being smart. "Something like that." I sniffed.

"S'okay, Dre. That happens to everybody."

She hugged me. "The thing is, nobody knows what those lines are but you. That's why it's awesome that feelings and thoughts are *invisible*. They're like magic. Nobody knows the truth but you, okay? You're safe."

"Okay." I sniffled some more.

"So you do what you think is right. And remember, if it gets too bad, just close your eyes."

"'Cause then it's like it never happened," I finished for her. "Jenny, I probably haven't told you this lately, but you're smart."

"I know," she said. "It's my secret weapon." She gave me a long look. "And Dre—just because it's not gonna happen for me, doesn't mean it's not gonna happen for you."

"What?" I asked.

"You know."

I shrugged. I knew exactly what she meant. "Jenny, it's *not* gonna happen for me."

She shook her head and pointed at herself. "No billionaire's gonna buy *me*. 'Cause I'm a whore, Dre, and I don't even feel bad about it. But you're different. You're doing this to take care of your brother. You're actually a good girl. Mr. Suit knows that. I can tell."

"He's not going to buy me," I said miserably.

"He might." She grinned at me and shrugged. "Crazier shit's happened, that's for sure."

"What about you and Cole?"

"I am going to suck him as dry as I can—him and his wallet."

I finished drying my eyes, and she linked her arm through mine. "You ready?" she asked.

I nodded.

"Then let's go bat some billionaires around like cat toys," she said and gave me a wicked grin.

OUR LITTLE GROUP was quite popular that evening. Everyone wanted to have a drink with the two gorgeous billionaires and their super-hot, mysterious dates. Even Evie seemed impressed. "You own part of the Thunder?" Evie asked, her flat chest pressed out toward Cole. She was looking at him as if he was some sort of rock-star, farm-team-owning Greek god.

"Yeah, he does," Jenny said, stepping forward in front of Cole. She thrust out her much more formidable chest, as if daring Evie to come closer.

Evie was about to say something back when Todd interrupted. "Are you flirting with the best man's best friend?" he asked his fiancée. They were both slurring their words a little; the cocktail 'hour' had been going for three hours straight.

Evie tossed her hair and narrowed her eyes at him. "Sorry, baby," she said in what sounded like her version of a sexy voice.

"Old habits die hard."

"You mean once a slutty sorority girl, always a slutty sorority girl?" Todd asked, grinning at her.

"That's exactly what I mean." She grabbed his tie and pulled him in for a quick, hot kiss. Todd lifted her up, and she wrapped her legs around him. They headed to a dark corner for some serious making out and grinding.

"They're drunk," Cole said and laughed.

"They're *happy*," I said, surprised. I turned to James. "They're actually good together."

James stood up taller and watched them making out in the corner, a bemused look on his face. "He likes her slutty sorority girl act. You just might be right," he said.

Meanwhile, sparks were still flying in our little circle. "You are so hot when you fight for me," Cole said to Jenny. He took another sip of his martini and looked at her with hooded eyes.

"That wasn't even a fight," Jenny said. She tossed her hair. "If you want to see me throw down, just bring that bitch back here."

Cole looked impressed. "That's so hot—that's the *bride*, Jenny. You gonna fight the bride for me?"

"I would, baby," she cooed, pressing herself against him. They started seriously making out then, with Cole's hands all over Jenny's ass. James and I just looked at each other, somewhere between mortified and amused.

Celia Preston was not impressed, however. She motioned for us to come over. We both took large swigs of our drinks before we went. "Who is that girl with Cole Bryson tonight?" she asked, watching them dry-hump next to the bar.

"That's Jenny," James said matter-of-factly. "They're dating."

"If that's what you want to call it." Celia turned to me. "Do you know this Jenny? She seemed excited to see you."

"I met her last night. We went out for after-dinner drinks," I said, watching James out of the corner of my eye.

"We met them," James said, nodding. "For drinks after dinner."

"Is he bringing her to the wedding?" Celia asked, scowling at them as they became more entangled.

"I hope so," James said. "Otherwise, Todd and Evie will be the only ones having inappropriate physical displays in public." James pointed them out in the far corner, still playing Slutty Sorority Girl and Her Jealous Boyfriend.

Celia frowned. "I think I should have had more substantial food served at this thing," she said mostly to herself.

"Live and learn, Mother," James said. "Live and learn."

WE SNUCK OUT after Celia was interrupted by one of her friends, asking about which red wine on the list had the most antioxidants.

I winked at Jenny on the way out, and she gave me a thumbs-up. Cole still had his hands on her ass.

"I think he really likes her," James said as we slid into the car. "I don't think he's pretending."

"What's not to like?" I asked. "She's gorgeous, she's young, and she's smart." He looked at me skeptically. "No, James—she's actually really smart. One of her many talents is hiding it."

"My brother and Evie were also entertaining tonight," James said.

"You know what? I think they're actually in love," I said. "Todd seems really excited about getting married. And Evie definitely seemed into him tonight… if he can live with what happened and accept her for who she is, maybe you can, too."

James snorted.

"I'm just pointing that out to you," I said in a know-it-all voice.

"We'll see," he said. At least it was something.

I sighed. "I have to deal with my mother." I gave Kai my mother's address in East Boston, and he sped silently through the night. "I wish we could just go home," I said. "I mean—your home."

James put his arm around me. "Do you want to tell me what's happening?"

"Nope," I said. *Because then you'd try to fix it, and it's my cross to bear.*

James sighed and sat back. "What do I have to do to get you to trust me? This is safe," he said, pointing between us. "You can tell me anything. It's not like we have to hide anything from each other."

"I'll trust you when you trust me," I said. "I seem to remember you have some things you're keeping to yourself." I thought he would move away from me then, but instead, he pulled me closer.

"The things I'm keeping from you I've kept from everybody," he said. "You shouldn't take it personally."

"Same for me," I said. "There's just some stuff that no one else needs to know."

"But what if I want to know?" James asked. He tucked my hair behind my ear. "What if I want to know who you are?"

"So you can fire me again?" I asked. He narrowed his eyes at me. "I'm kidding—*relax*," I said.

"And I feel the same way about you... but James, don't you kind of wonder what the point is? We're only going to know each other for another week." The thought made my heart lurch.

James looked down at our entwined hands. "Maybe the point is that we care about each other, even if it's just right for now. I don't care about too many people, Audrey. It's a very short list."

My heart lurched again, and I grimaced. *Don't tell me things like that,* I thought.

"I care about you, too," I said.

*Stupid, stupid, stupid,* I fumed at myself.

He kissed my forehead. "Then that's reason enough."

Kai pulled up outside my mother's building. "Saved by the bell. I guess we can't talk anymore—we're here," I said, relieved.

"I'm going in with you," James said.

"I need you to stay here. I have to do this by myself." I looked at my watch: it was nine o'clock. My mother was definitely drunk and most likely belligerent at this hour. It was nothing I wanted James to see. "Please."

"Is it safe?" he asked, nodding toward her run-down apartment complex.

"This is where I grew up. It's my mother. I'll be fine—and I'll be right back." Kai opened the door for me, and I got out.

"Audrey." I leaned back down to look at him. "I'll be waiting for you."

I sighed and quickly headed up the stairs to my mother's entrance, not looking back at the car. I didn't want him to be here, near the ugliness my mother always caused. I knocked on her door but there was no answer; the lights were on, though, so I tried the door. It opened, and I took one last deep breath of clean air before I went inside.

There she was at the kitchen table, next to an overflowing ashtray, smoking as if she were going to the electric chair. "Hey, Ma," I said through the haze of smoke.

"Well, if it isn't Little Miss High and Mighty. You're looking fancy," she said. "Nice of you to finally show up." Her hair was long and thin, with bleached ends and long, oily-looking roots. She'd been pretty once. Now her skin was red and mottled from too many Boston winters and too many Marlboro Lights.

"You were waiting for me?" I asked.

"You know I got into an accident today. You know they towed my car and that I don't have any money."

I would have felt bad for her then, had I not known any better. She didn't want my sympathy. She wanted my money.

"No offense, Ma—but how is that my problem exactly?" It wasn't what I should have said. But the half-empty bottle of Jack Daniels on the table and the fact that she'd tried to take money from New Horizons today pushed me over the edge.

"I don't know why a hooker thinks she's better than her own mother. At least I worked an honest job," she said. She had that nasty tone in her voice, the one that said she was just itching for a fight.

"You haven't had an honest job in a long time," I reminded her. "Last time I checked, your job was drinking, smoking, and trying to get by on other people's money."

She looked up at me, a triumphant smile on her face. "At least I'm not gettin' by on other people's dicks."

"Yes, you are," I said. It was sad, but her words didn't even faze me anymore. "You have one nasty man after another up here, and that's how you pay your rent and buy your cigarettes."

"What do you know about it?" she snapped.

"I know all about it. I'm a whore, too," I said flatly. "It takes one to know one."

She stood up, her hands curled into fists, ready to come after me. It certainly wouldn't be the first time, but I didn't want to get into it with her tonight. I wanted to defuse her and put her on the back burner of my life, where she would stay out of trouble for the imminent future, maybe forever.

As usual, I was doing a crap job of that.

"How much do you need," I said. It was a statement, not a question.

"Two thousand dollars," she said. She uncurled her fists, but she didn't bother looking like she was sorry.

"I can give it to you, but there are conditions," I said, pacing around the grimy kitchen. "First, do not *ever* go and try to get money from New Horizons again. That money is for Tommy. *Your son.* He needs it more than you and me put together. That's why I'm working so much. Please don't ever do that again. Promise me."

She nodded. I wasn't sure if I could believe her, but there wasn't anything I could do about that right now.

"Second, you can't ever go to my office again. My boss would have fired me today, except I'm on a job."

She snorted and lit another cigarette. "That boss of yours thinks her shit doesn't stink. I had a mind today to tell that beaver chomper—"

"Please don't call her a beaver chomper," I interrupted, "and just don't ever go there again. She said she'd fire me if you do. She meant it. If you want to keep crashing your cars up, getting bailed out of jail, and borrowing money for the rest of your life, I sort of need a job, okay? So lay off."

"Fine." She blew out a cloud of smoke in my direction.

I didn't know what I'd ever done to her to make her hate me, but she did. She didn't hate Tommy—she didn't take good care of him, but she at least ruffled his hair occasionally. But not me. Maybe it was just a complete and utter lack of love that I felt from her.

She was like the sun on a sub-zero day: she was there, but she gave no warmth. It was as if I'd come along and ruined her party just by being born, and now I had to pay. And pay. And pay. I took out my wallet and handed her the cash. It was the only money I'd kept from the advance. It was supposed to go toward rent, but there was nothing I could do about that right now.

Except go back to work.

"Bye, Ma," I said.

She stuffed the money into her pocket and nodded at me. "See ya. Have fun in that fancy outfit." The way she said it made me feel dirty.

I couldn't wait to flee the smoke and everything else. I threw the door open, eager to breathe in the fresh air.

And there stood James Preston on the landing, just standing there, waiting for me.

# JAMES

I caught a glimpse of the mother. She was about Audrey's height, but that was where the resemblance ended. I saw a barrel chest, stringy bleached hair, and a face that had seen too many Tequila Sunrises.

"Hey," Audrey said, closing the door behind her quickly. "I told you not to come up."

"I wanted to be here if you needed me," I said. I pulled her to me protectively as we headed down the stairs.

"Did that go okay?" I asked. I had no idea what "okay" meant in this circumstance, but it was the only thing I could think of to say.

She shrugged. "It was typical. It was fine."

"What does that mean, Audrey?"

She slid into the car and sighed. "Can I please have some bourbon?"

"Of course." I poured her a glass and watched her take a shaky sip.

"You know, I thought I'd never drink. After growing up with my mom the way she was." She shrugged. "But my mother taught me what it actually means to *need* a drink."

I poured myself one and clinked her glass. "Cheers to that." We watched the city lights as we sped from East Boston back through the Financial District. "Audrey. I know you don't want to tell me what your mother wanted, but I wish you would."

She stared out the window, the tension obvious in her shoulders. "She just needed money. Her car got… towed. That's all."

"Does she always ask you for money?"

"She doesn't always ask, James."

"Ah," I said. "So she's an alcoholic, and she's a problem."

"She's an alcoholic, and she's a problem." She smiled at me bravely. "Just another sob story from your friendly neighborhood escort."

I put my arm around her and pulled her to me. I didn't know what to say, so I said nothing. I just held her close and hoped that made it a little better.

I MADE LOVE TO HER again that night, slowly. We didn't say a word. I understood her body now, what she wanted, and all I wanted was to be inside her. We came at the same time. As I spent myself into her she called my name again. It left me with a deep ache, a yearning. I didn't know what that was, and I didn't know what to do with it. So I just wrapped myself around her as if she were mine, holding her from behind while we slept.

But she wasn't mine. *It's like a timeshare, baby. No one gets to own me. You just get to stay a while.* Her words echoed in my head as I drifted off to sleep. I hated those crude words. I hated the truth behind them...

I woke up the next morning pressed against her, hard again. She moved closer in her sleep, but I rolled over, not letting my erection overtake my thoughts. Today was the day of the rehearsal dinner. Tomorrow was the wedding. Then, Eleuthera.

Then, no more Audrey.

I looked at her naked back, rising and falling with her breath. She was too young to have dealt with everything that had been thrown her way. I hadn't let myself really dwell on the fact that she was a hooker. *She was a hooker.* I wouldn't even let myself imagine all the men she'd been with.

*Probably not as many women as you've been with, asshole,* I thought. That was true. And I'd only ever had feelings for one of them.

Now, two.

But when I thought about Danielle, what had happened... I shuddered. I couldn't let anyone down like that again. I didn't trust myself with another person's heart.

*Fuck,* I thought, and rolled back over. My erection pressed against Audrey, demanding and fierce. But what was I going to do? Move back to Boston so I could date my escort? Relocate her to

California so I could put her up in a condo and see her whenever I liked, keeping her from my family and the rest of the world?

My family would never accept her, even as the fake orphan/ graduate-school student she was pretending to be. Even buoyed by that lie, she wasn't good enough. If they found out she was an escort from a destitute family, they would hate her. My mother would make her life a living hell.

Audrey's background didn't matter to me—neither did my family's opinion. But they would never treat her like a Preston. Even if I could accept that, it would be cruel to ask her to.

My head was spinning. I pressed my forehead against her back, trying to block out my swirling thoughts. *This is why I didn't want a relationship,* I thought. *Too many fucking issues.*

She woke up then, turning over to me and smiling. "Hey," she said, a blush creeping up her neck.

The only escort in the history of escorts who blushed. She was adorable.

Any thoughts I'd just been having about issues vanished when she smiled at me like that. "Hey," I said and leaned down and kissed her.

She looked at me, sheepish. "I really need to brush my teeth."

She went to get up, but I grabbed her arm. "Don't," I said. "Don't go."

Audrey looked at me, confused for a second, and then settled back down on the bed. She moved her body against my hardness. "Ah," she said. "Do you need some services rendered, sir?" she wrapped her hand around my hard length and squeezed.

I sucked in my breath, hard. Maybe if I buried myself in her again, an answer about what to do would present itself.

Even if it wouldn't, I had to get back in there.

I kissed her again urgently. "Yes. But I'm going to be the one doing the rendering. Lie back," I growled.

AUDREY'S PHONE KEPT BEEPING while she was in the shower. I went into the steamy bathroom to tell her and also as an excuse to watch her.

"Audrey. Your phone." I could see her glorious silhouette, her ass and thighs tight and muscular. My cock stirred again. *Down boy,* I thought. We'd done it twice already this morning. We had to get dressed and eat at some point, even if I never wanted either one of us to leave that bed again.

"I'll get it in a minute. Thank you," she called, rinsing her hair.

I dragged myself out of the bathroom, away from her, her phone still in my hand. It was a funny looking old thing, with a keyboard you could pull out. It beeped again.

I wanted to check it to see if it was her mother.

*You want to check it to see if it's a guy,* I thought. She hadn't mentioned any sort of a relationship, but then, why would she? It beeped again. I could still hear her in the shower.

I hit a button and the screen lit up.

It was a message from someone named Reina. *Your mother came in this morning and withdrew money,* it said. *The manager had to ok it. I'm so sorry.*

The fact that it wasn't a guy was where the good news ended. Was this from a manager at Audrey's bank? Or something else? I put her phone down and paced for a minute. Audrey had given her mother money last night. But maybe it wasn't enough, or maybe something had happened that wasn't to her mother's liking.

I remembered what Audrey's face looked like yesterday afternoon when she'd been on the phone in front of the museum. Pale, cold, and furious.

Furious. Audrey was gentle, but something had made her beyond angry.

I immediately called Kai. "What's the name of the place Audrey had you take her the other morning? Where her brother lives?"

"New Horizons, sir. In South Boston."

"I'll be down in five minutes. Have the car waiting."

# AUDREY

"*Audrey*," James called.

"Huh?" I asked. There was soap in my ears. I was using his Argan oil body wash on every available surface of my body. It smelled like him and literally made my mouth water.

"I have to run out." I thought that's what he said, anyway.

Maybe I shouldn't have used so much in my ears. "Okay," I responded.

"Okay," he called. "I'll be back in an hour. Have some coffee."

"Okay," I said. I wanted to add *babe*. Or *honey*. Or *I love you, please don't leave me*. But common sense told me that would be very stupid, so I just kept rinsing.

"Audrey." He opened the shower door a little and I was careful not to splash him. "Did you hear me? I wish I could come in there, but I have to run out. I'll be back soon." He leaned in and gave me a quick, hot kiss that melted my insides. His hair got sprayed with water, and he gave me a devilish smile, closing the door behind him and leaving me.

Thinking about that smile, and what he'd done to me earlier that morning with his mouth, made me pant. Which made me get water from the shower in my mouth. Which made me cough.

Which was the only thing that made me glad he was gone. I hacked and spluttered, getting out of the shower and wrapping an enormous, incredibly soft towel around myself. I dried my hair, combing it out carefully as I went. Then I searched for my phone in James's room, but he must have stuck it somewhere. I'd just ask him when he got back. I grabbed the Wharton T-shirt he'd been wearing yesterday off the floor and put it on, inhaling the smell of him. Then I padded out to the kitchen, in search of coffee, wishing that I lived here with him and that this was my real life.

*My real life.* I'd never met my father. My mother told me that he was her boyfriend, and that he'd stuck around at first after Tommy was born. Then she'd gotten pregnant with me, and then he was gone. I always hoped he'd come back but he never did... and he never sent a child support check. He was probably not a great guy.

But when I was a girl, I'd pretended that he was a king. That he'd sent Tommy and me to live with my mother to hide us, because we were important, and he was protecting us. In my fantasy, he came back—and I discovered that I'd been a princess all along. He took us to live the lives we were always supposed to have: our *real* lives, which were orderly and beautiful and perfect.

I looked out across the sunny kitchen. James's apartment was sparkling and immaculate. It was orderly and beautiful and perfect. James was perfect. This was that royal life I'd always imagined and was never meant to have.

Yes, it was true that I loved James. I did. There was nothing I could do about that now.

But it was now truer than ever that I had to protect my heart.

"YOU MADE BREAKFAST?" he asked an hour later. He threw some things on the counter and swept me into his arms. He was so much bigger than me, I felt protected with him wrapped around me. "That was nice of you."

He kissed me deeply, and I got shaky from it. The raw energy between us was almost overwhelming. I ran my hands down his chest, feeling the muscles underneath his shirt. It should be criminal to be so gorgeous, with all those muscles and that wavy, steel-colored hair; it wasn't fair. He ran his hands down me, too, kissing me hungrily.

"You make me crazy." He rested his forehead against mine and held me close. I could feel his erection spring up against me. "I can't control myself when you touch me."

"You touched *me*, boss," I said. "I was just standing here making French toast."

"French toast?" He pulled back and looked at the stove hopefully. "That's my favorite."

"I know."

He looked at me, a curious smile on his face. "How did you know?"

"You ordered it at brunch. And you ate it in about two seconds."

"So you've been paying attention," he said, impressed.

"I'm just trying to earn my keep," I said. I kissed him on the cheek and smiled, vowing to keep all the wild thoughts and emotions going on inside of me at bay.

"Oh, you've earned it," he said, his eyes flashing at me and that devilish grin coming back. "And then some. You're absolutely my most valuable employee."

"Ha," I said, blushing with a mixture of pleasure and disappointment. I didn't want to be his employee. I wanted to be his girlfriend. I was, however, pleased that I was pleasing him. I plated some French toast and set it on the island. I poured him coffee, black, like he liked it, and a glass of fresh-squeezed orange juice. I also set out some blackberries and strawberries. I looked at the spread, impressed. Expensive clothes looked better. Expensive food did, too.

He sat down and looked at the meal before him. "This is lovely," he said. "Thank you, Audrey."

"It's my pleasure. I like taking care of you," I said and blushed a little more.

There was an expression I couldn't read on his face. "I like it, too."

I sat down next to him and he intermittently rubbed my back while he ate. "Do you want some more coffee?" He nodded, and I grabbed his mug. I spied his cell phone and wallet on the table as I headed toward his fancy coffee machine. "Hey, is that my phone?" I asked. It was with his things. I grabbed it and flipped it on.

"Yep," he said. He gave no explanation as to why he'd had it.

There was a text message from Reina at the center. I read it and kept my back to him while I made his dark roast, feeling a cold rage descend on me. *My mother had stolen from Tommy.* I made myself push that fact to the side for now: I would deal with her later, when I could.

"Did you take my phone for some reason?" I asked.

"Yes."

"Did you read this? The message about my mother?" I asked. I held my phone up, but I didn't turn around to face him.

"Yes."

"Do you want to tell me why?" I was angry not only about the message itself, but also the fact that he'd read it before me. The fact that he'd read it at all.

"Come here." I went to him, bringing his coffee and my phone. My guard was way up, on high alert. A man looking at your phone only meant one thing—he'd been snooping. I put the coffee down, and he pulled me onto his lap. I sat there stiffly. "Don't be mad at me, Audrey."

"Why did you have my phone?"

"It beeped when you were in the shower."

"You told me that. When I was in the shower."

"It beeped again." He wrapped his arms more tightly around me.

"So?" I asked. I had nothing to hide from him except for my fucked-up family. Still, he shouldn't go through my things.

"So I read your text message. I'm sorry."

"I wish you hadn't," I said, pulling back to look at him. "Just like I didn't want you to come in my mother's apartment last night. Some things just aren't your business. There's some things I don't want you to see. You have to let me decide what to share with you. That's called having boundaries."

His blue eyes burned into mine. "What if I want it to be my business?" He didn't sound sorry. He was challenging me.

"James. Tell me first why you read my text." I wanted to hear the truth from him.

He rubbed his face. "I wanted to know who it was from," he said, looking away. "I wondered if you had a boyfriend you weren't telling me about."

I laughed. "You think I have a boyfriend?"

He looked at me then, a mixture of jealousy, embarrassment, and defiance clear on his face. "Do you?"

Boyfriends were on my list of outside interests, of which I had none. "No," I said. "There's no one." *There's only you.* "I'm not sure why you care, though."

"I already told you last night. I care." He wrapped his arms around me a little tighter. He didn't say anything else, and I felt both angry at him and a little sorry for him. I was an *escort.* Having a boyfriend should seriously be the least of his worries about me, on a very long list.

"I'm sorry, Audrey."

It sounded as if he meant it, and I forgave him instantly. "It's okay," I said. I leaned down and kissed him tenderly. I ran my hands through his thick hair before I pulled back. "I'm telling you the truth, though. You have to trust me—and I have to know that I can trust you to do that. If you want to know something, ask. Don't go behind my back."

"I do trust you—I was being juvenile. And insecure." He looked so baffled by that I almost laughed. "It was a dick move. I won't go behind your back again."

I nodded and then held up my phone miserably. "I still have to deal with what my mother did."

"I already dealt with it."

"Huh?"

His eyes searched my face. "Before. When you were in the shower. Before I promised not to go behind your back again," he said, sheepish.

"I read the message, and then I had Kai take me to your brother's place. I handled it, Audrey. You don't have to worry. Although you do have to sign some paperwork from New Horizons that removes your mother from the account." He gently moved me off of him and grabbed some papers. "You should do it now. We can scan them and email them in. They're under strict instructions not to release any more funds for any purpose."

He held the papers out for me, but I couldn't take them. I just stood there, shocked, not understanding. "What did you do?"

He looked me in the eye. "Your mother had withdrawn all the money you'd deposited for your brother. I went there and took care of it. And then I went to see your mother."

"You did *what*?" I felt relieved, angry, and ashamed all at once.

I couldn't picture James in my mother's filthy apartment, her walls yellowed with nicotine. I didn't *want* to picture it. I covered my face with my hands, as if that could block the image out.

"Audrey. Your brother is taken care of. That's the most important thing." He came toward me and gently took my hands from my face.

"How did you know where he was?"

"Kai."

I nodded numbly.

"And then I had him bring me to your mother's apartment, because I wanted to make this okay for you. I spoke with her and gave her some money just to tide her over for now. You need a break. You've been dealing with this alone for a long time. I wanted to help."

"You can't help me," I said. I sat down shakily on the couch. Tears sprung to my eyes. It was too much. I couldn't have him in my life like that—especially when I was only going to know him for another week. I had to handle my problems on my own. I couldn't get used to relying on somebody else. That was only going to lead to big trouble.

"I'm like a cowboy," I said, wiping my tears away roughly. "I can't have help. It makes me weak. Do you understand?"

He looked surprised and confused. "A cowboy? No. I don't get it." He sank down next to me and took my hands in his. "Please explain what you mean."

I sniffled. "I read somewhere that good cowboys sleep on the floor when they come home after a long trip. They do it so they don't get used to sleeping in a bed again. That way, when they go back out to herd, it's not that bad—they're still used to being uncomfortable."

"So... you're the cowboy," he said. "And I'm the bed."

"That's right, James," I said. "I'm the cowboy, and you're the bed. I have to sleep on the floor—I can't get soft. I can't have you taking care of my problems and making everything all comfortable and squishy. Because after next week, I'm back out there, sleeping on the hard ground. And if you're too nice to me, it's just gonna hurt that much worse."

"You need to stay rugged," James said, playing along. "You don't want you to throw your back out or worse, lose your edge."

"Right?" I said, sniffling again. "No one wants that."

"No one wants that." He paused for a second, watching my face. "So maybe you shouldn't go back out there." He pulled me into his arms and held me close, kissing the top of my head. "Maybe you should just stay."

# JAMES

Only idiots put all their cards on the table and hoped for the best. And yet here I was, cradling her in my arms, asking her to stay with me.

She sniffled yet again and sat up, pulling back from me a little, straightening her shoulders and regaining her composure. "You're sweet," she said, and I could tell from the tone in her voice that she was dismissing what I'd just said to her. She didn't know if I meant it, and I couldn't blame her. So she was giving me a pass to act as if it meant nothing.

*Take the pass, James,* I thought. *Until you can get your head on straight.*

Expert actress that she was, Audrey turned the conversation around fast. "What on Earth did my mother make of you?"

"She thought I was... pleasant," I lied. *She asked me if I was paying you enough, and why I couldn't find a 'real' woman.* "I told her that she can't ever take money from your brother's facility again."

"I told her that last night. She doesn't care about anything other than what she can get away with."

"That was the impression I got, unfortunately," I said.

Audrey grimaced. "I can't believe you went and saw where she lives. And talked to her. I'm so embarrassed."

I reached out and grabbed her hand. "You have nothing to be embarrassed about. She's not you. You're nothing like her—and by that I mean you're honest, caring, and kind-hearted."

"I can't believe that she'd do that to my brother. I mean, I can—'cause she's done it. But still." Her tears had dried up and she had a resigned look on her face. "I should probably do that paperwork." She grabbed it, and I went and got her a pen.

She started signing the documents that would remove her

mother as a signatory on her brother's account. "How much did you pay New Horizons?" she asked without looking up at me.

"It doesn't matter."

"Of course it does. You're paying me a ridiculous amount for these two weeks. We'll just deduct it from that."

"No, Audrey. We won't."

Now she looked up at me, her jaw clenching. "How much money did you give my mother?"

"I'm not telling you that, either."

"You have to," she said. "I'm paying you back, James. I don't want this on my conscience for the rest of my life. My mother's *my* cross to bear—not yours. I don't want her having anything to do with you."

"We don't have to argue about it right now. Okay?" I asked. She finished signing the papers, and I pulled her back to me, placing her head against my chest. "Just let it go," I said.

"You have to promise that I can pay you back. It has to be even between us," she said. "Otherwise, I'll feel like a user. Not just a whore."

"Stop it," I said, anger flashing through me—not at her, but at her circumstances. "You're doing what you're doing for the right reasons. You don't have to be ashamed of the choices you've made. Protecting someone you love is the most important thing you can do."

She looked at me stubbornly. "I'm not ashamed. I just want you to promise me."

"I'll promise you anything, Audrey."

"Good. I feel better already," she said, finally relaxing and nestling against me. "Promise me I'm the cowboy."

"You're the cowboy, baby," I said. "I'm the bed."

Taking me by surprise, she hugged me. "Thank you, James. Thank you for helping my brother. You're a good person."

I lifted her chin in my hands, and I kissed her softly on the lips. "No, I'm not."

"You're wrong," she whispered. "I'm the cowboy, and I say you're wrong." She ran her hands through my hair again. "So... you've seen some of my really ugly skeletons now. I seem to remember last night you said you had some in your closet, too.

Wanna share? So we can balance the ugliness between us?"

I looked out the window. It was a beautiful, sunny June day. "Do you remember what I said? About the fact that you don't want to know?"

"I think that was my line, James." She traced my jaw with her finger. "But you don't have to tell me if you don't want to. I understand."

I looked over at her then. The thing was, she did understand. She was the one woman I'd met in decades with whom it was easy. Even though it wasn't easy. Audrey was the only woman I'd met in forever that I felt connected to.

"I LOST SOMEONE close to me. A girlfriend."

"I'm so sorry. When was this?"

"A long time ago. The summer after high school." I rubbed my face. I hadn't talked about this ever, really. Maybe a few words to Todd when he asked me if I was okay. He'd been so young when it happened. I don't think he understood how it wrecked me.

"Her name was Danielle. We'd dated our senior year at Philips Andover. I'd never met anyone like her before—she was a scholarship student, from a very different background than me. She was brilliant. And open. And kind." I smiled at the memory of her.

"She sounds lovely," Audrey said. "What happened?"

"She was going to Brown in the fall, and I wanted to change my plans and follow her there. My parents didn't approve. I'd been accepted to Harvard. That's where my father went, and that's where my father wanted me to go. They were against the relationship, anyway. Her family was lower middle class, nobodies from Tewksbury. Actually, they were really nice people—I'm still in touch with them. Which means they still send me a Christmas card.

"But just because I thought she was wonderful and her family was great didn't mean that she was acceptable to my parents. The fact that she'd gotten a full-boat scholarship to Brown for biology didn't earn her any points, either. She didn't have the pedigree. They wanted me to attend Harvard and end the relationship. I fought with them about it the whole summer.

"One night Danielle came over, and my parents were horrible to her. Really vicious. They told her that she was breaking our family apart by trying to get me to follow her to Brown. Which she wasn't—that'd been my idea. But knowing my parents the way I do, I just sat there. There was no use fighting them. Danielle became hysterical and left."

He paused for a beat. "She got into a car accident that night, Audrey. On her way home. And she died."

Audrey sat there, holding my hand and looking white with shock. "I'm so sorry." She looked as if she was going to cry for me. "But you can't blame yourself for that. She got into an *accident*. You didn't cause it."

"I did nothing to defend her that night. My parents told her she was unacceptable to our family. It was like they'd gutted her. And then she left, sobbing. I never heard someone cry like that before." The memory of it still haunted me.

"There was a thunderstorm, and the police said the visibility was bad. She hydroplaned and went off the road, into a guardrail. That never would have happened if she were calm—I know that. And she had her whole life in front of her. I took that away."

"James." She took my face in her hands. "You can't carry that guilt around with you forever. It was an accident. Yes, she was upset. But it wasn't your fault. Your parents must feel horrible about it, though."

I looked out the window again, trying to calm the sharp edges I felt inside of myself. It was like this every time I thought of Danielle. There was so much regret it physically hurt.

"My mother said it was fate." My voice sounded dead to my own ears.

"She did not," Audrey said. "Please tell me that's not true."

I shrugged. "She was appropriately mournful to begin with. She went to the service, said all the right things. She donated an obscene amount of money to the scholarship fund Danielle's parents set up in her memory. My mother is a master at putting on a show.

"Still, I knew she was relieved. And at Christmas that year I drank myself into a stupor and accused her of as much."

"And?" Audrey asked.

"And she told me that I was lucky. That Preston luck and fate had given me an out." The memory's sharp edges of pain dulled to a flat hate.

"And I thought my mother was bad. Celia's fucking unbelievable," Audrey said.

I laced my fingers through hers. "She sure is," I said.

"DID YOU LOVE HER?" Audrey asked me a little while later. We were still sitting on the couch. The only thing we'd done was send the paperwork in and then settle back down, holding hands.

"It was a long time ago, but I know that I did. It was first love. Nothing else is quite like that," I said. "Do you know what I mean?"

She nodded slowly, her gaze directed out of the window. "I do, James. I do."

"THAT'S ENOUGH DOOM and gloom for one day." Audrey sat up straight. My head was in her lap, and she'd been playing with my hair. I couldn't remember the last time that sitting with someone, talking to them, and having them play with my hair qualified as an event for me, but this did. And this particular event had stretched past lunch.

"Are you hungry?" I asked.

"I'm always hungry."

I sat up and smiled at her. "Me, too. Why don't we just go down the street? Sit outside, have a late lunch, and drink some wine?"

"That sounds perfect." She kissed me on the nose and went to get up but I stopped her, grabbing her hands.

"Thank you for listening to me today," I said. "I've never spoken about what happened before. I never even told Cole. It's something that I buried a long time ago. You're the first person I ever felt comfortable with enough to talk to about it." I tucked her hair behind her ear.

She smiled at me, flushing with pleasure. "Thank you for everything you did for *me* today—even though I'm paying you back—and thank you for trusting me enough to tell me about Danielle. You *can* trust me, James." She laced her fingers through mine. "You've shown me that you've got my back. I have yours. You need to know that."

I leaned up and kissed her then, tasting her sweet mouth. It was as if nothing else mattered to me anymore. My business back in California was a blur—it was like that was someone else's life. All those worries, that rhythm, were far from me now. I hadn't even called in to yell at my assistant Molly today. All I cared about was Audrey in this moment. As far as I was concerned my family could be damned, except for Todd. And I could already tell he knew what she meant to me.

"Let's go eat. It's a beautiful day out."

"Wait," I said, not ready to let her go. "I need something from you first." I kissed her again, our tongues connecting.

I got hard as soon as that happened.

This was uncharted territory for me. Not the erection, obviously. It was just that sex wasn't all I needed—I needed *her*, and I didn't know what to do with that. I couldn't articulate the need any further. I didn't know what to ask her for.

But Audrey knew exactly what to do. She showed me that she needed me, too.

She climbed onto my lap and straddled me. She said nothing, but she removed her shirt and mine swiftly, kissing me with an urgency I hadn't felt from her before. She stood and pulled off her leggings and then undid my pants, lifting my ass up and pulling them off, not saying a word.

She knelt on the floor below me. I ran my hands down her beautiful, smooth skin, and she took my cock in her mouth, licking and sucking. I leaned back, overwhelmed with the sensation. She took me all the way down her throat, sucking hard.

"Oh my God, Audrey." I threw my head back against the couch. I almost exploded in her mouth right then. I moaned, just wanting to fill her with me. She swirled her tongue around my tip and cupped my heavy balls. "Oh, fuck yeah—that's good." I fisted my hands through her hair, caught up in the moment. I almost came like that, hard in her mouth, but it wasn't what I wanted. I wanted *her*. I wanted to give her pleasure.

I wanted her to scream my name.

"Audrey," I said, my voice thick, "Come here." She sat up and straddled me again, taking my now-enormous cock and rubbing it against her wet slit. She threw back her head, like it felt good, as she rubbed against me.

"Baby, I need to be inside you," I said. "Now." She positioned herself above me, and all at once, took me in her, hard. We both cried out. Then we started rocking against each other. It felt so good. I was in so deep. I grabbed her ass and bounced her on my hard length, up and down, over and over.

"Oh my God, James. Oh my God."

"Tell me I'm the only one," I said. The sensation of having her on me like that, of being inside her so deep, was making me crazy. I squeezed her ass. "Tell me you're mine." Her breasts bounced in front of me and I buried my face in them, licking and sucking her nipples. I wanted to own her body. I wanted to leave my mark on her like a brand, so that no one else ever touched her.

I fucked her harder.

She moaned as I thrust into her again and again. "I'm yours. There's no one but you," she cried out. She arched against me, close to her release.

"Come for me, and say my name." I was about to explode. I put my fingers on her clit and stroked it relentlessly.

She arched her back and cried out, her body wrapped around me like a vise. "James, oh my God. *James*. Come in me. Come in me, baby. I need to feel you."

*I fucking love you,* I thought and came in a torrent.

# AUDREY

James had literally fucked my brains out. Good thing I'd sent that paperwork in while I was still lucid. Now my mother couldn't take any more funds from New Horizons. At least there was one less thing to worry about.

I couldn't have forced myself to worry about anything right now, anyway. James held my hand as we walked down Newbury Street in the early afternoon heat. We were lazy and loose, and I swear to God, we were in love. That's what it felt like, anyway. I was in love with him, my billionaire in his jeans and T-shirt, his sexy steel-colored hair mussed up from our recent lovemaking. I was in love with him, and I was positively drunk on it.

We went to Stephanie's on Newbury and he ordered a bottle of Chardonnay. I looked at the menu. "Would you like some crab cakes?" I asked him, and he started to laugh.

"What?" I asked, confused.

"I hate crab cakes," he said.

"You ate them the other night!"

"I only did that for you," he said. "You were trying to take care of me, and I wanted to be… nice."

"Well, you suck at being nice," I said. The waitress came, and I ordered a beet salad, a blue cheese burger, and a side of macaroni and cheese.

"I'll have the same," James said, not even looking at the menu, and handing it back to the waitress. He squeezed my hand. "You always get the good stuff."

"Except for the crab cakes," I said huffily.

"Don't be mad at me." The sunlight played on his face and I saw how relaxed and gorgeous he was right then. Well, he was always gorgeous. But relaxed? Not so much.

"I can't remember the last time I felt this happy," he said.

I looked at him again. Tears came quick to my eyes, and I mentally retracted them. *I've never been this happy,* I thought. That warmed me and burned me all at the same time. "Me neither," I said and smiled at him bravely.

"We have to be at the rehearsal relatively soon," James said, still holding my hand. "And the wedding's going to be an all-day affair tomorrow. But then I get you all to myself—well, almost—but I can't wait to go to the Bahamas now. I was dreading it before. Now I can't wait. I get to hang out with you in a bikini."

"I've never been to the Caribbean. I'm really looking forward to it."

He reached over and squeezed my hand. "You're going to love it."

"It'll be interesting to spend a whole week with your family." I was dreading that now more than ever.

"We're getting a villa on the edge of the resort," James said, "so everyone can leave us the fuck alone."

"Do you promise?" I asked.

"I'll promise you anything, Audrey."

WE WENT TO TRINITY Church for the rehearsal. James was wearing a light-grey suit with a lavender tie, and I was wearing a pale lavender dress. "You look stunning, and we match. It's perfect," James said. He held my hand as we walked through the church doors.

"It *is* perfect," I agreed. I'd seen his tie and picked out my dress right afterward; we looked as together as I felt like we were. We walked into the main chamber of the church, and the beauty of it took my breath away. Sunlight streamed through the stained-glass windows, and the ceiling soared high above us. It was fit for a fairy-tale wedding. I could imagine Evie coming down the aisle in a pouffy princess dress, her pale face behind a veil.

Thinking about it made me sad.

James leaned down and kissed me on the cheek. I looked up at him, flustered. Being in the church with him like this was making me feel an uneasy longing, followed closely by dread. "What?" he asked, watching my face.

"This is just stunning," I said, turning away from him. "I've never been in here."

"It's something, isn't it?" Celia Preston asked, coming toward us. She eyed us suspiciously, taking in our clasped hands and co-ordinating outfits. "You two are looking very… matchy," she said, and she didn't sound pleased. Celia was wearing another Chanel suit, this one black-and-white checkered. Her face looked as if it had de-puffed nicely.

"Mother," James said icily, giving her a slight bow.

"Hi, Mrs. Preston," I said in what I hoped was a casual, friendly way. I was trying to balance out James's formal coldness. After what he'd told me, I didn't blame him for how he felt about her. But now more than ever, I needed to step up my performance. He'd helped me, and I wanted to help him. I needed to make this easier for him. "You look so pretty."

"My swelling from the filler went down, just as expected," she said.

"I have to go up front," James said to me, nodding toward Todd and the rest of the wedding party. "Will you be okay?"

"I'm fine," I said. I smiled at his mother bravely. "Your mother and I can watch."

"Great," James said, giving his mother a warning look. "This shouldn't take too long. I hope."

"James—it's your brother's night. Let it take as long as it needs to," Celia said. She motioned for me to follow her to a pew closer to the front, and I obeyed. Of course I obeyed—I wasn't about to argue with her. I sat down next to her, careful not to get too close.

"So," she said, arranging her skirt and turning her unnaturally smooth face to me. "James seems more enraged with me than usual. I assume you told him about our conversation about grandchildren at tea."

*That, and he told me you made his high-school girlfriend cry so hard she hydroplaned her car into a guardrail and died.*

"I might have mentioned it to him," I said carefully. "But I had no idea how upset he would get."

"Did he talk to you about the trust?"

I did not care for Celia Preston, but I did admire her ability to be direct. I didn't want to tell her the truth, but I didn't see a way out. "He did," I admitted.

She sighed and sat back a little. "He's never understood my perspective—he takes moral offense to it. But that is limited thinking on his part. What James doesn't understand is that having a family requires an enormous sense of duty. One must put one's family before oneself. You have to protect it. Your family is all you've got in life, Audrey."

She gave me a quick look. "Oh—sorry dear, I forgot that all your family's dead."

"No, you didn't," I said.

She gave me a terse smile. "You're right. I didn't."

I wanted to roll my eyes at her but I didn't dare. We sat there in silence for a minute, watching the priest discuss the ceremony with Evie and Todd. James stood behind his brother, his arms crossed tight against his chest, glaring at his mother.

"James doesn't approve of Evie," Celia continued. "But what he sees as a lack of a personality and good judgment, I see as an opportunity."

"How's that?" I asked.

"She has the proper family and the proper pedigree—her parents met at Tabor Academy. She has a trust fund. She registered at Shreve, Crump & Low, and I didn't even have to tell her to. She's an appropriate addition to the Preston family."

Everything that Evie had, I didn't. Celia was telling me in no uncertain terms that I was an inappropriate candidate for the Preston family. And she didn't know the half of it. She'd thought Danielle—of the full-boat biology scholarship to Brown and the poor but respectable family—was bad. Next to me, Danielle was like the Patron Saint of Louis Vuitton.

"I know everything there is to know about Evie," Celia said.

I looked at her doubtfully, and she raised an eyebrow at me. Her filler had absorbed enough so that it actually lifted a little. "Oh, but I do—I know that she tried to sleep with James."

I must have looked shocked, because Celia looked triumphant

and patted my knee. "Todd tells me everything, dear. Unlike James."

"So—why do you want them to get married?" I asked bluntly.

"Because she's easy to control, of course." She smiled at me. "Evie loves money more than anything. She and Todd have signed an airtight prenuptial agreement. If Evie cheats, Evie gets nothing. If Evie tries to divorce Todd, Evie gets nothing. If Evie wears a blouse I don't like, Evie gets nothing. Just kidding about that last one. But close enough." She watched her son holding Evie's hand, still talking to the priest.

"I think Evie loves him," I said. I was surprised to hear myself defending her, but still.

"You're a funny one, Audrey," she said. "But I agree: Evie does love Todd, at least right now. Right now she's a bride, and they're the center of attention, and they're having wild sex. She'll get bored eventually. In a normal situation, that could be a problem. But I'm here. And I can take care of her."

"Don't you think Todd's capable of taking care of her? And himself?" I probably shouldn't have been so blunt, but I was following her lead.

She shook her head. "Not Todd," she said. "Todd's too nice. He needs to be with someone that I can take care of *for* him. I haven't told her yet that I know about the incident with James, but I can dangle it over her head if and when I need to."

"But if Todd already knows, who are you going to tell?"

"Everyone else," she said and smiled. "Their children. Her cousins. Her mother. Her friends. And I'll tell them all that James refused her and said she was a bony, disgusting whore."

"Well, hopefully you won't ever have to do that," I said, mildly appalled.

"We'll see," Celia said and shrugged. She sounded as if wasting that information might be a disappointment.

"Mrs. Preston, I appreciate you being forthcoming with me… but why are you telling me all this?"

"Because I don't want you to take this personally," she said. "I can tell that James has feelings for you." I started to protest but she held up her hand to stop me. "You might not see it, but I'm his mother, and I know him best. Even if he wishes that weren't true.

"Now, you've been very direct with me, and I appreciate that. So I'm doing the same for you. Your relationship with my son can't go on past the trip to the Bahamas. You have to call it off with him after that. I can tell that you're good for James. But that isn't the only thing that matters in my world. I have an enormous responsibility to my family. James's children are going to be some of the wealthiest people in the country. They have to be able to handle the duties that come with that sort of privilege—and their parents have to be able to help them do that.

"James needs someone who can help him, Audrey. Someone who can guide him and make his life easier. He doesn't need someone to babysit."

I swallowed hard. She was actually making sense to me, and that was scary. I could only imagine what she had said to Danielle, so many years ago. Celia Preston was being polite right now. Her actual wrath would be terrifying. *That poor girl*, I thought. James had been her first love, and she'd been so young.

"I know you care about James, Audrey. You want what's best for him. Think about what I'm saying to you."

She paused for a beat and turned to me. "And between you and me? If you go quietly, I'll make it worth your while." We watched as Todd and Evie knelt in front of the priest.

"I'll keep that in mind," I said.

"You do that, dear," Mrs. Preston said.

"WHAT WAS MY mother whispering to you about?" James asked me as we headed toward the car.

"Oh, you know. This and that. Stuff. Things."

"What sorts of things?"

"Things that would make you mad," I said. I grabbed his hand. "Things that we should only talk about while we're having alcoholic beverages."

He slid into the car next to me and scowled. "Was it the same stuff? About how exclusive our family is?"

"Sort of," I said. Since Celia had ended her diatribe, I'd been struggling with how much to tell James. I decided that the whole truth might push him over the edge right now. He was still so raw from telling me about Danielle. I would tell him everything his mother had said, but not the night before Todd's wedding. He would be too angry. Tonight and tomorrow needed to be about the happy couple, not crazy, vindictive, and cunning Celia Preston.

"She was just talking about Evie. Why she thinks Evie is a good fit for your family." James snorted, and Kai drove through the Financial District on the way to the waterfront. The rehearsal dinner was at Il Pastorne, one of the most exclusive restaurants in Boston.

After a few minutes sitting in traffic, Kai pulled up outside of the restaurant. As he went to open the door for us, I saw something on the sidewalk that made me pause. A flash of a familiar blond head, badly in need of a root touch-up. "Oh, shit." I turned to James. "That's my mom out there." Kai opened the door, but I didn't get out. I watched her for a second. She was smoking and pacing out in front of the restaurant, inspecting all the town cars pulling up to the curb.

She was waiting for me.

"I'll deal with her," James said, but I stopped him.

"No, let me." I jumped out of the car.

The last thing I needed right now was for Mr. and Mrs. Preston to see that my supposedly dead mother was alive and well, smoking like a fiend outside of their son's rehearsal dinner. "Hey," I said, rushing up to her and looking around, nervously. "What're you doing here?"

"Nice way to greet your mother," she said. I grabbed her elbow and dragged her to the car, shoving her inside. "Ow."

"Shut up," I hissed and slammed the door behind me. She was giving me a defiant look, and James was watching her face. "Ma, I would introduce you to James, but I heard you met him yesterday."

"Hello, Mrs. Reynolds," James said, a mask of courteousness on his face.

She nodded at him and almost looked abashed. Almost.

"James, do you mind if I speak with my mother alone? I'll be in in just a minute."

The look he gave me was annoyed, resigned, and not at all surprised. "Sure. But if I don't see you in five minutes, I'm coming out to get you." He gave me one last look. Then with a curt nod to my mother, he slid out of the car and slammed the door.

My mother blinked at me, her eyes beady in her puffy face. "He's bossy, huh?"

I just glared at her. "Kai, can you circle the block?" He pulled out silently and headed down the street. I ducked down low, thankful for the tinted windows.

"You—ashamed of *me*," she said and snorted.

My mother had all the nerve. "Do you understand that I'm on a job? I'm working. I can't have people from my outside life dropping in on me. I could get fired. If Elena gets wind of this, I *will* be fired."

"I don't really think you need to worry about that. Do you?" She looked at me slyly.

"What the fuck are you talking about, Ma? Are you drunker than usual?"

"I am not drunk. But I had a visit from your friend yesterday. He's bossy, but he's generous. I think he likes you."

"Just shut up. Please."

She shook her head, that smug look intact. "He gave me money, Audrey. *Lots* of money. Just so I'd leave you alone. So you could be *happy*. That's what he said!" She chuckled at this. The fact that someone wanted me to be happy was amusing to her.

"How much," I said flatly.

"Twenty thousand dollars!" she said. She clapped her hands together in glee. "I needed a break so bad. And he gave it to me like it was nothing. It was chump change to him, Audrey. There's a lot more where that came from." She licked her lips, and I felt nauseous. I almost threw up right there, in the back of James's hired Mercedes.

"Please stop," I said.

"Oh honey—I'm just getting started."

I looked up at her, sick with dread. "You can't do this to me." I felt as if I were under water, my words coming out muffled and strange. The world was crashing around me like tumultuous waves, the undercurrent fierce and scary. My mother was dragging me down again.

"All I'm gonna do is ask him for a little more money," she said.

"He already gave you money. To be *kind*, Ma. Do you even understand what that means?"

"He's got more to give. He didn't even blink." She paused for a second, her beady eyes studying me. "I bet he'd give *you* a lot more than that."

"He's already paying me. Through the service."

"He'd give you more. I know he would."

"I don't want more. I don't deserve more—and I don't make it a habit of trying to suck the people around me dry."

She smiled again, triumphant and absolutely petrifying in her dull cunning. "But you've been sucking him dry. That's what you do. I bet those fancy people back there don't know he's paying you to do it, either." She took in my lavender dress, my flawless makeup, and the designer bag Elena had lent me. "I bet they don't know you're a hooker. I bet he doesn't want them to know."

"I fucking hate you." I stared at her brazenly. I'd thought it a thousand times, but I'd never said it out loud before.

She didn't even wince. "You owe me. I brought you and Tommy into this world. Your father left me because of you kids. And now I have nothing."

"You disgust me," I said, my chest heaving in anger. If I hadn't had to go pretend to be a real person at a very fancy rehearsal dinner in approximately two minutes, I would have thrown myself at her and scratched her face. I was beside myself with fury.

Underneath that, her threat was like an undertow, threatening to drag me out to sea. I couldn't let her do this to James.

I no longer cared what she did to me.

I had to protect him.

"Ma." I made myself calm down. "I can give you more money. A lot more." She watched me, saying nothing. "I just can't do it now. After next week," I said, nodding. I would give half to Tommy and half to my mom. I didn't even care anymore. I would do anything to get her to leave us alone.

"What if I don't want to wait? What if I think my daughter's tricking me? And no way you'll be able to give me as much as Mr. Fancy Pants will." She jutted her chin out at me. "He's filthy rich. Him and his family. I can just imagine how much they'd give me to keep quiet. To not tell the papers that you're a hooker."

I swallowed hard. "How did you find us tonight, anyway?"

"It was in the gossip column at *The Tribune.*" She shrugged. "Just fancy rich people, flauntin' their money, is all. While the rest of us starve."

I looked at her barrel chest, thinking of all the cartons of cigarettes she'd inhaled into it over her lifetime at fifty dollars a pop. "You're hardly starving. And the last time I checked, no one owed you anything."

She jutted her chin out at me. "I don't like your holier-than-thou attitude, girl. Never have."

"Just put it on the long list of things you don't like about me," I said, my eyes narrowing. "But I'll give you all the money you want. I mean it. It's a lot."

Kai pulled back up in front of the restaurant. I could see James waiting for me on the sidewalk, his hands stuffed into his pockets. "Kai, please take my mother home." I turned to her. "If you leave us alone, I'll give you almost all of it," I said in a small voice. "Some of it has to go to Tommy, though."

She nodded. She'd already stolen close to six thousand dollars from New Horizons this morning, so maybe that curbed her attitude. A little. "I'll think about it."

"You do that." I looked at her, and suddenly I didn't want to get out of the car. I wanted to go back to East Boston with her. Back to her desolate apartment where I'd been raised. That was where I belonged. When I was younger I couldn't wait to leave that place, to be on my own. To try to do better. But I didn't belong to better. The filth kept coming back up to claim me. I should just give in to it, let it drag me back down, where the people I cared for couldn't be tainted by me.

"Your boyfriend's waiting for you," my mother said, motioning toward the car door. James was right outside, looking antsy.

"He's not my boyfriend," I whispered, still sick.

"You might want to tell him that. You better go."

# JAMES

"*What* did she say?" We were standing on the sidewalk near the restaurant, looking out at the view of the harbor. Audrey was tense beside me, her face pale and resigned. I rubbed her back, trying to make her feel better.

"She just wanted to... check in."

"Is everything okay?"

"No. Nothing's ever okay when it comes to my mother. But it *will* be fine."

I pulled her against me. "She wants more money." Audrey nodded stiffly. "How did she know we were here?"

"The *Tribune*."

"How much does she want?"

Audrey shook her head again. "She wants whatever she can get her hands on. Don't worry about it—I took care of it."

"I was pretty generous with her yesterday," I said, watching the boats go by. "That was probably a mistake. I didn't take into consideration... how far she might go." I laced my fingers through Audrey's, feeling sad and angry on her behalf. Even though I should know better from personal experience, I was still surprised that a mother could be so indifferent to her child.

Or maybe it was just because it was Audrey, and I couldn't understand how anyone would want to treat her that way.

"You mean you didn't take into consideration that she would throw me under a bus? That she would jeopardize my job? Then you underestimated her. Or maybe you overestimated her," she said. "She doesn't care about me. Look what she did to Tommy this morning. She doesn't care about anybody but herself."

I pulled her to me. "Your mother is almost making my mother look half-decent."

We both laughed. "They're quite a pair," Audrey said. She

sighed and looked up at me. "James… my mother might try to pull something. She threatened to."

"What?" I asked, but I already knew.

"Tell your family about me. Expose us. Blackmail anybody and everybody she can."

"She won't do that," I said. "I won't let her get that far."

"You can't give her any more money," she said. "She won't ever stop. I'll pay her—I already promised I would—but she has to understand that you're a one-and-done. Otherwise, she'll keep coming back." She looked at me, anxiety and stubbornness playing out on her face. "Promise me."

"Not yet—I can help you. We'll figure it out." I looked back at the restaurant and sighed. "We have to go in there. Dinner's going to start, and I don't want to call attention to us."

"Don't you want me to just go?" she asked. "If I leave now, she won't be able to do anything else. Cause any more trouble. I'm worried, James. She'll stoop as low as she can. I don't want your family finding out about me, and I don't want her near any of you… because she could do anything, and it would be horrible."

"Of course I don't want you to go. Don't be ridiculous." I kissed her on the forehead, careful not to mess up her makeup. She looked beautiful. She'd dressed so carefully for the occasion. I'd watched her pick out her jewelry, selecting the perfect earrings, scowling at her reflection in the mirror until she felt confident with her choices. When we'd walked through those church doors together, and I turned to look at her, my heart had just about stopped.

"I have a bad feeling about this." She exhaled shakily. "Can you imagine what your mother would say?"

"I don't care." I grabbed her hand, and we headed in to dinner. We'd been gone long enough. I didn't want my mother getting fidgety, or worse, curious. I didn't like the way she'd been talking to Audrey at the church—I shouldn't have flaunted our togetherness last night at the Gardner like I had. I needed to protect Audrey from my mother, to shield her.

Both my mother and her mother needed to back off and leave her alone.

Leave *us* alone.

Audrey hung back, stopping before we went in. "I don't want you to get hurt, James. I don't want to drag you and your family down. I think I should just go." She pulled away from me, like she was going to run.

"No. Stop," I said, holding her firmly. Panic rose inside me. "I'm the one who hired you. You *can't* drag me down—we're in this together." I pulled her to me. "We're going to handle your mother, and then we're going to handle mine. And once we stop panicking, we might even be able to enjoy it. I don't want to do this without you. Please don't go. Don't even say it again."

Her eyes searched my face. "Don't you want me to, though? Think about it." I could tell she meant it. She thought she would be sparing me.

"Are you hearing anything I'm saying?" I felt myself getting angry, and I struggled to control it. I didn't want to hurt her any more right now. Her mother had been bad enough. I would have Kai just take her back to the apartment to free her from the rest of the evening, but I was worried she'd be gone by the time I got back.

"No, I don't want you to go. I want you with me. And I want this to be the end of the discussion. Can you do that for me? Can you put on your game face?"

We just looked at each other for a beat.

"Of course," she said finally, relenting. She fake-smiled at me.

"Fake-smile more. Put your back into it," I ordered. Her smile widened, and the actress was back. "You're good. You're really, really good."

She gave out one last shaky sigh. "You're not so bad yourself," she said, making herself grin at me.

FOR BETTER OR FOR WORSE, Cole and Jenny were at the rehearsal dinner.

"Dre!" Jenny whooped, coming up and giving Audrey a jiggly hug. "This place is frickin' amazing!"

Audrey smiled at her, but the smile was laced with worry. "It's gorgeous. Just like you—you're looking really good, Jenny."

Jenny tossed her curls and modeled her gold-lamé dress. "Coley bought it for me."

"Coley?" I asked, raising my eyebrows at my friend. "For real?"

He slapped me on the shoulder hard. "For real, bro. So shut up." He dragged me to the long table where my entire family was seated, along with Evie's family, all sorts of cousins, and friends. My father sat at the head of the table, resplendent in a suit, my ice pick of a mother at his side. I deposited Audrey with Cole and Jenny at one end of the table and went up to where Todd and Evie sat looking happy and excited. I grabbed a glass of champagne from a passing waiter, and I raised it.

"I'd like to make a toast," I said. All eyes turned to me except for my mother, who was watching Audrey and Jenny with a thinly veiled look of distaste on her face. But Audrey was watching me, a smile on her face now that looked real. She nodded at me in encouragement.

For once, I wanted to do something nice. I was tired of all the ugly. There'd been too much underbelly today. I had to be positive... for once.

"My baby brother is all grown up," I said and patted him on the shoulder. "And I'm happy to announce he's marrying the woman that he loves. Evie, I know that you love my brother. I do. Seeing you two together for the past week has been inspiring. I expect good things for you in the future." My mother had turned to me now, most likely surprised. She was probably waiting for the other shoe to drop.

"So I'd like to toast the happy couple. Cheers to your wedding tomorrow, and for a lifetime of happiness to follow." Everyone cheered, and I leaned down to Todd. "I mean it," I said and gripped his shoulder. "I'm happy for you."

He gave me a surprised smile. "Stop," he said sheepishly.

"Don't make him cry," Evie said teasingly. She beamed at Todd. "He's so alpha tonight." They started kissing, and I took that as my cue to leave quickly. I sat down next to Audrey and pulled her face into my hands. I gave her a long, lingering kiss, for the moment not caring about all the radar in the world.

Maybe my mother would see that I was happy for the first

time. Maybe she would soften toward Audrey.

Maybe… but probably not.

*Hope is a four-letter word*, I thought, but I pulled Audrey close to me anyway.

COLE DRAGGED ME to the bar after dinner. The girls had gone to the ladies' room. "Dude," Cole said. He ordered two bourbons.

"Yes, dude?" I asked. "Actually—aren't we too old for that now? We used to say that at Wharton. It makes me sad to hear it come out of my mouth now. It's like I'm an old-timer."

"An old-timer who's ready to settle down?" Cole asked.

"Do you have to go there tonight, Coley?"

"Fuck you," he said good-naturedly and had some of his drink. "You know you've got an emotional boner for that girl on your forehead though, right?"

"An emotional boner? I didn't know they existed."

"It's like a heart on your sleeve, but bigger and more obnoxious," he said, laughing at me. "And you totally have one."

"She offered me a crab cake today, and I didn't eat it."

"You've fucked her, though. I can tell. Like, fifty times this week I bet."

I shrugged. "Not fifty."

"Then Jenny and I are winning."

"Haven't you been to work?" I asked him, simultaneously disgusted and impressed. He was probably exaggerating. Probably.

Cole shrugged. "Nah. I did a conference call. But this girl is like a drug for me. I can't keep my dick out of her."

"Does that qualify as an emotional boner? Or are you two just sort of disgusting?"

"I don't know," he said and rubbed his eyes. For once, my friend actually looked perplexed. "I seriously can't keep my hands off her." He looked back at me. "Is that love?"

"It sounds sort of like it… but it could just be lust," I said.

"There's definitely lust."

"Do you *like* her?"

"I'm fucking crazy about her," Cole said. He had that baffled look again, and I patted him on the shoulder. I watched as Audrey and Jenny came back toward us, both of them laughing. Audrey looked happy and almost relaxed.

"Dude," he said. "Put your emotional boner away. It's embarrassing."

# AUDREY

Jenny told me that she'd had sex with Cole earlier today while they were out shopping, and it almost made me forget about the awful scene with my mother. And the story about Danielle. And Celia Preston's offer to pay me to go away.

Which was saying something.

She wanted to tell me about how her assignment was going. We'd gone to a bathroom at the other end of the restaurant to avoid James's family and anyone else connected to the wedding.

"He's frickin' crazy," she said, applying blush to her face with a pouffy brush. She added lip gloss and fluffed her hair. "I swear to God, I've never been with someone who wants to have this much sex. He can't keep his hands off me."

"Even in the dressing room at a fancy store?" I asked.

"Yeah. He totally thinks he's above the law, right? It's a billionaire thing—he thinks the rules don't apply to him.

"He just followed me when I was trying this dress on. We weren't in there for two seconds, and he pinned me up against the wall. With the sales clerk right outside! He had to lift me up so they couldn't see our feet together. And he fucked me like crazy. I had to slap my hand over his mouth though 'cause he's a yeller when he comes. Real loud, Dre. Real loud. And he likes me to do this thing with his balls—"

"Jenny—I don't need to know the thing about his balls!"

Jenny fanned herself. "Fine. But I'm gettin' hot just thinking about it. I should be exhausted, but I'm not. Jesus. He's worse than Loospy and Fat Vinnie put together."

"Do you *like* him?"

"Are you kidding me? This is the best time I've had with a John, *ever.* It's like we're the same person. Except he's rich, and he's a guy. And that thing with his balls."

"Huh," I said.

"Huh is right." She turned to me and inspected my face. "Mr. Sex in a Suit is a little romance-y tonight, Dre. He's got it real bad. I almost feel sorry for him. Did you bat him around like a cat toy last night?"

I decided to spare Jenny the actual ugly details of the past twenty-four hours. "I might have… a little."

She nodded at me, a knowing look on her face. "It worked. You better watch it. I know that look he's got."

"Jenny, stop."

I paused and then said, "What look is that, exactly?"

She rolled her eyes at me. "I think he might be in love with you. I'm just sayin'." She shrugged. "He doesn't look like he's pretending anymore."

"That only happens in the movies."

"Then I'll come over and film you," she snapped. "Jesus, Dre. You gotta loosen up a little. Sometimes good things happen to good people."

"Huh," I said.

"Huh is right. Let's go. We don't want your Mr. Suit to cry because he misses you… and Coley's hand hasn't been on my ass in more than five minutes. My butt's gettin' cold."

"WHAT'S GOING ON with Cole and Jenny?" I asked James when we were driving home.

"I have no idea," he said. "Last night I thought it was just physical. Tonight I don't know. What does Jenny say?"

"That they have sex non-stop."

"That's what Cole said, too."

"So that's good," I said. "They're enjoying each other." *I wonder what's going to happen afterward,* I thought. *If it'll become a regular thing.* I didn't say it out loud; I didn't want the conversation to circle back to us. It was something I wasn't prepared to face.

"They're coming to the Bahamas," James said. All of a sudden he was shaking with silent laughter. "I think Todd's rewarding me for my good behavior all week. My mother's gonna have a fit."

"I'm surprised Evie's allowing it after Jenny tried to fight her last night."

"Her cousins think Cole's hot," James said and shrugged. "They voted for eye candy on the trip."

"Speaking of eye candy, I'll make sure to tell Jenny to pack thong bikinis," I said, grinning and feeling pleased. Being around my friend always made me feel better. I was glad she would be there next week just for that selfish reason, but the added benefit of her parading around in front of the Prestons in a minuscule bikini warmed my heart.

The downside, of course, was that Jenny wasn't the most inconspicuous person, and I still had to pretend to be a legitimate, aboveboard graphic design student from New Hampshire. I also had to get her to stop calling me "Dre" somehow.

He linked his hand through mine. "This just keeps on getting better and better."

"After the past twenty-four hours, there was really nowhere to go but up."

"True," he said. "Your mother didn't come back tonight, though. That's an improvement."

"I know." Still, I couldn't shake the feeling that she wasn't done with us. My mother was relentless. That's how she'd lived this long on nothing of her own. "I'm worried about it, though."

He put his arm around my shoulder and pulled me to him. "We just have to get through the next twenty-four hours. Then we're getting on a plane and getting out of the country. It's going to be okay."

"Okay," I said, wanting to believe it.

There were a lot of things I wanted to believe right now.

I WOKE UP BEFORE James the next morning. His broad chest was rising and falling in his sleep. I just lied there and watched him. I had so many emotions going on inside of me right now, it was hard to keep up. But one thing was certain.

I loved him, and I had to do what was right for him.

I got up and went out to the kitchen to make coffee. I needed to think straight. Today was the wedding; I had to play my part of loving girlfriend. That would be easy—too easy.

The problem was just about everything else.

My mother wanted to blackmail him and his family to keep quiet about the fact that I was an escort. A tabloid scandal like that might not do too much to injure James individually; he was a single billionaire, and he could do as he liked. Public opinion probably didn't mean that much to him, anyway. But his family—his mother—was a completely different story. Having her proper family associated with prostitution would ruin the Prestons' spotless reputation.

She would never forgive me for that. Worse, she would never forgive James.

So my mother was a threat and a problem. Celia Preston was both of these as well. She wanted me to disappear from James's life after next week. She offered to pay me to go away. She'd made it crystal clear that I was not Preston material—and that was based on the moderately respectable and completely false profile I was using for this job.

If she found out I was a whore, she might do something far worse than make me cry really hard and then send me on my way.

Also, what she'd said was still ringing in my ears. *James's children are going to be some of the wealthiest people in the country. They have to be able to handle the duties that come with that sort of privilege—and their parents have to be able to help them do that.*

I'd barely graduated high school. I had an alcoholic, grifter mother and an absent father. I lived in an apartment in the bad part of the city, and I was lucky to be there.

Also, there was the fact that I was a whore.

I swallowed my coffee. It tasted bitter, but I made myself drink it, anyway. I was not in a position to raise wealthy trust-fund children and help guide them through the duties that came with that sort of privilege. I got excited about James's super-fluffy towels; his fancy coffeemaker was like a ride at Disney World to me. I didn't have the experience or capacity to live in his world, or attempt to raise a family in it.

But it was this train of thought that brought me to my biggest problem. James was my *John*. Just because Celia Preston, my mother, and Jenny thought he cared about me did not make it true. Just because I hoped against hope that he cared about me did not make it true. He was paying for me to pretend I was his girlfriend. He was paying to fuck me.

The fact that he'd let me play with his hair yesterday afternoon and that he'd told me about his dead girlfriend did not a relationship make.

I was in love with him. That fact was as clear to me as the sun coming up outside. But I couldn't let my feelings cloud my judgment. I had to protect myself a little, too. Otherwise this was going to hurt too badly. I wished I could put a shield around my heart, so it wouldn't break all ugly and uneven when this was over…

Because that was the thing. James had told me he cared about me. But that was it. He'd held my hand. Our lovemaking had been totally intense—but how did I know he felt what I felt? Just being close to him made my heart feel as if it was going to burst. When he was inside me, I felt like I was going to weep because I finally felt complete.

I'd had a lot of sex. Too much. But none of it had ever made me feel anything close to the rush of emotion that I felt when I was with James. He'd been so tender with me, so loving, that it felt as if it was more than just sex for him, too.

But he hadn't said a word about the future. He'd said he cared about me right now. And that was something, and I would cling to it when he was gone, but it was only what it was.

If he felt more than he was saying, it made it even worse.

"Hey." He'd padded out to the living room in his sweats and nothing else. Of course, my traitor heart stopped when I saw him.

"Hey." I got up and went to him. I ran my hands down his gorgeous chest and kissed him deeply. Because he was only mine for right now. And I wanted to remember all of it, every feel, every detail of him, for when I was alone again. Which would be all too soon.

# JAMES

"Can you do my cufflink?" I asked. I could manage on my own, but I wanted her to touch me.

Audrey clasped it and straightened my tuxedo jacket. "You look amazing," she said, beaming at me. "I didn't think you could look any hotter than you do in a suit. But wow."

I laughed and ran my fingers down the pale lace of her dress. "You look stunning. I never knew I liked yellow until now." Her hair was up in an elegant bun. Her gown was long and strapless, with beading along the waist. She looked like a princess. You would never know that she lived in a piss-poor tenement apartment in Southie. She wore the gown, jewelry, and flawless makeup regally, as if they were hers from the beginning, not some borrowed finery from her madam.

My gut twisted at the thought.

"What?" she asked.

"Nothing," I said, more casually than I felt.

"Are you nervous about the ceremony?"

"Not really—it's more like adrenaline."

She nodded and let out a shaky breath. "Me too."

"Are you ready?" I asked, and she nodded. "Oh wait—I have something for you." I grabbed a turquoise jewelry box from my dresser and handed it to her.

"What's this?" she asked. Her voice was a little shaky.

"Just a necklace," I said, watching her face. "I saw it yesterday when we were walking down Newbury Street. I had the concierge pick it up for me." I'd seen it in the window, and I'd immediately wanted to buy it. It was beautiful and understated. It was a gift, but it was a selfish one: I wanted her to have something on her body from me. So I would always be touching her.

"I thought you might like to wear it today." She opened the

box and pulled out the delicate gold chain. There was a pendant attached, with two interlocking diamond-encrusted gold rings.

"It's so beautiful." She sounded touched.

I went behind her and fastened it around her neck. "I just wanted you to have something from me." I came around to face her, and I was suddenly embarrassed. My emotional boner was at full mast.

I was going to kill Cole for ever saying that to me.

She reached out and stroked my hot cheek. "James—I love it. I'll never take it off."

"It's beautiful on you." I smiled at her, pleased. "We should go. Happy occasions in my family don't come around that often—we don't want to miss any of it."

The attendants in the lobby stopped and stared at us. "You look amazing, Miss Reynolds," one of the girls called. Audrey smiled back at her shyly, pleased.

"I figured they'd be saying that to you," she said.

"No one's even bothering to look at me, babe," I said. "You're too stunning."

Kai was waiting for us outside. It was a beautiful June day, the weather lustrous and bright. I held Audrey's hand and led her to the car, careful of her long gown.

"If I may say so, Mr. Preston, Miss Reynolds is looking particularly lovely this afternoon," Kai said stiffly.

I smiled at him. "You *may* say so, Kai," I said, "and I agree."

When I slid into the car next to her, I looked at her smooth skin in the sunlight, her hand clasped around the necklace I'd given her.

My whole world was centered around her now. Everything else—everything that had seemed crucial to me only last week—was muted in the distance. The thought had been creeping up on me, but now I knew it all at once, sitting and watching her like that.

She smiled. "What?"

"What do you want to do after next week?" I asked her bluntly. I hadn't planned on asking it, but there it was.

"What do you mean?"

I tightened my grip on her hand. "What do you want to do when we get back from the Bahamas? About us."

She looked down, and I could see how flustered she was. "I don't… I don't know what to say."

"Do you want to keep seeing me?" I asked. My temples were pounding hard. *Fuck. What if she said no? Why the fuck was I doing this to myself?*

The thing was, women never said no to me. Never. As in not once. But that was for a different reason than the one I was looking for from Audrey.

"Of course I do," she said, the words coming out of her all in a rush.

I felt relieved until she looked up at me, her eyes dark and sad. "I just don't know if we should."

"Because of your mother?" I asked.

She nodded miserably. "Yours, too."

"What did she say to you yesterday?"

"Honestly, you don't want to know right now."

Anger flashed through me. "I don't even care anymore," I said flatly. I could pay Audrey's mother off, and I would shield Audrey from mine.

*If* that was what she even wanted.

"I'm tired of them both. We're adults. We can handle them."

The car pulled up at Trinity Church; it was unfortunately close to my apartment. Now that I'd finally started it, I wasn't ready to let the conversation end. I wanted to know where I stood. But we had to go in. The ceremony was going to start soon, and I had to go out back with my brother.

"We'll finish this later." I watched her until she nodded her assent.

"Audrey." She looked up at me, her face a mask. "Smile."

I DEPOSITED HER with Cole and Jenny, who were both looking very fancy and freshly fucked, in a pew toward the front of the church. I headed back toward the rectory, giving curt nods to my mother and father.

"There he is," Todd said when I came around the corner. "I was hoping you weren't going to jilt me."

"Ha ha," I said. I pushed all the bullshit in my head to the side and smiled at my brother. "This is your day. I wouldn't miss it for the world."

"Good," he said. There were nine of us back here; Evie had wanted an insane number of bridesmaids so Todd had to ask as many cousins and friends as he could, just to match her.

"Are you ready?" I asked, slapping him on the back.

"I'm past ready," he said. "I've been wanting to marry her since the day I met her. I just want her to be my wife, already. I can't wait."

"You get to be married forever," I reminded him.

"I know. But when you finally figure out what you want, you're pretty ready for forever. You know what I mean?"

THE ENORMOUS CHURCH was packed with guests. "How many people are here?" I whispered to Todd. We were waiting in the front of the church for Evie and her bridesmaids to come out.

"I think Evie said it was close to five hundred."

I let out a low whistle. "Jesus, Todd."

He smiled at me. "That's another good thing about not being involved in the planning. Just one more thing I didn't want to know."

I winced a little at that, thinking about what I'd told him about Evie. I'd never apologized to him about it.

"Todd, we never talked about that night again—"

"Jesus, James. Stop." He looked at me, incredulous. "Not only is now not a good time, but speaking of timing—look, I'm here, right? I'm obviously over it. You should be, too."

I laughed a little, and then I grinned at him, impressed. "Did you just out-big-brother me?"

"Yes," he said, grinning back at me. "Yes, I did. Now shut up and let me get married, already."

The music started. My parents had gone back and walked down the aisle first, followed by Evie's mom. Then one after another, Evie's sinewy cousins and friends came down the aisle. I was relieved and grateful that Todd had spared his groomsmen that tradition; we'd been able to enter through the side door and stand with him at the front. I could see Audrey in her pew. I smiled at her, fighting the overwhelming urge I had to wave.

She smiled back at me, making my heart stop. Cole saw us and grinned at me from farther down the bench—I really had to stop being such a little bitch. He was going to be relentless on this trip otherwise.

Finally, the wedding processional started. Everyone stood. Todd clasped his hands in front of him, looking expectant and happy. I admired him. He knew what he wanted, and he was going for it—no matter what I or anyone else had said.

My little brother had bigger balls than I'd thought.

Then came Evie, in an enormous crystal-encrusted dress. I was surprised she could lug it down the aisle, bony as she was. Her father walked beside her, tall and proud, ready to give her away to one of the richest families in Massachusetts.

Evie reached us and beamed at Todd from behind her veil. He clasped her hands. She looked absolutely thrilled. Maybe she really was sincere, I thought.

If Todd could forgive her, maybe I should, too.

The priest started speaking, and I turned my attention to him. Until a few moments later, when I saw a flash of pale yellow.

And I turned to see Audrey hustling down the aisle and out of the church just as fast as she could go.

# AUDREY

"*Hey*, Dre!" Jenny pulled me in for a hug.

I was relieved to be next to her, to be distracted by her gorgeous dress. "You are stunning," I said. She was wearing a long, jewel-toned mermaid gown, fitted to every inch of all her luscious inches. Her hair was also up in a bun. Large emerald earrings sparked on her ears. She looked classy and almost regal.

"Aw, thanks Dre. I guess I clean up okay," she said, beaming at me in pleasure. "Cole bought the dress for me this morning. And the earrings." Her skin looked flushed and glowing, like she had a very good-looking fever.

They must have had fun shopping again.

"That was nice," I said to him. He was looking sharp in a black suit.

He gave me a big grin. "It was my pleasure. Jenny looks beautiful." They clasped their hands together, and Cole moved in for a quick kiss. I moved away from them a little; it was suddenly getting hot in our aisle.

When Todd and his attendants came out, I tried not to stare at James. Tried and failed. He was so handsome in that tux, his huge shoulders visible under it, his steel-gray hair tousled to perfection. At one point he smiled at me, and my heart stopped.

I was going to have to give him an answer about what I wanted to happen after our trip. And even though I knew exactly what I wanted, I still had no idea what the *right* answer was.

"I still can't believe he ate that crab cake, Audrey," Cole said, pulling me from staring at James.

"Huh?" I asked.

"The crab cake you fed James. That first night I met you," he said. "He *hates* crab. Loathes it."

"I didn't know," I said, sheepish. "He didn't say anything."

Cole looked at me for a beat. "He must be completely in love with you."

I just sat there, gaping, my mouth opening and closing. I felt them both watching me, a deep blush creeping up my neck.

"S'kay, Dre," Jenny said, patting my arm. "It's gonna be okay. Close your mouth—you look so pretty, you don't wanna get drool on that dress."

"I didn't mean to make you upset," Cole said, his brow furrowed. I decided there and then, in spite of how he'd tried to take me home that night and what Jenny had told me about the thing with his balls, that I liked him.

"You didn't make me upset," I said. It came out like a stammer. My heart was pounding in my chest.

"Dre doesn't think it's possible that he has feelings for her—she doesn't believe in fairy tales. She's a *realist*," Jenny said, making it sound as if I were some sort of brain surgeon.

"Of course it's possible," Cole said, but now he had eyes only for her.

"Oh, Coley," she said, throwing her arms around his neck. They started kissing again.

I moved a little further down the pew. It was getting *really* hot now.

On one hand, I wanted to believe that Cole knew what he was talking about. That James was in love me—because that would be my wish come true.

On the other hand, I hoped he was wrong, and that James wasn't in love with me—because that wouldn't be the best thing for James. *I* wasn't the best thing for James.

The thing was, I still didn't even know what he wanted.

The enormous church was packed, the pews filled with beautifully dressed people. The music started and the Prestons led the wedding processional. Mr. Preston looked dapper in his suit; Mrs. Preston looked like a glittering, illicitly smoothed matriarch from hell in her long, silver-beaded gown, secured at the waist with an enormous diamond broach.

The nine bridesmaids were next—first Evie's cousins, Meghan, Michelle, and Sarah, their biceps popping as they clutched their bouquets. The bridesmaids' dresses were simple—black, strapless and stunning. Then Evie came down the aisle with her father. She looked so beautiful I almost cried. She smiled at me as she swept past, and I saw real joy on her face. I hoped that Celia was wrong about them, that this happy phase wasn't going to pass into a boring one and then into a dissatisfied one. Evie *did* love Todd. Maybe she loved his money more than she loved him, but I was positive that there was at least some real affection between them. I hoped it was enough to make them happy, and enough to last. I found myself crossing my fingers on my lap, my palms sweating, rooting for them.

Evie reached Todd, and they clasped their hands together, joy apparent on his face. My heart soared as I saw that even James was smiling at them.

But then I heard something behind me, and the soar turned to a plummet. A muttering, when we should all be silent. I turned and saw a familiar figure charging down the aisle—stringy bleached hair and a barrel chest shoved into a cheap black spaghetti-strapped sundress. The kind with the elastic visible on the outside. I cringed, wishing I could unsee my mother crashing Todd and Evie's society wedding.

"Jenny," I turned around and whispered. "I have to go. It's an emergency. Tell James I'll meet him at the reception."

"What?" she asked me louder than she should. People turned to stare at us.

"It's my *mother*," I hiss-whispered.

"Oh fuck, Dre. Go. I'll cover for you."

I ran down the aisle in a flash and a panic.

"HELLO, MRS. REYNOLDS," I whispered to her, grabbing her from the pew she was trying to slide down, away from me. "Got ya." I grabbed her arm, hard, and dragged her with me.

"That hurts," she said, her voice loud.

I dug my nails into the puffy flesh of her arm. "Shut the fuck up, right now, or you get nothing. And I'm gonna make this hurt a lot worse." I dug my nails in further. Wedding guests were watching us, surprised and shocked, but I didn't dare stop.

I hustled her out into the bright sunlight and dragged her to the side of the church; I couldn't risk standing out front. This was already worse than I could probably recover from. I turned to her. "Why are you here?" I was surprised to find myself on the verge of tears; I should have been all cried out where my mother was concerned.

She raised her hands at me in exasperation. "I told you yesterday: I need money. These people have it, Audrey. They have more than they need."

"But it's *theirs*," I wailed. "Just because they have it doesn't mean they have to spread it around. I'm sure they give to a lot of charities. But their money has nothing to do with you."

"I'm not getting their charity." She looked at me stubbornly.

"That's because you don't deserve it," I said. "You don't need charity, Ma. You maybe need a job. Or a hobby."

She sneered at me. "Look at you in that dress. Pretending to be something you're not. Who do you think you are?"

I shrugged at her, defeated. "I'm no one, Ma. I just don't think what you're doing is right. James already gave you twenty thousand dollars. He paid for Tommy to stay at the center for I don't even know how long. He's a good guy. You trying to punish him for hiring me isn't fair."

Hot, ugly tears sprang to my eyes again, and I struggled to hold them back; I had to go to the reception, and I had to be presentable. "I already told you I'd give you money. I can, a lot of it—two hundred thousand dollars. The rest is for Tommy. But you have to get out of here right now. 'Cause otherwise I'll never get it."

Her eyes almost popped out of her head. "That much?"

"Yes, that much. But not if I get fired first."

I just wanted her to go, but she wasn't budging. Not yet. She grabbed her cigarettes out of her purse and lit one. She exhaled and looked at me, her foot tapping. I could almost hear the wheels turning greedily in her head. "That's fine to start with," she said. "But I want you to tell your boyfriend that I need a salary. That money ain't gonna last forever."

"He's not my boyfriend, and he's not putting you on salary."

"I beg your pardon," said a voice from behind me, making me jump, "but I would say that I'm at least a *candidate* for boyfriend at this point."

I sighed and turned to James. The sun was hitting him from behind, making him look like some lit-up action hero, showing up just in time to save me from my mother's evil clutches. I cringed—I didn't want him here, rescuing me, anywhere near the filth that was my mom. I wanted him to take the sun and his billions of dollars and go back where he came from, safe from me and my ugly world.

"You're just my *date*," I said, raising my eyebrows at him and trying to keep my tone light.

He shrugged but smiled at me. "I feel so used."

"You two are cute," my mother said, blowing smoke in my direction and then turning to James. "And I'm gonna tell your parents just how much it warms my heart."

"That's not a great idea," James said, his tone changing dangerously. I watched as he drew up to his full height, the easy humor leaving his face.

So this is what it looked like when James Preston was really pissed. I would have to remind myself not to make him angry—even though it *was* pretty hot.

My mother shifted, just a little, as if she was on her guard now. "I wouldn't try anything, if I were you," she said to him. "Even if you don't let me talk to them today, I *will* get to them. After I talk to *The Tribune* and anybody else who'll listen."

"You're not going to do that," James said, watching her icily. "Because after I went and saw you yesterday and gave you a very generous amount of money out of the kindness of my heart, I called an old friend of mine. Who used to be Boston PD. Now he does private detective work."

"Is that so?" My mother tried to appear disinterested while smoking her cigarette down to the filter.

"I now have *him* on salary, Mrs. Reynolds. He was thrilled with the amount and promised to be hyper-vigilant when it comes to your case. He assures me that any probation violations you commit will be promptly reported to the East Boston PD. He did a quick search online and said that he already had a lot of material to work with, actually."

"Really," she said, but I could hear the bluff in her voice. "So what?"

"So *what* is that if you keep harassing my girlfriend or come near my family, I'm going to have him turn in his lengthy file immediately." He held up his fancy cell phone, which was as large as a Pop-Tart. It glinted in the sun. "He's in my contacts, Mrs. Reynolds. And he is ready, willing, and able to send you back to county as soon as I instruct him to."

She snorted and stubbed her cigarette out. "You're a real prick, you know that? Masquerading as a gentleman. Just like Little Miss Whore over here in her ball gown. You two deserve each other."

"Yes," he said as she huffed and walked away. "I know that."

# JAMES

*When* I'd seen her leaving the church, I only had one thought: *No.*

Then I'd found her with her piss-poor excuse of a mother, and I'd tried to make everything okay. We watched as her mother hobbled off into the afternoon, lighting another cigarette immediately and muttering to herself.

I held out my arm to Audrey. "Well," I said. "Sorry about that."

"You're kidding, right?" Audrey asked.

"No. That's your mother. I shouldn't have spoken to her like that."

She stopped dead in her tracks. "Oh, hell yes, you should have. She showed up here to ruin the wedding. She was in the church, James. She was going to make a scene."

"I'm still sorry."

"Is it true? About the detective you hired?"

"No," I said sheepishly. "But I know someone who can do that. I just wanted her to leave you alone."

"Thank you," she said. "You've been too good to me."

"Not as good as you deserve," I said. "I should have just threatened her to begin with. Then she wouldn't have gotten so greedy." I sighed and pulled her to me. "Let's just forget the drama for now. Your mother's been handled." *One down, one to go.* "Let's go to the reception. Both of our mothers have left me in serious need of a drink."

"Is the wedding over?" She peered at the church, looking crestfallen.

"Close enough. I don't think going back in there right now is wise. Let's just head to the Plaza." I called Kai; he pulled up in less than a minute.

"So, you left *during* the ceremony?"

"I gave the rings to my cousin. He handled it," I said, shrugging. "I don't even think Todd noticed."

"What about your parents?"

"I didn't check in with them, Audrey. I don't care."

She reached over and squeezed my hand. "James. What your mother said to me last night... you would care about it."

"I don't care what my mother wants," I said. "I care what *you* want. And you still haven't told me." I watched her profile, flustered but still perfect. "Tell me what you want, Audrey."

She fidgeted, and I sighed while I waited, my headache coming back. I put my hand on her thigh. I wanted her to feel me, to remember what it was like to have my hands on her.

"What I want and what you need are two different things." She put her hand over mine. "Does that make sense?"

"No," I said. "No, it does not." It didn't make sense, and it sounded like a thinly veiled letdown. My head started to pound. We pulled up outside the building, and I led her in, waiting for her to talk. The Plaza was splendid, decorated with every care for Evie and Todd's reception. I noticed none of it, walking through the ornately decorated lobby and heading straight for the bar in the ballroom. We were the first guests here—we had the place all to ourselves.

"Two martinis, please. Hot and dirty."

Audrey raised her eyebrow at me. "I've never heard you order that before."

"I'm just trying to keep you interested," I said, fighting to keep my voice even. I felt like I was about to lose something, and I never lost. *Fuck.* This could not be happening to me.

She had the upper hand and I had... nothing.

"Of course I'm interested," she said, a soothing sound in her voice. The actress was back, trying to calm me, trying to give me another pass.

"Audrey. Don't. I need to hear something from you that makes sense." The bartender handed us our drinks, and I took a long sip.

She leaned back against the bar and exhaled, as if she was either frustrated or defeated—or both. Then she turned and played with my jacket, putting her mask aside and looking at me with those big, honest *Bambi* eyes of hers. "I'm sorry," she said. "I'm just trying to keep it together right now. There's just a lot… to consider. It's not just about me."

She pressed herself against me, and I felt myself growing thick and hot against her, like I always did. This time, though, my arousal was almost painful. I didn't know what she wanted, and it was cutting me. I leaned down and kissed her, parting her lips and deepening the kiss, my tongue searching for hers.

She pulled back. "I have to do the right thing for you. *That's* what I want."

I kissed her again, running my hands over her bare shoulders delicately. I needed to show her what the right thing was. I grabbed her hand and put it on my cock. It throbbed against her.

It may have been crude, but it was honest. I needed her.

"James." She tried to pull away, but I stared down at her, willing her not to, as I grew harder still against her touch.

"Don't pull away from me. Ever." I meant that in more ways than one.

Other guests were starting to arrive, so I quickly grabbed her hand and brought her down the back hall. I found the coat-check room. It was June, so the room was empty. I pulled her inside and pressed her up against the wall, my erection fierce and accusatory against her now.

"I need you," I said. "Do you understand that?"

Her face, raw and open and honest, stared up at me. "Is this just sex? For you?" Her voice came out in a hoarse whisper.

I took a step back from her, wounded. I motioned to the air between us. "*This* is not just sex. And it hasn't been, even from the first time." I paused for a beat. "For me."

Something softened in her eyes, and she pulled me to her. She undid my pants quickly, almost desperately. My cock sprung free, and she stroked it between both of her hands while I fumbled with her long beaded gown. "Just unzip it." She turned around, and I undid her dress; it cascaded in heavy waves to the floor. She stepped outside of it and put her back to the wall, spreading her legs for me. "I want you."

I knelt before her, ripping my tuxedo jacket off. I took her delicate lace underwear and roughly shoved them to the side. Then I spread her legs a little more and kissed her cleft. She moaned and I circled her with my tongue, licking and sucking her clit.

"I need you inside me," she said desperately, grinding down on my face. "I need your cock." I sucked her harder, feeling her body bunch up and clench around me. She fisted her hands through my hair, and she came, hard and quick, crying out and shaking above me. I stood, my pants undone, and hitched my hard length against her slit. She was so wet, so ready for me, I started to get dizzy. "Do you want me?" I asked breathlessly against her ear.

In answer, she grabbed the tip of my cock and put it inside her. She looked up at me. "Fuck me, James. Please. I need to feel you inside me."

I lifted her up a little and adjusted my hips so that I was pinning her against the wall. Then I slid all the way into her, all at once. Her tight body stretched around mine, and she cried out, a mixture of pain and relief in her voice. "That's it, baby," she said. "That's what I wanted." She leaned down and kissed me fiercely, and I pounded into her, my thrusts as ragged as the emotions inside me.

I entered her deeper and harder each time. She arched her back, and the underwear I'd pushed to the side chafed against me, driving me wild. I was blind inside of her, pounding, seeking my release urgently. I held her shoulders, pumping into her over and over, my hands scraping over her breasts, still encased in her lace bra. I was so close, so out of control.

I wanted to fill her with me.

"Oh my God," she said, her body starting to quake and clench around me. "James." Then she threw her head back and cried out loudly as she shattered. That pushed me over the edge; I clung to her and pounded into her desperately, exploding into her.

"Audrey," I cried, clinging to her.

I set her down gently, both of us limp and shaky. I looked down and saw her face against my chest. Her eyes were shut tight.

"I love you," she whispered against me. "I just want you to

know that." I could feel her shaking. I held her to me, just loving the feel of her body against mine, the joy her words brought.

"And James."

"What, baby?" I asked, staring down at her gorgeous face, her eyes still scrunched up tight.

"I quit."

# AUDREY

At the reception, I tried Jenny's trick of thinking of it like a movie. If it was bad, she'd said, pretend you were watching it and that it was happening to someone else. If the movie took a turn for the worst and got really scary, just close your eyes, she said. Then it would be as if it never happened.

After James made love to me, and another powerful orgasm had wracked my body, I knew what I had to do. *This is the part where the heroine tells the hero that she loves him, and they live happily ever after*, I thought. Unfortunately, this wasn't a movie. This was my life, and there wasn't a happy ending in sight.

I closed my eyes tightly.

"I love you," I whispered against James. "I just want you to know that." He held me close as I shivered, pleasure mixed with misery pulsing through me.

"And James." I wouldn't look up. I kept my eyes closed, my face against his chest.

"What, baby?" he asked.

"I quit."

I ran away after that, as quickly as I could, back to my apartment. But even though I was miles away from him now, I could still feel his hands on me. I could still imagine the feel of my face against his chest.

I wrapped my arms around myself, trying to keep the pain that encircled me at bay. I sat at my window and stared out. The morning broke, hazy and humid. The sun rose up over the sky, and still, I didn't move. I thought I saw a limousine crawling down my street, but I might have imagined it. Limousines did not frequent my neighborhood.

In any event, I knew it wasn't James. He was probably on the plane by now, on his way to the Bahamas. And I was here, in my run-down Southie apartment, where I would always be.

Because I knew now what I'd known last night. This was where I belonged. I didn't belong to better. Between my mother and his, the opposition was too intense. The chasm between us too wide.

Because I loved him, I had to protect him.

From me.

# JAMES

I had someone from the hotel come up to pack my things for the trip. And Audrey's things. I didn't even let myself think about it.

I stared out the window at the hazy-looking morning, seeing nothing. I was too obsessed with the pain I was feeling. With the *why* of it.

Why she'd told me she loved me. And why she'd left.

I'd tried to run after her out of the Plaza, but I had to put my damn pants on first. By the time I'd dressed, she was gone. And I was left wondering just what the hell I was supposed to do now.

Todd stopped me on my way out of the lobby. He looked alarmed. "Are you leaving my *reception*?" he asked. "And what the hell happened back there at the ceremony? Why'd you run out?"

I watched the cars going by outside, itching to call Kai and go search for Audrey. The thing was, I didn't even know what she wanted. "I'm not leaving," I told him, fighting the very real urge I had to do just that. I had to find her and talk to her, but this was also Todd's wedding, and I was the best man.

And I'd already sort of run out of the ceremony.

"And the ceremony… I just had to go to the bathroom."

"The bathroom," Todd said, looking at me with flat incredulity.

"That's right," I said. "But I'm here now. And I'm not going anywhere. I promise."

"Where's Audrey?"

"Taking a break," I said, my voice ice.

My brother watched my face. "Is she coming back?"

I shrugged.

"Do you want a drink?"

"Not just one," I said, clapping him on the back and following him inside.

And now, not just one drink and only three hours of restless sleep later, I was still wondering if she was coming back.

But I was pretty sure I knew the answer to that.

I sighed and finished my coffee. Then I called Kai and told him to meet me out front. Now.

"WHO IS IT," she mumbled when I buzzed ten minutes later.

"You're kidding, right?" I asked.

She didn't answer me. A fuzzy silence filled the air while my temples pounded from the combination of my hangover and a dull, aching anger.

Then the monitor went blank, and I just buzzed again. And again.

SHE FINALLY RELENTED and let me up. "This is getting old," I said, pacing her apartment. "Didn't I just chase you here the other day?"

"That one was your fault," she said. The skin around her eyes was red and puffy, as if she'd been crying. I wanted to reach out and touch her face, but I didn't dare. I had no idea what was going on with her right now. Just like I had no idea what made her run from me last night.

But in no way did that mean I was done with her. Not even close.

"I thought you'd be gone by now," she mumbled.

"They pushed the flight back. Everyone was too hung over to make the earlier one." I made a big show of looking at my watch. "The flight's leaving from Logan at eleven. I'd like you to be on it."

She looked at me, her shoulders sinking down, as if I was asking too much. Part of me wanted to take what pride I had left and leave. But she was still wearing the necklace I'd given her last night, her fingers twined tightly around it. That gave me hope.

"Audrey. We had an arrangement," I reminded her. "I want

you to come with me on this trip."

"Why." Her voice was flat.

I ran my hands through my hair in frustration. Any small shred of patience I had left was being ground down to dust. "Is this… a hormone thing?"

She rolled her eyes and flopped down on her futon. "It's nothing that simple," she said. She sounded both miserable and resigned.

I paced the length of her apartment. "You have to come on the trip. For a few reasons," I said, my voice firm. "Not the least of which is our agreement, and the fact that my parents think I'm finally in a relationship. I have another whole week to get through. You're my buffer, remember?"

She didn't look up at me. "I'm the wrong buffer, James."

"It doesn't matter if you're the wrong buffer. That's not what we're talking about."

"That's what *I'm* talking about," she said.

"I don't know what you want from me," I said, my voice rising. "You said last night—"

"Stop," she said, cutting me off. "I don't want anything from you."

I felt as if she'd punched me. I stopped pacing and looked at her: her face was pale, and she was hanging on to that necklace for dear life.

I took what I hoped was a steadying breath.

"I guess I need to remind you that we have a contract, Audrey. I expect you to perform your part of the bargain. If I remember correctly, you were planning on paying me back some of the funds I'd forked over toward your… family expenses." A blush crept up her neck at my words. Even though I knew I was hurting her by what I was saying, I didn't stop. "I'm expecting you to follow through."

Part of what made me successful in business was that I knew how to motivate people, even when the motivation was ugly. So now I was ugly-motivating Audrey. I was hurting her to get what I wanted. At this point, I didn't care—I just wanted her to get on the damn plane. I'd work on my manners then.

Maybe.

"Fine. Of course I need to pay you back," she mumbled.

"You can change at my place, but we need to hurry," I said. "Oh, and Audrey—"

"Yes?"

"I want you to know something. For the remainder of our contract, I will no longer be needing the full range of your services."

# AUDREY

Kai studiously avoided looking at me as James led me to the car. I sank down into the back of the Mercedes SUV, defeated and resigned. I'd hurt James, and now James was hurting me.

*He would no longer be needing the full range of my services.* It was like a slap across the face. I should tell him he'd finally figured out the way to execute a bitch-slap, but that would require speaking to him.

I sighed and looked out the window.

"What's the matter?" he asked. "Besides the fact that you're back in this car with me?"

"You're kind of being mean," I said. "I'm just pointing that out to you."

He said nothing. He just looked out the other window, away from me.

His words and his dark look hurt. But maybe that was a good thing. Maybe I could distance myself from him, and this would all work out for the best for the both of us.

Maybe.

BACK AT HIS PLACE, I showered, changed, and made sure I had everything I needed.

"We're all packed—everything's ready to go. Do you have your passport?" James asked.

I nodded. I took a long last look around his apartment, mentally saying goodbye to it. When we got back from our trip, I would be going home.

"What?" he asked.

"Nothing," I mumbled, shrugging. "This is the last time I'm

going to be here, is all. I just want to remember it."

James closed his eyes as if he were trying to ward off a headache.

"I'm sorry," I said. "I'll just stop talking."

"I'm the one who's sorry," he said, opening his eyes and coming to me. He grabbed my hands, and I looked at him, a mixture of hope and fear coursing within me. "About last night. I didn't get a chance to tell you—"

"S'okay," I said, abruptly pulling back from him and cutting him off again. "Don't even worry about it."

His steel-blue eyes flashed with what looked like hurt for a second, but then he put his billionaire all-business face back on. It was like I could see him closing himself off from me. He straightened himself up to his formidable height, his enormous biceps accentuated by the snug fit of his T-shirt. "Let's just go, Audrey. We've got a plane to catch."

JAMES AND I WERE SILENT on the way to Logan and as we went through security. Being next to him and not holding his hand was awkward; the absence of his touch was palpable.

Celia and Robert Preston were in the waiting area, as were Todd and Evie, Jenny and Cole, Evie's cousins and their husbands, and a crowd of other people who I'd glimpsed at the ceremony last night.

Celia rose up as soon as she saw me. "Audrey, dear, we were worried you weren't going to make it. What happened to you last night?" she asked. "I would have asked my son at the reception, but he avoided me like the plague, as usual."

I felt James stiffen next to me. "I wasn't feeling well, Mrs. Preston. I'm so sorry I had to leave—I missed everything. James said it was extraordinary." I fake-smiled at Mrs. Preston and decided then and there that I needed to throw everything I had at her this week: James had protected me from my mother, and I needed to protect him from his.

"You're better this morning?" She looked at us shrewdly, probably noticing that we weren't holding hands for the first time ever.

I reached over and grabbed James's hand, squeezing it. "I'm much better, thank you. I'm really looking forward to this trip."

She smiled at me tightly and went to sit back down. But then stopped herself. "Oh, I meant to ask you—who was that strange woman you were talking to yesterday at the church? She caused quite a stir in the back, I understand."

The fake smile was still plastered to my face. I hung onto it and James's hand for dear life. "She was just some woman who wandered in off the street—I didn't want her interrupting the ceremony. So I helped her out."

Celia Preston managed to raise one eyebrow slightly, and her gaze shifted to her son. "And you left your brother's wedding to go help Audrey with this random stranger?"

James shrugged. "I wanted to make sure Audrey didn't need me. Turns out she didn't. She handled it all on her own."

"How impressive. You almost make it sound as if Audrey's an actual adult." Celia chuckled meanly and sat back down.

That's when they called the flight; I exhaled in relief. "Saved by the bell," James muttered under his breath. Then: "I really hope there's a fully stocked bar on board."

THE PRIVATE PLANE was impressively luxurious, of course. The chairs were wide and comfortable-looking, with plenty of space to spread out. James quickly said hello to Todd and Evie, and I hugged them both in congratulations. Then he dragged me all the way toward the back of the plane, far away from his parents.

At least we were still holding hands.

Jenny and Cole flopped down across the aisle from us. Cole was wearing enormous sunglasses on top of his head and a polo shirt, his black hair artfully wild and spiky. Jenny was wearing a fedora, a black jumpsuit, and a frown—directed at me.

"Where'd you run off to last night?" she asked. "We had to watch James drown his sorrows in about ten bourbons."

"I had a thing," I said, still forcing a smile on my face.

She frowned at me some more then turned to James. "Hey,

James. Wanna switch seats for a minute?" He nodded, probably relieved to break our stony silence. Jenny turned to me as the flight attendant went through the safety presentation. "What's the matter with you two?" she whispered.

I leaned over to check that James and Cole couldn't hear us; they were deep in conversation. "A lot," I admitted. "I'm thinking I just need to be his escort. No more feelings. It's too messy. There's too much at stake." *Including my sanity,* I thought. *Not to mention my heart.*

*And, most importantly, James's whole future.*

She raised her eyebrows at me from under her fedora. "He was a mess last night at the reception, Dre. Seriously. He was miserable without you. And he still looks like that today—like he has an emotional hangover. You need to make that right."

I picked at some imaginary lint on my skirt. "I don't know if I can do that, Jenny."

"Dre." Jenny waited until I looked up and met her eyes. "Don't you try to fool me. I know you have bona fide feelings for that man."

I looked at her defiantly. "I thought you said thoughts and feelings were invisible, Jenny. No one's supposed to be able to see them."

"They're not invisible when they're written all over your face," she snapped.

We just looked at each other for a beat.

"I'm trying to do the right thing," I said. "For both James and me."

"Did you talk to him about how you're feeling? Did he tell you what *he* wants?" she asked.

I shook my head no. "He tried to. But honestly, I don't want to know. Because no matter what he says, I know I'm not the best thing for him."

Jenny squeezed my arm. "You're such a good person—one of the best people I know. When're you going to give yourself a chance?"

"A chance for what?" I asked miserably.

"To be happy," Jenny said.

"I *am* happy. At least I know what it feels like now," I mumbled.

She frowned at me again. "If you love him—and I'm guessing that's what you mean—you've got to give him a chance," she said.

"I can't, Jenny." I felt as if I might cry. "I'm just trying to keep this from going from bad to worse. Bad is where I'm at. I love him, and he's totally out of my league. His mother hates me, and she'll never accept me into their family. My mother's already tried to blackmail him. That's why she came to the wedding. It's not like we're ever going to be one big, happy family."

I took a deep breath. "And it could get so much worse—that's why I don't even want to know how he feels. What if he loves me back, huh? It'll never work out and that would break my heart. Or what if he *doesn't* love me back? Then *that* would break my fucking heart. You get it?"

"I get it." Jenny sighed. "But you gotta stop this overthinking. And you gotta let him have a say. Otherwise you'll never find out."

"Find out what?" I asked.

"Who he *is*, Dre." Jenny looked like she pitied me a little. "If you don't let him tell you how he feels about you, you'll never get a chance to know. And that might seem safe and perfect, in that little airtight container that you're trying to create for yourself, but it's not right.

"I know you: you want everything in order. You want to take care of Tommy and keep your Mom out of trouble and keep James up on a pedestal. But that little airtight container's not big enough for you, girl. It's not big enough for you to have a *life*."

"Huh," I said. I picked some more imaginary lint off my skirt. Jenny knew me better than I wished she did. "Have I told you lately that you're smart?"

"You have," she said and smiled. "So if you think I'm so smart, you listen to what I'm saying. You gotta be brave here. Desperate times call for desperate measures. And maybe some liquid courage."

She hit the button above us and an attendant appeared instantly. "We'd like two large glasses of alcohol," Jenny said. "Any kind you got. This being such a fancy flight and all, I'm sure it's all good."

# JAMES

The plane ride passed in a blur. Cole and I drank bourbon and talked about sports. He must have sensed that I needed to keep things on an even keel; he didn't even bug me to switch back to my old seat so he could be next to Jenny.

We got to the island, and although I was sure it was beautiful, I didn't really notice. I'd been to a dozen beautiful islands before. I didn't give a fuck. Audrey was like a prisoner next to me, silent and resigned.

We'd just checked in when I heard my name. "James!" I turned around to see Todd waving at us. "Drinks poolside tonight," he called, giving me the thumbs-up. It was still early, which meant Audrey and I had a few hours to ourselves.

I didn't know whether to laugh or cry.

We walked through the resort's property, and although I supposed it was sufficiently luxurious, I noticed none of it. All I could think about was Audrey. I didn't know what was going on inside of her—I had no idea what she was thinking—and it made me feel off-kilter.

She'd told me she loved me… had she meant it? She'd been so distant from me in the hours since then, it was as if she was someone else.

The valet brought us to our villa, which was an enormous, ornate pink-stucco house with a wraparound porch. We went inside, and he assured me that our luggage and all the liquor I'd requested would arrive shortly. We had a butler assigned to us, but I dismissed him immediately; I only wanted to be alone. I wasn't even sure I wanted to be with Audrey right now.

I had the sinking feeling she was getting ready to tell me something I didn't want to hear. Again.

"This is amazing," she said, walking through the house. "It's so pretty."

I looked at her then. She had a full, printed skirt on and a tank top. Her hair was pulled back in a low ponytail. She looked casual, young, and so beautiful it cut me.

"Audrey." She looked up at me. "I can't do this. You have to tell me what's going on with you."

A shadow crossed her face. "James… let's just get through today. There's been so much going on."

"Did you hear from your mother again?"

"No," she said. "But I know I will."

I reached out and grabbed her hand, pushing my wounded pride out of my way. "I'll help you with her. You know I will."

She smiled at me, but she pulled her hand back quickly. "I have to do it myself."

I sighed in frustration. "Is this the cowboy thing again?"

"Sort of." She stepped back. It was as if there was some sort of chasm in between us now. Even if I reached out, I wouldn't be able to get to her.

"I'm going to go check out the rest of the place and take a quick shower," she said. And just like that, she was gone.

The butler buzzed then, bringing in the booze I'd requested. His timing was the one upside thus far today. The only one.

TEN MINUTES LATER, Audrey called to me from the bedroom. I went in, gripping my bourbon. I wasn't sure if I was going to get Jekyll or Hyde right now.

I stopped short when I went into the room. She was naked on the bed, her glorious body spread before me. "I know you said you didn't want my services anymore." She looked up at me and ran her hand down herself, skimming her breasts. Her nipples were hard and erect. "Would you reconsider?"

I just looked at her, dumbfounded. I took another swig of bourbon.

This was going to be a long day.

"Are you fucking kidding me, Audrey?"

She sat up immediately, as if she were surprised by my tone. "No."

"You think I want to have sex with you? Right *now*? After the way you've been acting?"

She crossed her hands in front of her chest, trying to cover her nakedness. "I thought… I thought it would make it better. Like we could get back to what this was supposed to be." She looked up at me defiantly. "Services requested and services rendered. You're paying for it, remember?"

A cold rage descended on me, and I had to fight to calm myself. I wanted to throw the glass I was holding; I wanted to hear it shatter and smash. But I stopped myself. One of us had to act like an adult.

"Audrey," I said, trying to keep my voice under control. "Do you feel as if I've mistreated you?"

Now a blush started to creep up her neck. She grabbed the comforter and pulled it around her, as if to shield herself from me. I thought I saw a flash of sadness or regret in her eyes, but it was only there briefly. "No," she said. Her voice was strained, like she was trying to keep it even.

"Then why are you doing this to me?" I asked.

She winced then. "I'm not doing this to you, James. I'm doing it *for* you." It looked as if she might cry, but she was still trying to sound defiant.

"Audrey," I said, "what the fuck does that even mean?"

Her face crumbled then and she looked sad, defeated. "I meant what I said last night. About loving you," she said, miserably. "But I wish I didn't."

I sat down on the bed heavily. I took another sip of my drink and looked at her wounded face. She was clutching the necklace again and I took that as a sign. A sign to be brave.

"Well, it would suck if you didn't mean it," I said. "Because I love you, too."

She didn't look at me. She just reached over and grabbed my hand, holding on for dear life.

"JESUS, AUDREY," I said, cradling her on my lap. "You don't have to cry."

"But I *do*," she wailed, blowing her nose as she rested against my chest.

"The fact that we're in love," I said, savoring the way the words felt on my lips, "that's a good thing. Not something to get hysterical over." I ran my hands down her back, thrilled and relieved to have her back in my arms, the walls between us finally coming down.

"But you *can't* love me back," she said, blowing her nose again, "It's going to ruin *everything*."

"In what screwed-up universe does this ruin everything?"

"In yours," she said. "Your screwed-up universe. No wait—mine."

I took a deep breath and pulled her in closer. "Can you please start making sense? I don't understand what you're saying."

She sighed and nestled in closer to me. "James, I love you. I do." She looked up at me, her face honest and afraid.

"I love you, too," I said. It felt so good to say it out loud. Joy surged through me, and I hugged her to me. Audrey's eyes were still shining with tears, but these looked happier. I leaned down and kissed her, my feelings for her overpowering and fierce.

But she pulled back. "What?" I asked. "Why are you pulling away from me?"

"I don't want you to love me."

"Why the fuck not?" I asked hotly.

"Because I'm not good for you, James. I can't be with you like that."

"Of course you can."

She shook her head. "I'm an *escort*, James. That's a fancy word for hooker, in case you didn't know."

"I know exactly who you are. I couldn't care less what you've done."

"Well, good for you," she said, moving a little farther away from me. She dried her eyes. "Your family would have a very different opinion, I'm guessing."

"Good for them. They can call me to complain about it. Trust me, I won't answer. They can have a hell of a time expressing their dissent to my voicemail, which I never check."

She sighed, sounding frustrated. "I don't think you've thought this through."

"And you have?" I asked, challenging her.

"I have," she said, looking at me levelly. "And no matter how many different ways I picture it, this doesn't work out."

"Then you're a pessimist," I said. I pulled her back to me.

"James… really. What about your parents?"

"I'll deal with them," I said. "We don't owe them any further explanation—about your mother, or your background, or anything else right now. It's not their business. And we're not ready to tell them anything. We might never tell them."

"Babe," she said, a hopeless look on her face. "I didn't tell you what your mother said to me. And she said it when she thought I was a legitimate, above-board art student. Not an escort."

I waited, my temples beginning to pound again. "What," I said, not bothering to make it a question.

"She told me she wants us to break up after the honeymoon. She said that your children are going to have an incredible amount of money and society responsibility, and that they need parents who can help them with that."

The pounding in my head got worse. "And she said you're not capable of that."

"She didn't say that." Audrey shrugged against me. "She didn't have to. I'm *not* capable."

"First of all, that's not true. You're perfectly capable. Second of all, I don't care what my mother thinks. I never have."

Audrey looked up at me. "I don't believe that."

"What do you mean?" I asked.

"I think you understand what your mother is saying, even if you don't want to. And I feel exactly the same way," she said. "Your children are going to be some of the richest kids in the country. You need someone who can help them—with private schools, charity drives, organic foods, stuff I can't even begin to imagine. That's not me."

"You can learn all that stuff," I said.

"I think we're getting ahead of ourselves here," she said. "The point is, your mother says I'm fine for right now. After that, I need to be gone. And she doesn't even know what I really am." She looked up at me miserably. "She offered to pay me off, James. After this trip. I would never take it, but I just thought you should know."

"She's going to pay, all right," I said, mostly to myself. I was quiet for a minute, running it all through my mind. "Audrey. Do you want to take the money and just go?"

"Of course not," she said. "But I think she's right—I *don't* think I'm good for you. I don't even know what you want from me."

"All I want," I said, pulling her to me, "is you."

"Don't say things like that," she said, her eyes filling with tears even as she settled against me. "*Don't.* I'm the cowboy. You're the bed. This is gonna end badly." She blew her nose again.

"Audrey," I said. "Please stop talking. And sniffling. You're the cowboy, remember? Cowboys don't sniffle."

# AUDREY

I'd lied to Jenny: I'd told her I'd be brave and that I'd be smart. But lying naked and waiting for James was not brave, and it was not smart. It was, however, all I had. It was my last-ditch effort to make him just a John and to save him from me.

It hadn't worked. He had shown me who he was. And he had told me that he loved me.

When he said it, it was the best thing that had ever happened to me and the worst thing that had ever happened to me. I didn't know whether to laugh or cry. So I cried. A lot.

And then he'd held me, and I'd tried to tell him that it wasn't going to work out, but he'd just kept holding me.

After a while, we just snuggled together on the bed and fell asleep. Neither one of us had slept much the night before. I nestled into his arms, feeling protected and for once in my life, absolutely happy.

I woke up a little while later in my normal state: absolutely petrified about the future.

"Hey." James opened one eye and looked at me, a smile spreading over his face. "Hey—I love you."

I couldn't help it. It was contagious; a huge smile broke out over my face, too. "Hey. I love you, too." We grinned at each other, and I kissed him then, hungrily. But as soon as I thought of the word "hunger" my stomach started howling loudly.

"We need to eat," he said, still grinning at me. "Does my girlfriend want to have an early dinner by the pool?"

Even though I would berate myself for it later, I couldn't wipe the stupid smile off my face. James's happiness was infectious; his easy joy at our newly declared feelings was palpable. "I would love to," I said.

"Okay," he said.

"Okay," I said.

Our truce must have been patently obvious, because Cole smiled at us in approval when we finally made it out of our villa. We went to the restaurant by the enormous infinity pool; he and Jenny were sitting at the bar.

"I see some people who look like they had sex and made up," Cole called, grinning at us.

"We didn't have sex," James said. I could see how Cole thought so: James's skin was flushed and glowing, a happy smile on his face.

"You didn't?" Cole asked. He looked impressed. "You might as well put a ring on it, bro. You're done for."

"Cole, leave them alone," Jenny said, and she punched him playfully. "You two go have lunch and then come swimming with us." She stood up and winked at me. I noticed she was wearing a crop top and a minuscule, black bikini bottom. Her curvy, luscious body was on full display. Cole was staring at her ass, a worshipful look on his face.

"I'm glad you two look happy again," she said. They turned and headed toward the pool, holding hands; I noticed that Jenny was indeed wearing a thong bikini like she'd threatened. Cole put his hand firmly on her ass, and she turned and winked at me again before putting her aviator sunglasses on.

I had to hand it to Jenny: she was certainly batting Cole Bryson around like a cat toy. And he appeared to like it. A lot.

"Don't you dare look at her in that bikini," I said to James accusingly.

"I would never," he said, laughing. "But I might have to buy you one of those."

WE HELD HANDS all through our meal. I was so relieved to be with him again, to feel our connection back. Even though it had only been one night, it had been the longest one of my life. I didn't let myself think about all the bad things that were on the flip side of my feelings for him. I couldn't bear to spoil the moment.

Everything was perfect if I could let myself ignore almost everything but James. I'd never seen him so happy before, so relaxed. For once, I wasn't going to be the one to take that away from him.

We ordered margaritas, fish tacos, and a curried vegetable rice. We ate every morsel. "I think I'm going to sink when I get into the pool," James said, pushing his empty plate away.

"It was worth it, though," I said. "Yum." He grabbed my hand and beamed at me. Heat shot through me at his touch, the way I felt under his gaze. But just when I thought nothing could burst my bubble, Celia Preston's slim figure cast a wide shadow over our table.

"Mother," James said by way of a greeting. "How inconvenient of you to show up and ruin a perfectly decent meal."

"You two look much happier," she said, ignoring his comment. She eyed our entwined hands and empty margarita glasses.

"We are, Mother," James said. He looked up at her, his face clear and calm. "I've actually never been this happy."

If his directness shocked her at all, she didn't let it show—not even the slightest ripple moved across her face. Of course, that could have been the result of all the filler she'd shot into it before the wedding. I'd never know for sure.

"How lovely for you," she said. She gave me a filthy look.

I had a bad feeling I was going to hear about this from her later.

WHEN YOU VACATIONED with billionaires, no one worried about how high the bar tab was getting. The older guests, including Mr. and Mrs. Preston, sat under umbrellas, playing cards and sipping an endless supply of white wine. Mrs. Preston intermittently cast disapproving scowls my way, which I pretended I couldn't see in the glare of the tropical sun.

The rest of us drank rum punches, which seemed to be constantly served by the white-linen-clad waitstaff. By the time the sun started to set, there were a lot of extremely drunk, extremely rich people around the infinity pool. I almost wished there were a lifeguard on duty.

Not that I needed a lifeguard; I was hanging on to James as if he were my own personal flotation device. He had me pinned up against the wall of the pool, his arms wrapped around me, the crystal water splashing over his enormous, gorgeous chest.

It was actually his erection that had me pinned against the wall.

"You know we can't actually have sex right here," I reminded him as he leaned in to kiss me again.

"What?" he asked, smiling at me. "Oh, that." He pressed his hard length in between my legs, and I moaned—and then I thought better of it and swatted him.

"Stop," I said.

"I actually can't stop," he said, grinning. "You're so fucking hot in that bikini."

I laughed. "I appreciate that and all, but you need to calm down. So we can at least walk back to our room without people staring at your crotch."

"Then let's just stay here," he said, poking me again with it.

"I need to help you with that thing," I said, laughing. "It seems like it's gonna burst."

"Now, that's an offer I can't refuse," he said. He pulled away from me and went to my side. "I'll just need a minute to calm down. Then I'm throwing you over my shoulder and carrying you home."

I linked my hand through his. "Works for me."

We watched Cole and Jenny engage in a vicious battle with Todd and Evie for the biggest splash contest. In between jumps, they were doing tequila shots.

"Jenny seems like she's warming up to Evie," I said.

"Four shots of tequila will do that to you," James said.

Cole jumped up and did a massive cannonball, leaving an atomic blast of water in his wake. Jenny was clapping and jumping up and down on the side of the pool. When Cole came up from under water, she reached down to give him a high five. Instead, he pulled her into the pool, giving her a huge kiss.

"I think Cole's in love with her," James said out of the blue. "I don't know if he knows what that means, though."

"He's never been in a relationship?" I asked.

"Not one that lasted more than two weeks."

We watched them for another minute, their arms wrapped around each other, both of them carefree and happy. James turned back to me. "I want you to come to California with me when we get back."

"James, I can't—my brother, my mom, all the other stuff we haven't even talked through—"

"I don't care," he said, cutting me off. "We'll bring your brother with us. The rest of it will sort itself out."

"I don't know what to say."

"Then don't say anything," James said, shrugging. "Or just say yes."

HE DIDN'T CARRY me back to the room like he threatened to, but we did practically run there.

I let myself enjoy the moment. Maybe the hot sun was getting to me, or maybe I'd had too many rum punches. But I didn't let myself think about all the bad things in our way. I only thought of him.

"Oh my God, I need you," he said. He kissed me as soon as we made it through the door, his hands skimming my body, my bathing suit still damp against me.

Then he stopped. He ran his hands through my hair and looked down at me, his steel-blue eyes burning. "Please don't ever pull away from me again like you did last night. My fucking heart can't take it, Audrey. I mean it."

I bit my lip. "I know you don't understand, but I did that to protect you."

He took my face in his hands. "You're not protecting me by running away from me. I need you to stand by my side." His eyes searched mine. "Do you understand?"

"Yes, but—" I started.

"No buts," he said, dropping his hands from me and taking a

step back. "I'm telling you what I need. I love you. I need to know that you love me, too, and that you're going to stay with me."

"I can't promise you that," I said, feeling my buzz wear off instantly. My doubts returned, numerous and ugly. "I don't know if I can. What if I think that I'm not the right thing for you? I love you—I want you to have everything in life that you're supposed to have. And that's probably not me."

"Do you think I give a fuck," he spit out, "what my parents think? When I first realized that I had feelings for you, I was afraid. But not of them—I was afraid for *you*. I didn't want to ask you to be with me, because I knew they wouldn't treat you fairly.

"But now that I know you love me and we're together, I don't care—I'll let you make a choice about whether or not you want to subject yourself to their dislike, sure. Because that's fair, and that's your choice to make. But if you think I'm going to let you choose what's best for *me*, you're fucking crazy. Because I already know what that is. It's you. I choose you." He crossed his arms across his powerful, naked chest. "So there."

"What your mother said to me about the future makes sense, James," I said, holding my ground. "Your kids are going to have more money than *you* even have. Scary money. And I'm a fucking *whore*, James. People will find out about me. You can't let your kids have a whore for a mother." All of a sudden, the truth of what I was saying hit me, and hot tears spilled down my cheeks.

"Stop." He came back to me then, wrapping his arms around me, pulling me to his chest. "If we were lucky enough to have kids, and they were lucky enough to have you as a mom...they wouldn't care, Audrey. We'd teach them about the real world. In the real world, you have to make choices. Hard choices sometimes. But you do it to protect the people you love the most."

He held me fiercely, and I clung to him. "Because that's what a real family does. They would be lucky to have you, Audrey. And so would I."

# JAMES

"They would be lucky to have you, Audrey. And so would I."

Once I had put all my cards on the table, I held my breath. I loved her, and I wanted her to know it wasn't just for now.

I wanted a hell of a lot more than that.

"Is it okay if I cry again? For just a second?" she asked, clinging to me.

"One second," I said. "We are on vacation, after all."

She nodded against my chest. "I just didn't think," she said, sniffling. "I didn't know. I never even let myself hope—"

"It's okay," I said, stroking her hair. "We're together now, and everything's going to be okay."

After a second, as promised, she calmed down and pulled back from me, wiping her eyes. "I'm a mess," she said and laughed.

"You're a hot mess," I corrected her, my hands skimming down her skin again. Actually, she was freezing; our bathing suits were still wet, and she was covered in goose flesh. "I think there's a hot tub out back. Do you want to go in it?"

"That sounds good," she said. I grabbed her hand and led her through the house to the small, private, fenced-in backyard. There was a large hot tub back here and an outdoor shower. We both got in, and I hit the jets; the hot water felt amazing. I pulled her to me, resting my hands on top of her bikini bottom.

"No one can see us back here, right?" she asked, looking at the high fence. Before I even had the chance to nod, she'd undone the top of her bikini, throwing it casually to the side. Her breasts were round and luscious, her nipples hard from the chill. She had the faintest beginnings of a tan imprinted on her skin. She stepped out of her bottoms and threw those to the side as well, coming to me.

It had been too long. She must have felt it, too. The need.

Without a word, she leaned up and pulled my face toward hers, drawing me in for a deep, luxuriant kiss. Our tongues connected, and I got rock hard again. She quickly undid my swim trunks and pushed them down, grabbing my thick cock within her hands expertly, stroking me up and down in the hot, bubbly water. She took her other hand and cupped my balls lovingly, all the while twining her tongue around mine, making me wild for her.

I was so hard it almost hurt. "Poor baby," Audrey said, still stroking me. "All that crying I did, and you just needed some attention."

"I'm fine," I said hoarsely. "It was worth the wait."

She was working me with her hands, and I started to thrust against her blindly, not even really aware of what I was doing.

"I want to you feel you inside me—deep," she said. She let go of my cock and came next to me. She leaned over the side of the jacuzzi, so her ass was facing me, and her face was against the warm tile of the patio. "Take me from behind," she ordered.

I moaned before I even put myself against her. "I'm not gonna last that long like this, babe," I said, stroking her glorious ass. She spread her legs a little, ready for me. The bubbles in the hot tub rubbed up against my balls and my huge erection, and I positioned my tip against her slit, feeling the wetness that was all her. I slid my hardness against her, getting lubricated and so hard I was about to burst.

She reached down and positioned my cock. She slid me into her, at first easing just my tip in. And then she moaned, and with a few motions of her hips, made sure I entered her all the way to the base of my shaft.

It felt so good to be back in her, I almost came right then.

"Holy fuck," I said. She leaned back over the side so I was positioned right behind her, in balls deep. I grabbed her hips and her ass and began to thrust. Each stroke made me moan, her tight body clenching around me, my balls slapping against her and splashing in the water. Each thrust brought me closer to the edge of oblivion. She pushed back against me, and I put one hand on her back, holding her down, continuing to thrust into her deeply, almost savagely. I wanted to fuck her forever, and I wanted to come right then. I wanted her to turn around to face me so I could kiss her, and I never wanted her to get out of this position ever again.

"James," she moaned. "Oh my God. I want to feel you explode in me."

I thrust into her harder, deeper, our bodies crashing against the water and the stone. Her body was so tight, squeezing everything out of mine. I was relentless, driving into her deeper each time. Her tight body stretched to accommodate me, and she moved back against me. I grabbed her ass and squeezed. "Oh my God," I said, starting to spasm.

"James," she cried out, her body clenching and shaking around mine.

"I fucking love you," I said, and came in a torrent.

THE NEXT AFTERNOON, I rolled off of Audrey, breathing hard. "That was brilliant," I said. Now that we'd started having sex again, we couldn't stop. We'd been sneaking back to our villa whenever we could.

"What?"

"Us. Together. I think we're even better now that we're official." I trailed my fingers lazily down her naked shoulders, thrilled just to play with her long hair and touch her beautiful, smooth skin.

"You think?" she asked.

"I know," I said.

"Do we have to go to dinner tonight? Isn't everyone going to be too drunk by then?" she asked. "I wish we could just stay here."

I sighed and flopped on my back. Our entire party had been drinking all day, again. "Unfortunately, the Prestons do not get too drunk to do anything—we're high-functioning alcohol abusers. We should join them. Todd wants me to make an effort while I'm here."

"Okay. But I'm worried about the way your mother's been looking at me since we've been here," Audrey said, nervously. "I'm all over her bad radar. I can tell."

"I'll protect you from her," I said. "But Audrey, you should get used to it. She's not ever going to change."

"No," said Audrey, looking up at the ceiling. "She's not. And neither is my mother."

"You're probably right," I said, lacing my fingers through hers. "So let's just stay the hell away from both of them."

She smiled, and I traced the outline of her jaw with my finger. "I meant what I said, you know. About California. You'll love it out there. And Tommy will, too. The weather is perfect—except for the smog. And then there's the traffic. But we have all the best restaurants."

She didn't say anything for a beat, and my heart was pounding in my ears.

"Tommy is really happy at New Horizons," she said, tentatively. "I don't know what that would be like for him to move."

"We don't have to do it right away. You can come out for a few days, and we can look at facilities for him—we can find the perfect place. One that's close to my house."

Audrey was still staring at the ceiling. "But what would I do? Where would I live? And I'm guessing you don't want me to open the West Coast office of AccommoDating, right?" She laughed, but I could tell the discussion was making her uncomfortable.

"Audrey, you can live with me. And Elena can keep AccommoDating. But she can't keep you." I squeezed her hand hard.

"But I can't just live off you," she said, still not looking at me. "That's not a smart five-year plan."

"A small country could live off me," I said. "It's not really a big deal."

She looked at me then. "It's a big deal to me."

"Is this that cowboy thing again?" I asked, feeling the inklings of a headache coming on.

"Sort of," she said. She sat up. "It's just that… depending on someone else for everything isn't smart. You could get tired of me. You could get hit by a car. I have to take care of Tommy no matter what happens. You can't be my *job*, James."

I looked at her, letting the irony of that statement just hang in the air between us.

She swatted me and rolled her eyes. "You know what I mean."

"I'll make sure that Tommy is taken care of for the rest of his life. I know how important that is to you," I said. If I could give her nothing else, at least I could give her that peace of mind. "And I can get you your own place out there, if that's what you want."

"No—that's not what I want," she said quickly. "But I haven't said yes yet. I'm not prepared to ruin your life."

"I'm going to keep working on you. With sex and booze as a large part of my strategy this week, I plan on being victorious." I squeezed her hand again. "Listen, back to California—I know you like things to be even and fair. But I'm kind of out of your price bracket, Audrey. We can't go 'halfsies.' No one can afford to go halfsies with me. You just have to accept me for who I am and deal with the fact that I have money."

"I accept you for who you are," Audrey said, "but I can't pretend that's my reality, too, James. I have to take care of myself. You've been generous and good to me. But we've only been together for a week. You shouldn't be making promises about the future. You need to think it through."

"Do you doubt your feelings for me, even though it's only been a short time?" I asked.

"No," she said, "but that's a no-brainer. You're kind of the total package, James. And I'm—"

"Exactly what I've been looking for my whole life," I said. She looked at me, stunned and a little wary. "Listen to me, Audrey. My brother said something to me last week that made me think. He said that when you finally figure out what you want, you're pretty ready... to be... serious."

Actually, he'd said that once you figure out what you want, you were pretty ready for forever. But I didn't want to scare the pants off of her, as skittish as she'd been. "I've figured out what I want. I'm ready to be serious. So don't worry about me—you need to figure out what *you're* ready for."

She took a deep, shaky breath. "I want to be with you, James," she said. "More than I've ever wanted anything. But I've never had anybody I could trust in my life except Tommy. I've always taken care of myself. And I've kept my expectations about other people really low—that way it hurts less when they disappoint you. I want to trust you and be with you. But does it make sense to you that I have no idea how to do that?"

"Of course," I said. "I don't either. I guess you just do it by doing it."

"Huh," Audrey said.

"Is that a yes?"

# AUDREY

I bitch-slapped my common sense into submission, and I nodded at him. "Yes," I said. "That's a yes."

James pulled me into his arms, where I felt safe and loved, and I was almost shocked by the depth of his feelings for me.

I knew who he was now. I knew what happened next.

Even though it was scary to let myself be vulnerable, my love for him outweighed my fear. My feelings were like a riptide, a force of nature carrying me along. If I struggled against them any harder, I would go under and be lost. I knew that now. I'd tried to run from him, and it was no use. Turning away would only hurt us both.

I had to be strong, only in a different way than I was used to.

EVERYONE WAS DRUNK at dinner, and there were no signs of stopping. Cole grabbed a bottle of Patron and started pouring tequila shots, passing them down the long table. "Hair of the dog," he called. "This might be a boot-and-rally sort of vacation." I watched as everyone took a shot, including Mrs. Preston. She gave me a quick, sharp look afterward, and I was on my guard.

"I'd like to make a toast," Todd said and stood. "First of all, to Evie for agreeing to marry me. I would have been in sad shape if she'd said no." He leaned down and kissed her, and everybody whooped and clapped.

"Second, I'd like to thank my parents and Evie's parents for hosting such a beautiful wedding celebration. It was perfect in every way. Thank you for organizing and for, well, paying." Everyone laughed.

"Third, I'd like to thank my brother James for being my best man, and for taking time out of his busy schedule to actually go on vacation for once. I have a feeling I should really be thanking his girlfriend, Audrey, since James has never been this relaxed in his life. So cheers to James and Audrey. And cheers to all of you for joining us on this happy occasion. To the hair of the dog!" Todd said and knocked back his shot.

"The hair of the dog." Everyone clinked glasses and drank their tequila except for me. The way Celia was looking at me made me think staying sober was the right course of action.

Jenny leaned over to me after the toast. "Can we take a break?" she asked.

"Sure."

She grabbed my hand, and we walked from the oceanside restaurant to the main part of the resort. "I just need a little space," she said, looking back at the table. Cole was talking to Todd and James.

"Is everything okay?" I asked.

She shook her head. "No. No it is not."

I waited until we found a private bathroom; we went in and locked the door. Jenny was looking as lovely as ever in a black maxi dress, her skin bronzed and glowing from this afternoon. Her hair hung in loose curls over her shoulders. "What's wrong?" I asked.

"It's Cole," she said. "He told me he doesn't want me to go back to work after this." I just waited a beat, letting her talk on her terms. "He said he wants me to be exclusive." Her berry-stained lips turned down in a pout, and she blinked back tears.

"Is that a bad thing?" I asked. "You don't want to be exclusive?"

Jenny looked grim. "It's not that," she said. She gritted her teeth and then examined them for lipstick in the mirror. "It's that he said he'd buy me an apartment, buy me whatever kind of car I wanted, blah blah blah."

"Oh. Huh." I paused for a beat, trying to understand why she was upset. Jenny lived in a crappy studio apartment in Dorchester. She'd always wanted a rich John to buy her and set her up as a mistress. "And that's bad?"

"Yeah, it's bad, Dre," she said. "'Cause that's not what I want."

"What *do* you want?" I asked, confused.

"More." Jenny rolled her eyes at herself in the mirror. "Jesus, you'd think I was some kind of amateur. I shoulda never come on this trip."

I rubbed her arm. "It's okay, Jenny. But did you tell him how you felt?"

She snorted. "No fucking way. He told me he didn't want me to go back to hooking after this trip. So I told him to make me an offer I couldn't refuse, ya know? And he made me an offer I couldn't refuse. It was just the wrong one."

"I think you should talk to him," I said. "Just like you told me to talk to James. Remember? When you told me to be brave?"

"I'm not you, Dre. It's not possible to clean this up," she said, motioning to herself, "put it into a Volvo, and pretend it knows how to play tennis. Do you understand?"

I nodded while I watched my friend carefully blot her eyes. "I don't know if Cole cares about Volvos and tennis, Jenny. But I'm pretty sure he cares about you."

"Do not try to turn my airplane pep talk around on me," Jenny said, her voice jagged. "This is totally different."

"If you say so," I said, unconvinced. "But you had some pretty good advice. I'm just saying."

Jenny blew out a deep breath. "What about you and James?" she asked, changing the subject. "You looked a lot happier in the pool earlier. Are you all better?"

I nodded at her. "He asked me to move to California with him."

"I knew it," she cried. "I knew it! I could tell just by looking at him. You're gonna live happily ever after."

"I don't know about that," I said.

"I do." She looked at me levelly. "I know it's gonna happen."

"Jenny, I see the way Cole is with you. *I* think he's in love with you." I hesitated to say it because I didn't want to be wrong and make it worse. Still, I'd seen the way he looked at her. I believed there were real feelings there.

"I thought he was, too," she said, returning to her reflection and fluffing her hair. "But it must have just been that thing with his balls. I do it exactly the way he likes."

She smiled at me. "I'm not even mad at him, though. He's great. I'm mad at *me*. I think I got too inspired by my own pep talk. I'm the one who started hoping—and that was a dumb fucking move. If I hadn't hoped, I'd be psyched that I was getting a South End condo and a Range Rover. Now all I'm doing is crying." She blew her nose loudly.

"You should give him a chance," I said. "See what he has to say for himself."

"I'll think about it," she said and gave her hair one final fluff. "In the meantime, I need some liquid courage to keep up with these people. Rich people sure drink a lot, huh?"

MUCH TO MY CHAGRIN, we passed Celia Preston on our way back to the restaurant. "May I have a word with you, Audrey?" she asked. She looked at Jenny. "Alone?"

"Of course, Mrs. Preston," I mumbled. Jenny shot me a worried look but obediently headed back to the table; Celia was not someone you said no to. "What can I do for you?"

"You could start by doing what I asked," Celia said tightly. "And stop digging your acrylic claws further into my son."

"Excuse me?" I asked.

"You heard me. We agreed that you would break up with James after this trip. I want to make sure you keep your part of the bargain."

"Excuse me," I said again. "I never agreed to break up with James after this. You asked me to. I said I would think about it. You offered to bribe me. I said I would think about it. I promised nothing."

"You're going to promise me now," she said, her voice dangerous.

"No. I'm not." I shook my head. "I'm not going to do that, Mrs. Preston, even though that's not what you want to hear."

She grabbed my wrist painfully. "You listen to me. I told you before—I know you have feelings for my son. You need to do what's right for *him*. Don't be selfish, Audrey. Don't ruin his life by dragging him down with you."

"Just because I'm not wealthy like you doesn't make me a bad person," I said. "I think you're being a little dramatic."

"Being poor doesn't make you a bad person," Mrs. Preston said. "Being a hooker does."

I felt as if she'd punched me in the gut. Inside, I was reeling. Outside, I tried to appear unruffled. "I don't know what you're talking about," I lied. "Are you feeling well?"

"You know exactly what I'm talking about." Celia let go of my wrist and I rubbed it; she had a surprisingly strong grip. She studied my face. "I know all about you and your little friend in there," she said, motioning toward Jenny. "Don't look so surprised, Audrey—you're not the first whore I've had to keep away from my sons."

"What?" I asked, my voice coming out small.

"Once I realized that my son was going to fight to keep you, I did some investigating. Rather, I hired someone to do some investigating. When you have money, position, and means, you can do things like that, dear. I'm sure you wouldn't know. And I found out all about you. The fact that you're not an orphan, and you're not a student. I also found out about your mother and your brother. I saw the low-class neighborhood where you really live. I know all the little secrets you've been keeping," she said.

"My secrets are none of your business," I said. My voice sounded faraway to my own ears and I felt sick, remembering the limousine that had slowly driven down my street the morning after the wedding.

Celia sniffed in disapproval. "I disagree. You have to understand something." She looked at me levelly, her unnaturally smooth face a mask of superiority and disdain. "You could ruin my son's life. Just by being with him. Have you considered that he might hate me enough to do this to me? That he might pick you just to spite me—do you understand that, dear? Do you understand that isn't the same thing as love?"

"This isn't about you. That's not why he's with me," I said quickly. "James isn't spiteful. He's a good person."

"See?" Mrs. Preston said triumphantly. "You *do* love him—I knew it. That's a good motivator, Audrey. If you love someone, you should do the right thing for them. *You* are not the right thing for my son. He can't have anything to do with you going forward. Do you understand?"

"What if he doesn't care?" I asked. I sounded defiant but inside, I was crumbling. "What if he says what I am doesn't matter to him?"

Celia Preston paused just long enough to look at me with disdain. "Do you realize that if you have children, they will be like royalty in this country? Everyone will know about them—where they go to school, what kind of activities they enjoy. That their mother was a prostitute. Do you think that's what they deserve? Their lives ruined because you were too selfish to walk away? Do you think I want my son living like that? Married to a whore?"

I fought back my tears. I wouldn't let her know she was wounding me. That she was winning.

"I know underneath it all, you're a decent girl," she said, watching me. "You're ashamed of yourself. And you should be, Audrey. You're infected with poverty and filth. So don't ruin the man you love. Part of loving is knowing when to let go."

"Who did you ever love?" I asked hoarsely, my voice barely coming out.

Celia snorted. "I love my sons, Audrey. I love James and Todd both. And I want what's best for them. And that's not you, dear. I think you know that," she said and patted my hand. "Don't worry. I've made arrangements for you to fly back first thing in the morning. And I'm still going to give you some money, like I promised."

"What if I say no?" I asked.

"Oh dear," she said, "I wouldn't do that if I were you. Too many things could go wrong."

"What does that mean?"

"Use your imagination," Celia said wickedly. "I know I will."

"WHAT THE HELL happened back there?" James asked, looking at me in alarm. I must have been as white as a ghost.

"Jenny was upset," I said.

"And my mother?"

I could feel her eyes on me from across the table. "She just wanted to check in."

Dinner was already on the table, and I picked at my food listlessly. Holy Christ, Celia Preston had just scared me. Her thinly veiled threat had left my heart hammering in my chest, wondering what lengths she would go to keep me from her son.

I thought about that for a second. And then I dropped my fork on the table.

*Celia Preston has been scary since I first met her,* I thought, *but I've never been afraid of her. Until just now.*

"What's the matter?" James asked, his brow furrowed. "Do you feel okay?"

"No," I said. "No, I don't."

"Then let's go back to our room. I can have room service bring me something." He stood and clapped Todd on the back. "Audrey's not feeling well—we're going to turn in."

"Hope you feel better soon, Audrey," Todd called.

I hoped so, too. But I doubted it.

"WHAT IS IT?" he asked once we were safely inside.

"I don't know how much I should tell you," I said, pacing.

He stepped in front of me, and I stopped. "Tell me everything."

"Well, first of all, before I forget—Jenny's in love with Cole. He offered to set her up when we get back to Boston. He offered to buy her a townhouse, a car, the whole deal."

"Okay," James said, clearly confused.

"She's upset about it. She wants more. And she's mad at herself for having feelings."

"Okay," James said again. He still sounded lost. "I know Cole cares about her. I can see it on his face. I'll talk to him."

"Promise?" I asked.

"I promise."

"Okay. Moving on, your mother knows that Jenny and I are

prostitutes."

"Huh?" James asked, completely taken aback. "What the fuck?"

I started pacing again, and this time, James got out of my way. "She said she thought you had... feelings for me... and so she decided to have me checked out. She hired someone to investigate me, and she found out that I work for Elena. She knows about my mother and my brother. She found out about Jenny, too. She knows where I live." I shivered.

"And?" James asked.

"And she's sending me home on a flight tomorrow morning. And paying me to never come back."

# JAMES

My head was pounding. "You know I won't let you go anywhere—not without me."

"You should let me finish 'cause that's not all she said," Audrey whispered. A blush was creeping up her neck, which was never a good sign.

"What else?" I asked. Ice-cold fury was pulsing through me. My mother had crossed her final line with me. "What else did she say?"

She held up her fingers to count my mother's grievances, ticking them off like a list. "She said that I was going to ruin your life if I stayed with you. She said you were dating me just to spite her. She said that our children would practically be famous, and everyone would find out about my past. And that the kids would have to live with the fact that their mother used to be a whore."

"Audrey," I said, "we already discussed this."

She looked up at me and let out a shaky breath. "It's a little different when you hear it from a third party."

"She's not just any third party—she has an agenda."

"She told me her agenda was to protect her family. That's the only motivation she has, James."

"That's bullshit. She doesn't know anything about family. All she cares about is the *image* of family." I stopped her from pacing and pulled her to me. Her skin felt hot to my touch. "I told you she was never going to accept us. What does this change?"

She looked up at me. "She threatened me."

"What do you mean?"

"I asked her what she would do if I said no. If I stayed. She said that she would think of something." Audrey pressed her face against my chest. "She...she was a little scary, James."

I stroked her hair. "She can't do anything to you, babe. I won't let her."

Audrey looked back up at me. "What exactly do you think she's capable of?"

"I wouldn't put too much past her. But what do you mean? What are you worried about?"

"I'm not sure." She paused for a second. "But I know I don't want to tear your family apart."

"You can't tear my family apart—there is no *together* in my family. My mother is a nightmare; my father does nothing to rein her in. That leaves Todd and Evie. Todd already cares about you. Once he knows I love you, he'll welcome you into the family with open arms. Evie will follow suit. And that's enough for me, Audrey. I don't care about my mother. The worst thing she can do is disinherit me. You know what? I don't even care if she does. I went out and made my own fortune. I don't need her money, and I don't need her. I don't need anyone except for you."

I just held her for a second. "Can you live with that, Audrey?" I asked.

"I want to," she said.

"That's all I'm asking," I said, smoothing her hair. "But I think maybe it's time we scared *her* a little. She's past due."

THE VALET KNOCKED on our door the following morning at seven a.m. I gave him six crisp five-hundred-dollar bills. "Please tell Mrs. Preston that Miss Reynolds left as expected," I said, nodding at him. "Off you go."

"Why'd you do that?" Audrey asked, padding out to the kitchen in my T-shirt. She turned the coffeemaker on and squinted at me, clearly still half-asleep. "I'm so confused."

"I'm just looking for the element of surprise," I said. "It'll be fun to see my mother's expression at breakfast."

"You have a weird idea of fun," Audrey said and yawned. "You want some coffee? You're gonna need it."

My mother's face at breakfast wasn't as exciting as I'd hoped. Unfortunately, she'd injected so much filler into it before the wedding it couldn't move that much. "Good morning," I said to her at the buffet. I pulled out a chair for Audrey at her table, and I sat down in between them.

"Ah," she said, looking pointedly at Audrey. "I see you're determined to enjoy the rest of your vacation."

"We're planning on enjoying lots of things. And she's not going anywhere, Mother," I said, spearing a piece of cantaloupe off her plate. "Audrey's agreed to move to California with me after this."

"Is that so?" my mother asked benignly.

"Yes, that's so." Audrey was tense beside me, but I refused to let my mother get under my skin. I wanted to see her crack, just a little, but that was going to take patience. My mother was the Ice Queen. It was going to take a blowtorch to get her to melt.

And even the blowtorch method would require some patience.

"What are you going to do for work out there, Audrey?"

Audrey looked pale. "I haven't decided yet, Mrs. Preston."

"I'm sure you have quite a resume. You'll find lots of willing, ready, and able employers in California." She gave her an in ice-pick smile.

"That is *enough*," I snapped, furious. "The only reason we're still here is for Todd. I want you to know that Audrey told me everything you've said. You can be as horrible as you like. But you need to know from me—your son, who you claim to care so much about—that your behavior will change nothing. Audrey and I will simply cut you out of our lives and our future. That's your choice, Mother."

My mother turned to me, her eyes softening a little. "Please don't say things like that, James. You're always too harsh with me."

"You're the one who's been too harsh. I'm done. Audrey is part of my life now," I said. I grabbed her hand from the table, lacing my fingers through hers. "I love her. You can't scare her off, and if you don't treat her with the respect she deserves, you'll never hear from me again."

"James," my mother said, "if you choose to have a relationship with Audrey, I will support that. I didn't realize you were this serious."

She forced herself to smile at us. "I can be pleasant, see? You never give me any credit."

"That's because you don't deserve any," I said.

She nodded and clutched her mimosa, her hands looking old to me for the first time. "You might just be right about that, dear."

"WELL THAT WAS HORRIBLE," Audrey said after breakfast. "But at least she seemed appropriately chastened."

"Don't believe it for a second," I said. We were changing to go on a snorkeling excursion with Todd, Evie, Cole, Jenny, and some of the others; I would be happy to put some distance between my parents and myself right now. "My mother is a lot of things, but sorry is rarely, if ever, one of them."

"Do you think that was just for show?"

I considered it for a second. "Yes. More for me than for you."

"So where does that leave me?" she asked.

"By my side. Where I can keep you out of her way." I leaned down and kissed her on the cheek.

"Are you going to wear that black bikini again?" I asked. "'Cause I don't know if I can take you out in public like that."

She laughed. "Do you want me to wear a one-piece instead? Or a tankini?"

"Hell no," I said.

She went to change, and a few minutes later, she called to me from out back. I went out and found her in the outdoor shower, the water running hot and steam rising up around her. She was waiting for me in the very black bikini that I'd cautioned her about.

As predicted, I got hard just looking at her.

"Let me just take care of you now, baby," she said and got on her knees. She started to stroke my balls, which got heavy at her touch. "That way we can relax and enjoy the snorkeling." She undid my swim trunks and took me immediately in her mouth, licking and sucking my hard length until I couldn't see straight.

Five minutes later I came so hard I forgot my name. But not hers.

Never hers.

I PULLED COLE ASIDE down on the dock. "How's it going with Jenny?"

"Awesome. She's incredible. I've never met anyone like her."

I raised my eyebrows at him. "Are you talking about her in a sexual way? Or as a person?"

"I didn't realize it was necessary to parse this out," Cole said. "But I meant both."

"What's going to happen after this trip?" I asked.

"What's going to happen with you and Audrey?" he asked in a challenging tone. "I asked you first, if you'll remember. Back in Boston."

"I asked her to move to California with me," I said. "I love her."

"To borrow Jenny's phrase: Ho my frickin' God, James. I'm so proud of you." He clapped me on the back and grinned. "I knew it."

"Well, you were right," I said, grinning back. "Now I want to know if I'm right about you."

"Huh," Cole said. "This should be interesting."

"I think you have real feelings for this girl," I said. "I think you might just have an emotional boner for her."

Cole looked at me thoughtfully and nodded. "It's obvious, right? It's *big*."

"It's not as big as mine, but you can still see it."

"Ha," Cole said. He watched Jenny as she laughed and talked to Audrey. "I think I might be in love with her." His jaw clenched as he said it.

"She told Audrey you offered to buy her a house when we get back."

"That's right," Cole said. "I asked her what she wanted, and she told me she wanted a South End condo and a Range Rover. So I said done and done."

"What if that's not all she wants?"

"What do you mean?" Cole asked.

"What if she wants you to be her boyfriend?"

"I frickin' hope she wants me to be her boyfriend if I'm buying her a South End condo and a Range Rover." He looked at me, confused. "Is she upset or something? She wouldn't even do that thing with my balls last night."

"Cole, please—"

"No, but she always does it. And I didn't know what was wrong. She wouldn't tell me. And she's not usually like that. She's always open with me. And I mean *really* open—"

"Stop," I said, holding up my hands in mock surrender. "Please, *please* spare me the details. All I know is that she told Audrey what you offered her and that she wants more."

"More than a condo and a car?"

"Yes, Cole."

"Like what?" he asked, thoroughly perplexed.

"Like *you*. In the condo and in the car."

"I was planning on being in the condo and in the car," he said. "That's sort of the point."

"You should tell her," I said. "Just be really clear. Sometimes they need to hear it with an exclamation point."

"Sounds like you, bro," he said and gave me a lopsided smile.

# AUDREY

We snorkeled all afternoon, laughing and talking and enjoying the beautiful surroundings. I finally got a minute alone with Jenny on the boat when the others were in the water. The captain was out of earshot, checking his instruments.

"So, are things better with you and Cole?" I asked. They'd taken a long walk down the beach earlier. Since then, they'd been holding hands and kissing, looking very much together. "You two seem like you're being very *romantic.*"

"I decided to talk to him. Like you said." Jenny took her sunglasses off and stuck them on her hat, so I could see her eyes. They were brimming with happiness.

"Being brave was *your* idea, if I remember correctly," I said.

"That's right—'cause I'm so wicked smart," Jenny said and laughed. "He told me he *loved* me just now, Dre. He said he wants to move in with me when we get back."

"That's so awesome," I said, because no other word would do. Jenny was my best friend, and she was finding happiness that she thought she'd never have.

"It is pretty frickin' awesome," she agreed, her eyes still shining. "We can double date," she said, "and it'll be box seats all the way, baby."

"It's crazy, right?" I asked. "Who'd have thought?"

"Me," Jenny said. "This is where I get to say I told you so."

"You did," I admitted. Then I sighed. There was a black cloud hanging over me, in spite of the bright sunshine. "But it's not all fun and games, unfortunately—last night, after we went to the bathroom? Mrs. Preston cornered me, remember? She hired a private investigator to find out about me, Jenny. She knows that I'm an escort. She knows about you, too."

"She's evil," Jenny said, crossing herself. "I can't stand to be in the same room with her. What'd she say?"

"She threatened me and offered to pay me off to go away. You know. Pretty much what you'd expect."

Jenny snorted. "Did you tell James?"

"I did. He's furious," I said. "He told her this morning that I'm moving in with him and that he loves me."

"I just got the chills." Jenny ran her hands up and down her arms. "What'd she say?"

"Not too much. I don't think she wanted to make him any angrier," I said. "But just watch out for her. She's a barracuda."

"I can handle her." Jenny tossed her curls. "It's just too bad I can't use a spear gun on her bony ass."

WITH ALL THE SUNSHINE and the happy news about Jenny and Cole, I almost forgot about Mrs. Preston and her threats. Almost.

When we got back to the resort, James went with Todd and Cole to have a beer and smoke cigars. Wanting to give them some guy time I begged off, citing a desperate need for some shade. I was headed back to the safety of my villa when Mrs. Preston practically jumped out of the bushes and grabbed my wrist again.

"*Ow.* Jesus," I said. "Were you waiting to ambush me?"

"Something like that," she said, giving me her best fake smile. A shiver ran down my back. "Where's my son?"

"With Todd and Cole. But within shouting distance," I said. I wasn't sure if that was true, but she didn't know that.

"Why didn't you get on that plane this morning?" she asked.

I took a deep breath. "Because I love your son, Mrs. Preston. And he actually loves me back. I can't just leave him because you don't approve of me."

I looked at her for a beat. "I've listened to everything you had to say about how I'm not the right person for James, and I actually agree with a lot of it. But the thing is, Mrs. Preston, we really do love each other. When that happens, all the things you're supposed to do—like get on a plane and accept a bribe from your boyfriend's mother—those things don't make sense anymore. The only thing that makes sense is staying together."

She dropped my wrist, and I took a step back.

"I'm sorry to let you know that, despite what I said this morning, I still do *not* approve of your relationship." Celia studied my face. "My son might be more sentimental than I'd realized."

"Maybe he's just happy," I said, rubbing my wrist. "It's been a long time. I just wish you could be happy *for* him."

"He can't marry a hooker," she said matter-of-factly.

"We're not getting married," I said, refusing to let her under my skin. "We're going to live in sin first." I fake-smiled at her, and I meant it.

She drew herself up to her full height, as if she was preparing to make an announcement. "Audrey, I believed you had my son's best interests at heart. Now I see that you are letting him control you. Either that or you are too selfish to see that you're about to destroy him."

Fury bubbled inside of me. "I'm not being selfish. I love James, that's all. And he's not controlling me, Mrs. Preston—and you are not a candidate for that position, either." I remembered what she'd said about Evie: that she was perfect for Todd because she was easy to control.

"Oh, you've made that clear," Mrs. Preston snapped. "I can see now that you're a problem, and that you're not willing to work with me to become part of the solution. It's too bad. Because now you really will break James's heart."

"What's that supposed to mean?"

"It *means* that there is no way on God's green earth that I am letting a twenty-two-year-old hooker have a relationship with, let alone move in with, my oldest son. Something bad will happen to you, dear. These things have a way of working themselves out. It's Preston luck," she hissed.

All of a sudden the sunlight was too bright on my face; I felt dizzy, my world scrambled. Celia had told James it was "Preston luck" that his high school girlfriend had been killed.

"Holy fuck," I said.

She looked at me innocently, and an icy fear spread over my exposed skin. "Indeed. See you around, Audrey," she said.

I REALIZED LATER THAT, of course, she'd actually admitted nothing.

Celia had just confirmed my worst fears about her. I paced through the villa, jumping at every little sound. Finally James came back, and I unlocked the door for him. He was loose and happy; he looked sexy and tan and he smelled like beer.

He watched me pace back and forth, a quizzical look on his face. "Audrey," he said, "we're in paradise. You're supposed to be relaxing. It doesn't look like that's working out too well for you."

I clenched and unclenched my fists. "I ran into your mother on the way back here."

"Great," he said, rubbing his face. "What'd she do now?"

I stopped dead in my tracks. "You're going to think I'm crazy."

"My *mother* is crazy."

"She actually is, James," I said, fiddling with my hands nervously. "She threatened me."

"She threatened you yesterday."

"This was a real threat," I said, watching his face. "She said that I would never move in with you. That something bad would happen to me first. And that Preston 'luck' would take care of it."

James was looking at me but it was as if he wasn't seeing me.

"What?" he asked finally. "What were her exact words?"

I swallowed hard. "'*Something bad will happen to you. These things have a way of working themselves out. It's Preston luck.*'"

"Are you sure?"

"It's sort of branded into my memory by fear," I said.

"Holy fuck," James said.

"That's exactly what I said."

"SHE KILLED DANIELLE. Or arranged to have her killed…" James was sitting on the bed, still looking but not seeing. "I can't believe this."

"She didn't admit to anything, James. She just used that phrase, and it was like a lightbulb went off for me. But she doesn't know what you told me. And no matter what really happened, she *didn't* actually kill her—she was home with you when Danielle died, right?"

He nodded numbly.

"So it wasn't her. Not directly, anyway. Maybe she felt she was responsible for making Danielle so upset that night—maybe that's what she meant."

"My mother's not really a loose-ends kind of person. If she'd wanted Danielle… permanently out of the picture… I don't think she'd leave it up to chance," James muttered. He sounded sick. "I just hadn't thought she was capable of something like this. I underestimated her—or maybe I was overestimating her, now that I think about it."

"Do you think she hired someone? Or had something done to her car?" I'd run through the list of possibilities earlier as I'd paced, waiting for James to come back, filled with dread as I'd imagined the different scenarios.

James nodded. "Either one of those is a distinct possibility." His eyes finally focused on my face. "I can't believe I never considered this before. I feel sick."

"You were just a kid when it happened. And you can't blame yourself for not thinking your mother could have *killed* someone. That's not in the normal repertoire of maternal behavior." I shivered just thinking about it.

"And now she's threatening to hurt you." James reached out for my hand. "I'm so sorry I've dragged you into this mess. I can't even believe this is happening right now."

"That's because it's unbelievable," I said, squeezing his hand.

# JAMES

"*Should* we go home?" Audrey asked.

"Not yet," I responded. "The safest place to be right now is near her. She'll never do anything to jeopardize her own position. If we go back home, anyone could try to..." I let my voice trail off. I couldn't bear to finish the sentence or even the thought. "I can't even believe we're having this conversation. This is insane."

"We don't know for sure that she did it," Audrey said.

"As far as I'm concerned, she did it," I said, scrubbing my hand across my face. "We should let them know that we know. They need to understand that if they're playing hard ball, it's going to come back to them. And it's gonna hurt."

"They?" Audrey asked. "And *hurt*?"

"My father has to be involved in this. There's no way he didn't know. And yes, hurt." An image of Danielle crying that night, the night she died, flashed in my mind. Pain ripped through me then. She'd been so young, so full of promise and life.

And my parents had taken that away from her.

"What's our goal here?" Audrey asked. "Besides keeping me alive?"

I looked at her beautiful face, and I was furious. I couldn't believe we were having this conversation, but I pushed that part of me—the part that was reeling with both disbelief and pain—roughly away. I had to protect Audrey. I loved her, and I couldn't let anything happen to her.

Especially not at my mother's hands.

I had to show my parents that they were rapidly heading to the end of the line. *I* was the end of that line. And I was going to make them pay.

"Our goal is to show them that if they try to hurt us, we will destroy them," I said. "It's simple. This is war now, and I'm bringing the nuclear weapons."

Audrey looked at me warily. "What are the nuclear weapons, James?" she asked.

"The truth about Danielle. And a healthy dose of jail time to go with it. There's no statute of limitations on murder, last time I checked."

"I HAVE TO CONTACT Danielle's parents," I told Audrey a little later. We'd ordered room service and were spread out in our villa, which in the course of an hour had become a combination of tactical headquarters and bunker. I was afraid to let her leave. She seemed to be afraid, too, jumping at every noise and not straying from my side for more than a minute.

My fucking mother was going to pay for this. Hard.

"Her parents deserve to know what happened to her."

Audrey looked at me and frowned. "Don't you think we should have more facts before we call them? All we have right now are few off-hand comments from your mother and a bad feeling," Audrey said. "It's been a long time since it happened, James. Let's make sure we handle this the best way for everyone."

She stood up and started pacing again. "I had an idea," she said, wringing her hands together. "What if I go back to your mother and pretend to try and blackmail her? What if I tell her I've guessed the truth about Danielle? And that I want money to keep quiet—or in exchange for my silence, she lets me stay with you? Sort of like a blackmail quid pro quo?"

"If she wanted to kill you before, this will seal the deal," I said.

"But now I have something on *her*," she said. "And I can tell her I've made arrangements for it to go public if something happens to me."

I thought it through for a minute. "I don't know if she'll believe that."

"I'll make her believe it. In fact, I'll do something—write a letter, something like that—and show her that I've already made the arrangements. I'll tell her I've addressed letters to all the major

Boston news outlets, and that I've asked friends to send them for me if something happens. And I'll tell her the friends don't include Jenny, so she doesn't try to hurt her."

"Are you going to tell my mother you've told me all this?" I asked.

"No—not yet. I'll say I haven't said a word about my suspicions to you. Let her believe that I've spent some time thinking about it on my own, and I'm trying to leverage this for my own gain. That way we keep the element of surprise on our side."

"I don't know. My mother is shrewder than I wish she was," I said.

"Remember—I'm an *escort*. You do a lot of faking when you're an escort. Trust me, I can fake something this important." She looked at me and scowled. "You're the one who needs to put on an act. You look enraged. And even though you have every right to be, we have to play this just right. Even if it only buys us a little more time."

# AUDREY

I didn't ever want to talk to James's mother again, but I really didn't want her to kill me, either. I was taking a risk with the threat of the letters. *A calculated risk,* I kept telling myself, but I was still petrified.

Celia Preston could do that to you.

"I'm going to the bar," I told James. I was wearing a conservative black dress so that when she called me a whore, at least I'd be dressed like a lady. I held up an envelope. "This is what I'm going to show her. I drafted another one. It's in the bedroom. If she strangles me, please mail it to the *Tribune.*" I smiled at him, trying to make light of the situation, but James glowered at me as I stuck the envelope in my pocketbook.

"It's not funny," he said, his jaw clenching. "I don't want her anywhere near you."

"You said it yourself—she's not going to hurt me here. It's too close. And you can come, too, but you have to stay with Todd and Cole. And no glowering, at least no more than usual. We don't want your mother to know that I've told about Danielle. Okay?"

"Okay for right now," James said. He grabbed my hand, and I noticed how very sexy he was looking in his T-shirt and a pair of faded cargo shorts with flip-flops. I loved the man in a suit, but I loved him dressed casually, too. He looked as if he were a mere mortal, not a gazillionaire.

I think the point was I loved him.

"I love you," I said, stopping him before we went outside. I pulled him in for a deep kiss. "All this family intrigue is really messing with our sex schedule," I said, pretending to pout and keep our moods light. "I thought we were just going to be in bed this whole trip."

"I wish," James growled, running his hands over me. "But we have to deal with this. I can't have my mother even thinking about harming you. We'll try this tonight, but tomorrow, I'm calling Danielle's parents and alerting the authorities back home. They'll have to reopen the case as a criminal investigation."

I nodded at him. "Okay. Let's just see what your mother has to say to me right now."

AS THIS WAS A GROUP vacation, and as James's family liked to drink, everyone in our party was at the bar. The floor-to-ceiling windows had all been opened, so the warm night air spilled in. There was a breathtaking view of the ocean and the moon above it. *Someday,* I thought, *James and I will come back here and have a real vacation.* I clasped my fingers around the small, gold necklace that he'd given me before the wedding; I needed it to remind me to be brave. I loved James, and I had to protect him from his mother. Protecting myself from her was secondary—but if something happened to me, if she did something horrible, I knew it would break him.

We had to beat her.

He ordered us drinks, and I gave him a small kiss, leaving him with Todd and Evie and Evie's sinewy cousins, as I searched the room for his parents. They were seated near the indoor fireplace with several of the older guests.

I took a sip of my martini, hoping it would act as liquid courage, and approached their little group.

"Good evening," I said, barely able to contain the shakiness in my voice. Celia Preston was wearing an island-appropriate flowered tunic, white linen pants, and orange patent-leather gladiator sandals that probably cost as much as a mid-sized Hyundai.

"Hello, dear," she said, and I noticed she was drinking a martini, too. So she'd already had some liquid courage.

Not that she seemed to need any.

"May I speak with you for a moment, Mrs. Preston?" I asked politely. "It's about what we discussed earlier."

She smiled at me tightly and stood. "Of course," she said. She motioned for me to follow her to a small table at the corner of the bar, away from everyone else. I was afraid, but I knew she was too dignified and far too premeditated to throw herself across the small glass table at me right here in public. Still, a cold sweat coated my palms, and I felt positively queasy to be so close to her again.

"What is it, Audrey?" Her voice was ice.

"I thought about what you said this afternoon," I said. "About the Preston luck. I realized something. James had told me about his poor high school girlfriend, Danielle. He was explaining how hard it was for him to get close to a woman after what happened to her. Because that almost ruined him, Mrs. Preston. When Danielle died—I'm sure you know how difficult it was for him."

"For a senior in high school, he dealt with the tragedy admirably," she said.

"He said the same thing about you. That you did all the right things, made all the right donations." I paused for a beat. "The other thing I remember him saying, though, was how inappropriate you were privately. That you told him her death was a blessing in disguise. That you said the 'Preston luck' had saved him from a poor match. That really stuck with me," I said. "And then yesterday, when you mentioned Preston luck to me, I started to piece things together."

"Audrey, dear, that martini's gone straight to your head. You're not making any sense." She didn't look vaguely rattled, but I didn't let myself doubt my gut.

"The thing is, it hasn't." I took another big sip, which I desperately needed at this point. "You've threatened me several times now. And I finally believe that you mean exactly what you say. So I want to take you up on your offer.

"You offered to pay me. I accept. Except now, I'm dictating the terms. I will accept your payment, Mrs. Preston, in exchange for my silence on this matter. I've written several letters to the Boston media outlets—just in case something happens to me, you know? Like a head-on collision with a guardrail? That sort of thing. But if you pay me and you let me follow my natural path toward a happily ever after with your son, I will agree to never speak on the matter. Your secret will be safe with me."

Celia Preston smiled at me and drained her drink. "You know, dear, I have much more experience with this sort of thing than you do."

My stomach dropped while I waited to hear what she had to say. I drained my drink, too, wishing desperately that I could wave a waiter over. I already needed another one. I did not have enough courage for this.

"I anticipated something like this from you," she said. "You might be smart, but you're guileless. This was the obvious move, and I was expecting it. So in advance of our little impromptu meeting tonight, I called your mother, who is very much alive. We had an excellent conversation."

My mouth opened and closed a couple of times, but no sound came out at first. "What?" I asked. "What did you say?"

"I said I called your mother earlier this evening. She and I had a lovely talk. About your family, your brother, your *wretched* treatment of her. And of course, her desperate living situation and her myriad of financial needs." She smiled at me. "I explained to her that you were being difficult about parting ways with James."

"Did you explain that you have a nasty habit of killing the girls James loves? The ones you deem inappropriate?"

Celia gave me another unfazed smile. "First of all, I don't know what you're talking about. Second of all, we didn't get that far. What we *did* cover, however, was the fact that you recently had your mother removed as a responsible party for your brother at his facility. I don't think you had the legal right to do that, Audrey. So I told your mother I would have my attorney—who's excellent, by the way—look into the situation. And that you could be removed as his guardian permanently, and your mother could go back to being solely responsible for making choices for him."

She beamed at me while I tried to catch my breath. "I also told her I'd be happy to put her on salary in exchange for her silence about your profession, as well as the fact that you were ever anywhere near my son. She agreed with everything. She was very accommodating."

My heart was frozen, and I couldn't say a word.

I could feel James watching me from across the room; my face must be white, all the blood draining out of it. "You didn't do that," I finally said. It only came out as a mumble.

"Of course I did, dear. And that was just a warm-up. I can stop it all, of course, but you have to do everything that I ask. Including not telling my son a word that I just said."

She smiled at me in triumph as James stalked over to our table, his mouth set in an angry line. "What's the matter, Audrey?" he asked, looking at my face.

"Nothing," I responded, too quick and too sharp.

He turned to his mother. "What did you say to her?"

"She's quite capable of speaking for herself," Celia said calmly.

"Nothing. We weren't talking about anything," I said immediately.

James reached out his hand and grabbed mine. "Let's go."

I looked back at Mrs. Preston as he pulled me away. She was looking at me with an expectant smile on her face. "I'm assuming we're on the same page, dear," she said.

All I could manage was a nod.

# JAMES

"*Let's* stay and have another drink," Audrey said. Her voice was jagged. All I wanted to do was wrap her in my arms and hold her, but she looked wary. I ordered us drinks, and we went and stood with Todd and Evie.

"What's Celia's problem?" Todd asked, watching our mother.

"Nothing," Audrey said. She took a shaky sip of her martini. "She was just talking to me about graduate school."

Todd raised his eyebrows at that. "She probably wasn't that helpful," he said. "Mother's education consisted mainly of sorority rushes and mixers."

"She had some insight," Audrey said. I watched as she put her game face on, tight and intact. "But enough about that. How does it feel to be newlyweds, you two?" She reached down and twined her fingers through mine, holding on for dear life.

"It's so great," Evie said, linking her arms through Todd's. "We are enjoying every minute this trip. And then it's back to reality."

"Are you going back to work after this?" I asked.

"Oh, no," Evie said and laughed, her teeth a blinding white against her new tan. "We're buying a townhouse, and I'm going to be managing the remodeling, the decorating… and then we're going to try and start a family." Evie turned and grinned at Todd, as he squeezed her tiny frame against his.

"That's wonderful," Audrey said. Only I would notice this, but I could hear sadness in her voice, maybe mixed with a little envy. "You two will be wonderful parents."

"And you two will be a wonderful aunt and uncle," Todd said, beaming at her. "We're going to start our own family traditions. We can come out to California for Thanksgiving, you two can come to Boston for Christmas. Mother and father are being put on the back burner—they no longer get to boss us around. Evie's going to organize everything."

"As long as that's okay with you, Audrey," Evie said.

"I'll happily defer to you, Evie. I'm sure you're better at all that than me," Audrey said, and I could still hear that undercurrent of sadness in her voice. Her hand held mine in a death grip, and she drained the rest of her martini in one gulp.

"If you two will excuse us, it's past Audrey's bedtime," I said.

"Don't be such a baby," Todd said, looking at his watch. "It's only nine o'clock."

"We're still in that new relationship phase where we have to have sex every couple of hours," I said. "You old married people probably don't even remember that, right?" I grinned and swept Audrey up in my arms; I was going to pretend that everything was normal with us, even if it was clear to me that Audrey was about to crack.

"On that note," Evie said, laughing. "Just remember to get some rest, too! We're snorkeling the West End reef tomorrow."

"Good night," I called jovially. I leaned down to Audrey's ear. "Smile," I commanded.

She made her best effort at it. But inside, I could tell her heart was breaking.

"WHAT HAPPENED?" I asked when we were back in the safety of our room. "What on earth did she do to you?"

Audrey was pouring herself a glass of white wine. "I can't tell you," she said. Her voice was flat, dead.

I went over and stood next to her. Without asking if I wanted any, she poured me a glass and handed it to me. I had a sip and watched her face, which was drawn and pale underneath the color she'd gotten today on the boat. "You have to tell me. We're in this together."

"I can't be in *this* anymore," she said, her voice small and far away. "And your mother said that if I tell you what's going on, the deal I just made with her is off. And it's not even a good deal, James. It's not gonna end well, and I know it."

She looked defeated. My heart broke for her then, for her and Danielle both, what loving me had done to them. I pulled her to me. "This is on me. I should have known it wasn't safe...that I wasn't safe to be with."

She pulled back and looked at my face. "Stop it. Your mother is a monster. While we're at it, so is mine. We didn't make them that way."

I took her face in my hands. "Please tell me what she said. No matter what, I promise you, I'll make it better. If she doesn't want me to know, I'll pretend I don't. I'll deny it till I die. Just tell me."

"Your mother doesn't fight fair," Audrey said. I could see her visibly calming herself down, drinking her wine and taking deep breaths.

"Go on."

"I told her about the letters. I said that I was going to send them to the *Tribune. S*he didn't flinch. She wasn't even surprised," Audrey said. "She said it was an amateur move. And then she said she'd called my mother, and that she was having her lawyer look into having my mother reinstated as Tommy's guardian." She swallowed hard. "She said I didn't have a legal right to take her off his account at the home in the first place. She's started paying my mother so that she'll never go public with the information about me."

She looked up at me. "I had to promise her that I'd stay away from you, James. And that I wouldn't even tell you this. She said she'd take Tommy away from me. She'll make sure that my mother gets total control. And she'll do it, James. I know she will."

Even though she hadn't moved, I could almost feel her pulling away from me in her voice.

"She won't do that. I won't let her." I wrapped my arms around her. "I'm so sorry, Audrey."

"No. It's my fault," she said, her voice flat. "She told me I didn't belong. She gave me fair warning."

"She doesn't get to win," I said, holding her to me. "And neither does your mother, Audrey."

"I don't know. I don't see a way out of this."

"There's always a way out," I said, my mind churning. "We

have tonight to figure out what it is. Tomorrow, we're back with the nuclear arms."

"I'd be happy with a BB gun at this point," she muttered.

"One of my first business rules is, when it gets scary, stay in and push. That's not the time to back off. And also—it's okay to lie. There's something to be said for saying one thing and doing another."

"Ethical behavior is pretty much a non-issue for me at this point," Audrey said, watching my face. "What're you thinking?"

"I'm thinking," I said, "that we fuck with her a little."

Audrey looked at me expectantly, like that wasn't good enough.

"Or a lot, babe."

LATER, AS SHE SLEPT in my arms, I made plans. I ran my fingers up and down her smooth skin, relishing the feel of her. I loved her. She was mine; nothing my mother could do or say was going to change that. I thought of Danielle, of what had happened. I would never forgive my parents for what they'd done to her. My heart was closed against them forever.

To Danielle, whose life was taken too early, I sent out silent love and prayers that she'd gone on to a better place and that maybe she could forgive me. As I sat there in the dark, I tried to forgive myself. I had no idea who my parents were when I was eighteen. I had an inkling… but I hadn't realized the depths they would sink to in order to protect their precious, useless ideals.

I hadn't known they were capable of murder.

I watched Audrey's chest rise and fall. I was almost forty. I'd spent the last twenty years shielding myself from love, from feeling connected to another person. There'd been too much pain when Danielle died. I don't even think I'd realized what I was doing—burying myself in my work, developing an endless list of projects, dating women I didn't even like. But I didn't regret any of it except for the loss of Danielle. Because each step had brought me to needing to hire a date for my baby brother's wedding, and that date had ended up being Audrey.

Who was the love of my life.

"Audrey." I said. "Wake up."

"What?" she asked, alarmed, and sat straight up. "What's the matter?"

"Nothing," I said, still stroking her skin. "I just wanted to tell you something."

She lay back down, still half-asleep. "What is it?"

"I love you," I said.

"I love you, too," she said. She put her hand on my chest, tracing my muscle.

"You're moving to Los Angeles with me," I said.

"Yes. I told you I would. If your mother doesn't run me off the road first."

"And you're going to bring your brother."

"I have to, James," she said. "I can't leave him with my mother. We'll have to get all the legal stuff taken care of, and now we're gonna have to fight your mom's lawyer—"

"But we're going to take care of all of that. I want him to come too, Audrey. I know how much you love him. I just need to know that's still what you want."

"Of course it is," she said. "I wish it wasn't, because then I wouldn't have caused you all this trouble—"

"Stop," I said, cutting her off again. "Please don't ever say that again."

"Okay." Her voice was cautious. "Please tell me what's going on with you."

"I just want you to promise me," I said. "I don't want us to ever be separated again. I just don't want to waste any more time."

"Okay," Audrey said again, nestling against me. She was quiet for a minute, and I thought she'd fallen asleep. "What's it gonna be like?"

"What?"

"Living in your mansion in California," she giggled. "The way things are going, it seems like we're never going to get there." She yawned. "Like it's a fairy tale…"

I wrapped my arms around her. "Well, my house isn't a mansion—

not exactly. It's all one level, up in the hills. I have a great view when there's no smog. And I get all the sports stations, every single one. Even in my room." I smiled at her in the darkness, picturing her in my house. "You can have your own closet, and if you behave, your own shelf in the bathroom."

"If I'm living with you, I'm going to need more than one shelf," she laughed.

"Well, okay. You can have more than one. If you're good. What else is my house like... hmmm... I have a really big refrigerator."

"Bigger than the one in Boston? 'Cause that thing's huge," she said.

"Yes, it's bigger. And no offense, but Audrey, a Barbie mansion has a bigger refrigerator than the one you have in Southie."

"Ha ha," she said, punching me lightly. "But keep talking. Tell me what our life would be like."

"Well, we would get up every day, and then we could do a quick workout in my gym—yes, I have a gym—and then you'd make me breakfast. Preferably French toast because you're pretty good at that. And then I'd go to work—"

"And I'd go to work, too," she slipped in.

"Yes, of course you would. Or you can go to school full-time. Just don't let any of the students or professors ask you out. Then I'd have to fight them."

"That might be hot, actually."

"It might be. Yeah, it probably would be." We both laughed then, and it felt so good. "But seriously, that might be a great place to start. And then I could pick you up from school, and we could go visit Tommy. On the weekends, we can go to dinner. We can take Tommy to the beach or to the park—we don't have crap weather in LA. It's totally different. You can go outside all year. And we can go see the Red Sox games in Oakland when they play the A's. We can fly up in my private plane. We can fly to Hawaii for a long weekend. You can make me dinner every night."

"Ha," she said again, but she sounded pleased.

I paused for a second and traced her spine with my finger. I took a deep breath. "And then we can have kids, and you change their diapers—all of them, because I have a feeling that would be beneath me—and they'll go to all the best schools. We'll take them to Disneyland. We'll go watch their music shows and their plays, and they can play baseball and be awesome at it like their dad, and they will never like the A's, the Dodgers, or the Yankees, and if they are girls they will have beautiful, *Bambi*-like eyes like their mother. So there."

"*Bambi*-like eyes?" she asked, and giggled.

I blew out an embarrassed sigh. "Mock me if you will. Just promise me," I said, still stroking her back. "Promise me we are going to do all the things."

"I promise," she said, her face pressed against my chest. "I promise."

THE NEXT MORNING, Audrey brought me coffee in bed.

"I'm going to make a few phone calls," I said, "starting with Danielle's parents. Even though I don't have hard evidence, I believe my mother was at the very least involved in the accident somehow. I have to let them know. They still live in Tewksbury; I can look up the number."

"Are you sure you want to do this right now?" Audrey asked. "It's a pretty big wound to open up."

"We need their help. They're the only people my parents won't be able to pay off," I told her. "And they deserve to know, even if it's only that I *think* my parents were involved. I'm going to let them in on the plan."

"Are you going to let *me* know what the plan is?" she asked.

"Yes, but later. I want the element of surprise to go to bat for us."

"What about your parents?" she asked. "Are we going to confront them today?"

"Don't worry. They're on the list. I have plans for them."

# AUDREY

James was on the phone for what felt like forever.

"I talked to Danielle's parents. They're going to help us," he said when he finally came out. His face was drawn, and his eyes were red. "My mother's going to have a nasty surprise waiting for her when we get back."

He poured himself another cup of coffee. "I also called my lawyer. He's better than my mother's, by the way. He said that he'll get the paperwork prepared for you to become Tommy's sole guardian. You'll have to sign it when we get back, and then he'll start the process with the court. And I made a call to that private investigator, too—he said he was going to go to your mom's house today with a large file and a larger threat."

"But what if she tells Celia?" I asked.

"She won't. We're going to make her an offer she can't refuse. So she'll receive a financial incentive while simultaneously being blackmailed. It's win-win."

My heart sank. "I don't want her getting any more of your money..."

"I'd rather she gets it from us than from my parents," he said. "Plus, we can't just let your mother stay in that apartment, living like that, when there's more than enough money to take care of her. It's not right."

I wasn't going to forgive my mother so easily, either for what she'd done to Tommy or what she'd done to James. "It's exactly what she deserves," I said. "She doesn't seem unhappy to me. Just greedy. And scheming."

"Well, you're right. She *is* greedy. And she'll just come looking, threatening us again. I don't want to deal with that for the rest of my life, and I know you don't either. It's better to just manage her, Audrey. She's your mother. She's not going to change, and she's not going anywhere."

I sighed, understanding what he saying and wishing I didn't. "How did it go with Danielle's parents? That must have been such a tough conversation. It was so out of the blue."

His eyes looked hollowed out. "It was awful. I'm sure hearing from me after all this time was the last thing they were expecting."

"What did they say?" I asked. I couldn't even imagine.

"I spoke with her father. I told him that I didn't know the details, but that I believed my parents were directly involved with Danielle's death. That it wasn't an accident. I told him that you'd confronted my mother, and that she was threatening you, and that I needed his help."

"What did you ask him to do?"

"I told him to go to the police. That we'd be back soon," James said. His face was pale. I went to him and wrapped my arms around him. "He thanked me, Audrey—he said the way my mother had acted afterward had bothered him for years. He said he felt like she'd been relieved that Danielle was dead. He wants her to go to prison."

"And you?" I asked. "Is that what you want, too?"

"I'm pretty sure prison's too good for her," he said. "But it'll have to do." He paused for a beat. "We need to call your mother. To let her know that she's got company coming."

I held up my hand. "I got this," I said, picking up his fancy cell phone. "The farther I can keep you away from my mother, the better."

TODD, EVIE, COLE, AND JENNY were waiting for us down at the dock again. "Good morning," Cole called. He had a huge smile on his face, and so did Jenny. Since they'd professed their love for one another, I hadn't seen them *stop* smiling.

Even though my world was on the edge of veering wildly out of control, their enthusiasm was infectious. I beamed at Jenny and gave her a big hug. "You look gorgeous," I said, "and happy."

"I am. Everything's working out," she said, holding me tight.

"But I'm worried about you. Evie said Celia read you the riot act last night, and that you were wicked pale and upset after. What's going on?"

I shook my head and blew out a deep, ragged breath. "She's giving my mother a run for Mother of the Year, is all."

Jenny snorted. "You and James are good people. Maybe you were both adopted."

"I wish," I said.

WE SNORKELED ALL MORNING. The kitchen staff had packed lunch for us; the crew dropped us on a secluded beach with our enormous picnic basket and a cooler full of prosecco and beer. "I could get used to this," Todd said, sitting back on the blanket that Evie had set up and cracking a beer. "Sure beats filing Department of Labor compliance docs."

Cole smiled at him. "I don't miss compliance or due diligence, but I *do* miss my hockey team. But really, I have every thing I need right here." He threw his arm around Jenny.

"I don't miss work," Jenny said, deadpan. "I don't think I'm going back."

"You're not. You're retiring," Cole said protectively.

"I have about ten deals that have probably gone south in the past two weeks, and I don't even care," James said. He poured us each a glass of champagne and gave me a loving kiss on the cheek. I leaned back against him, trying not to stare at his tanned six-pack stomach, rising up tautly from his swim trunks.

"I'm sure you'll still have a booming empire to attend to when you get back," Todd said. "You always do. Audrey, are you going to transfer to a school out there?"

"I think so," I said. *I hope I make it that far,* I thought. "California would be a nice change of pace."

"I know—warm weather, can you imagine? Winter lasted forever this year," Evie said. It was true; there had been dirty snowbanks in Boston well into April. "Being down here's been really nice. It's so beautiful here. I'm glad you guys came—you're way more fun than my cousins. All they do is talk about their protein intake and their training schedules. And their screaming kids." She looked at Todd and wrinkled her nose. "That's not normal, is it?"

"No, honey, it's not," Todd said agreeably. "We won't be like that when we're parents. We won't talk about our kids all the time, and they won't be screaming, filthy little buggers like your cousins'."

"Of course not," she said. She was wearing a pink-polka-dot bikini, her collarbones tanned and on prominent display. "We have manners, and so will our children."

"We should come down here every year—and we won't invite your cousins. Or your screaming kids," Cole said to Evie.

"*My* children won't be screaming," Evie said defensively, telling the same lie all non-parents told themselves.

"Then it's a date," James said, lacing his fingers through mine. "Same time next year."

---

WE WENT HOME and showered before the night's festivities; Todd and Evie had arranged for dinner at the fanciest of the resort's restaurants. We had to dress up, which bothered me. Only because I was worried that I'd have to run away from Mrs. Preston in my spike-heeled sandals. And that I wouldn't get far.

James was dashing in a sand-colored linen suit; he wore a white shirt underneath, slightly unbuttoned, showing off just a peek of his gorgeous, tanned chest.

"Do we have to have to go right now?" I asked, fanning myself. "'Cause you look wicked hot. That tan is killing me."

"*Wicked* hot?" he asked, laughing. "Is my wicked hot girlfriend from Southie, or what?"

"She is," I said, grinning at him.

He pulled me to him and gave me a long, lingering kiss that took my breath away. I felt him stir against me. "Yes, please," I said and started undoing his belt.

James groaned. "No, thank you," he said, even though he'd sprung to life instantly underneath my touch. "We have reservations, and we have to go deal with my parents, remember?"

"Ugh," I said, forgetting all about undoing his belt.

"Ugh is right," he said. "But I'd like to pick that back up as soon as we get home, if you don't mind."

"I don't mind," I said and kissed him again. "Taking your clothes off is about the only thing that can keep my mind off of all our… more unpleasant business." I sighed. "That and thinking about your abs."

"That's what I like to hear," he said, beaming at me. "You're perfect, you know that? Now let's go, before I start trying to show you my abs."

AS SOON AS WE were back out in the sunlight, my heart started thudding in my chest. We had to face his mother again. James still hadn't told me what our strategy was going to be at dinner. He'd just instructed me to play along.

He looked straight ahead as we headed to the restaurant, gripping my hand. His easy demeanor of a minute ago was gone. He was almost a little scary right now, striding toward the restaurant in full-blown preparedness for combat.

"Audrey," he said when we got to the door, "I want you to remember something. This is about to be a show. Don't lose the plot, okay? Remember who the enemy is. And remember that no matter what I say in there, I will love you forever."

# JAMES

We marched into the restaurant, and Audrey's face was pale and concerned, just the way I wanted it to be. There was another long table with a white tablecloth; chandeliers and candles shimmered throughout the room. I was getting tired of these fancy dinners. I was certainly tired of my fancy parents, with their misplaced faith in their abiding superiority.

Danielle had been better, a better person than my mother, not the other way around. My mother needed to understand that. I wasn't sure she was capable, but I was going to try my damnedest.

I just had to make sure that Audrey and I were credible right now. We needed to be pitch perfect. My mother didn't miss much, and there was no room for error. The vacation was ending, and we were going back to the real world. Audrey was going to be a part of my world. I just had to make sure I got her there unscathed.

Mostly unscathed.

"Let's sit here," I said to Audrey, pulling out a chair across from my parents. Audrey nodded at me silently and didn't look at them: it was as though she couldn't bear to.

My father nodded to us over his bourbon, and I saw his eyes slip down to Audrey's chest. "Father," I said to him coolly, "eyes on me."

He gave me a dirty look and sipped his bourbon. "I was young once, you know."

"Really?" I asked, taking a seat next to Audrey. "I don't remember. It seems like you've been an old man forever."

He snorted at me. "You're in rare form tonight," he said, peering at me over his glasses.

"So are you. You've said more than four words." Per his usual, he grunted at me and turned back to the menu. Compared to my mother, my father was like a cardboard cutout of a person. He'd been forever in the background, a voice on the other end of a line from his office. I would always think of him as dressed in neutral tones, nursing a bourbon, scowling at the world from behind his Armani glasses. I'd often thought my mother had chosen him largely because he did what she said.

I wonder if he'd fought her about Danielle, or if he'd just fallen in line. Maybe she never told him, but he had to have guessed. My mother was a difficult woman. I wouldn't be surprised if he'd never said a word and just gone back to his office on the Monday morning after the accident, as though nothing had happened.

As though his wife had never killed a girl.

Celia swept in after that, in a blush-pink gown that ruffled at the neck, probably to mask the few existing lines she had left there. If she was surprised that we'd chosen to sit across from them, her face gave nothing away. Not that I expected it to. She was either so morally bankrupt that she was completely without remorse or her filler had settled in just enough that her face wouldn't really move for another few weeks. Either way, her smooth expression was just as I expected.

"Hello, James," she said. "Audrey."

Audrey nodded at her and looked away, and I settled in for what was going to be an excruciatingly long multiple-course dinner.

"HAVE ANOTHER DRINK," I said to Audrey in a low voice, just before dessert was served. "You're about to need it."

"Yes, sir," she said, motioning to the waiter. My parents had been civil during dinner, but little else. My mother had asked me to no avail about several business ventures. After finally giving up, she'd turned to my father to discuss their various upcoming social obligations.

After Audrey got her drink and we finished dessert, I stood abruptly. "Mother, we need to speak with you," I said. "Follow me." Both Audrey and my mother obediently followed me out to the almost empty lobby, where we grabbed a table near the fireplace.

"What's this about?" Celia asked. She gave Audrey a quick look.

"James can speak for himself," Audrey mumbled, still not looking at my mother. She'd barely said a word all through dinner, and now she looked tense and small against the enormous chair she was seated in.

I knocked back the rest of my bourbon and sat forward in my seat. "I wanted you to know something, Mother. Audrey told me last night about the conversation she'd had with you—about her brother and the fact that you called her mom. I want you to know that I'll be handling those issues going forward."

What looked like lasers shot out of Celia's eyes at Audrey. "I thought I told you to keep that between us, dear. I'd love to say I'm surprised, but…" She turned back to me. "I want you to know I was trying to protect you. From this girl and her lies. What else do you have to say, James?"

I gripped my glass so hard I was surprised it didn't shatter in my hand. "Audrey also told me about her… suspicions. About the death of Danielle, my high school girlfriend."

My mother watched my face. As always, hers gave nothing away. "Audrey told me the same thing. She said she believed I was *involved* somehow."

"That's what she's claiming." I saw Audrey look at me briefly, confused. My head was pounding. "You know I have some serious issues with you, Mother. But I don't believe you're capable of something that horrific. And I *don't* believe it. So I want you to know, Audrey and I are heading home tonight. And this will be the last time we see each other. I will take care of her and her family. I'll make sure that nothing about our relationship or her accusations about Danielle's death ever come out."

I took a deep breath. "Because although I believed she had feelings for me, I know now the truth: that she's a grifting, blackmailing whore. Just like her mother."

"The apple doesn't fall far from the tree, dear," my mother said, looking triumphant. "I've tried to tell you that a thousand times."

AUDREY DIDN'T SAY A WORD to me on the way back to the room. I didn't say anything, either. We could be followed or overheard, and I wasn't going to risk it.

Her face was still pale when we went back inside, her mouth set in a grim line. "I'm calling the valet to come and get us," I said. "Pack your things. Pack mine, too, if you can stand to."

She looked up at me, and I could see the wounded look on her face.

"Audrey," I started. "Let's wait to talk it through—let's get out of here while that performance is still fresh in my mother's mind. But you *know*."

"Know what?" she asked, slamming though the house and grabbing our stuff.

"That I love you. And that I'm sorry about the ugly things I just said." I went and wrapped my arms around her, pressing the full length of my body against hers. She wriggled against me, as if she were trying to get away. I leaned down and looked at her. "My mother isn't easily fooled, Audrey. I had to make that seem real. She has to believe that we're through and that you aren't a threat to her. So even though I hurt you, I did it to keep you safe. That's the only thing that matters to me."

She looked up at me. "Tell me you didn't mean it. Not a word."

"I didn't mean a word of it." I smoothed the hair back from her forehead and kissed her gently. "You know I didn't."

"It still hurt. It made me feel sick to hear it," she said.

"It made me feel sick to say it."

I released her, and she took a step back from me.

"I had to do that, Audrey. I had to take control of the situation. My mother's been running things for too long. We're going to have both my mother and yours on a short leash after this. And we're the walkers, babe. They're the dogs."

"I hope they don't turn around and bite us," Audrey said. "Those are some big fangs."

I DIDN'T HOLD HER HAND until the plane had taken off. I didn't want anyone to see us. Audrey was quiet, pretending to listen carefully while the flight attendant went through the safety presentation, inspecting her nails afterward and generally ignoring me.

"Can you please forgive me?" I asked. "I didn't think we'd get out of there, intact, any other way."

"I can forgive you. I already did," she said under her breath. "But if you ever compare me to my mother again, you can say goodbye to this." She motioned to her lower body.

"No," I said. "I am not *ever* saying goodbye to that."

She smiled at me a little, and I could tell it was reluctant. "You were just so *mean*," she said.

"I know. It was ugly."

"Do you think she believed it?" Audrey asked.

"I think so. I think my mother believes that the apple really doesn't fall far from the tree. She thinks that underneath it all, I'm just like her. Ruthless. Only interested in myself. And she's right," I said, throwing my arm around her. "Except that she hadn't counted on you. Now I'm ruthless, and I'm only interested in *you*. And I don't think my mother believes I'm capable of that."

"Of having a relationship?" Audrey asked.

"Of loving someone more than I love myself," I said. "Even though she's a parent, I don't think she knows what that means."

"Your mother and my mother deserve each other," Audrey said. "They should be prison roommates."

"I might work on arranging that," I said.

I'D NEVER BEEN so relieved to be back in Boston. Audrey must have felt it, too; she relaxed next to me as soon as we landed. Kai was waiting for us at Logan. He smiled at me and, as per my previous instructions, averted his eyes from Audrey.

"Kai, it's good to see you," I said as we slid into the back of the SUV.

"You too, sir, ma'am. Did you enjoy your trip?"

"We did. We mixed business and pleasure. It was productive," I said. "Did you miss us?"

"Of course," Kai said. "You two are my favorite clients. Especially you, Mr. Preston. No offense, Miss Reynolds—but you know how he is about you." He cracked a smile, and Audrey had a laugh at my expense.

"Ha ha. That's nice, Kai," I said, leaning back and pulling Audrey to me. "I'm not a favorite with a lot of people right now. It's nice to know I'm still capable of being liked. But you can let Audrey be your favorite—you can even smile at her from now on. Everyone likes her better than me, anyway. For good reason."

"What's that?" she asked.

"You're not a total prick," I said and grinned at her.

# AUDREY

"I still like you," I whispered to James. "Barely."

"Gee, thanks," he said, kissing me on top of my head. "Do you need to go to your apartment? To get anything?"

"I'm going to have to. And I need to go to New Horizons, and also call Elena. There's a lot I need to take care of. But I think I'd like some coffee first." I blew out a shaky breath. "I have to go see my mother, too. To make sure she understands the financial incentive/blackmail package we're offering her."

"It's a day of reckoning," James said, looking at his watch. "My parents are flying back tomorrow afternoon. Everything needs to be in place before that."

I looked at him, still not completely understanding what he had planned. "What do we need to do?"

"I'll call Danielle's parents, to see what they've done in terms of contacting the police. I'll probably have to follow up and give the detectives a statement. They'll want to speak with you, too. You'll have to tell them how my mother threatened you and exactly what she said with respect to Danielle. And then we'll go from there. I need to speak with my brother, to tell him what's happening. This is going to be very hard for him. And I have no idea if my father was involved or not."

James ran his hand over his face. He suddenly looked tired. "I don't know if they'll have enough to arrest either of them. They need probable cause—I don't know if the information we're going to give them will amount to that."

My head was spinning. "What if it doesn't?" I asked. "What if it *does*?"

"I don't know," James said. "But we'll be prepared either way."

"You're methodical. And smart," I said. "I'm just pointing that out to you."

He laced his fingers through mine. "That's what you're here for, babe."

WHEN WE HEADED Into the lobby of The Stratum, it felt as if we were coming home. I was so comfortable with James now, it was the opposite of the first time he'd brought me here. The attendants greeted us warmly, their faces open and familiar. When we got into the elevator, I started to laugh.

"What?" he asked.

"I'm just remembering the first time I was in here with you," I said. "I couldn't take my eyes off you—and your big hands." James lifted his hands up and examined them, as if for the first time. "And I kept wondering what you had going on underneath your suit."

"Well, you ought to know," he said. He leaned down and kissed me. "You're the expert in that department now."

"I was so annoyed that I was attracted to you," I said. "I thought it was inconvenient. Especially since you said you didn't want to sleep with me."

"Oh, I wanted to sleep with you," he said and tucked my hair behind my ear. "As soon as I saw you, I wanted you."

"It sort of took you a long time," I said, pretending to pout.

"I'm pretty sure we've made up for lost time," James said, his eyes darkening as he looked at me. I leaned up and kissed him, slowly, our tongues connecting. Heat shot through me, and I threw my arms around his neck.

"I'm ready for more now, though," he said. "You didn't come near me last night." Now it was his turn to pretend pout.

"That's because you said I was a grifting whore. Just like my mother. That's not exactly my idea of foreplay," I said.

"How about this instead," he said. As the door opened, he grabbed my ass and hoisted me up on him; I wrapped my legs around his waist, and he carried me toward the door, kissing me deeply.

I could feel him against me, hot and hard, and it caused a

familiar ache all through me. He punched in the code without looking.

I wanted him, but the hurt I'd felt last night bubbled up in me, mixed with the hot, heavy desire I was feeling. "Tell me you love me," I said.

"I love you. You know I do," he said, carrying me into the bedroom. He laid me carefully on the bed, then he looked around and smiled. "I don't think I've ever been this happy to be here before. I don't even hate Boston anymore. What have you done to me, Audrey?"

"Taught you how to relax and eat onion rings in bed. Went to Fenway Park with you and drank beer. Oh—and I popped your swan-boat cherry," I said and shrugged. "All the important things."

He knelt on the floor before me and kissed me, gently at first. Then the kiss deepened, and I felt myself open up to him. I hadn't realized it, but I'd been balled up inside myself, like a fist, after what he'd said last night. But now I clung to him, forgiving him, trusting him.

He pulled back from me for a second. "Tell me you're mine," he said. "Say it."

"I'm yours," I said. "I love you so much."

"I want to see you naked with that tan," he said, stripping my clothes off roughly. "It's been too long."

"It's only been a day," I said, laughing, but I felt it, too. The need. "James—I was hurt last night. It was stupid, because I understood what you were doing. But still."

He'd already managed to take my clothes off, and I looked up at him, as naked and vulnerable as I could be. "It's hard for me not to believe… the bad things about myself."

"But you shouldn't believe them," he said, his eyes burning into mine. "You're the best person I know, Audrey."

"Thank you," I said, trying to keep my voice even. I didn't want to cry and ruin our sexy moment—I was aching to have him inside me. "I trust you, James. It's real. And I… I trust you with all of me." I ran my hand down my naked body as his eyes raked over me, making me flush with heat. As he watched, I started playing with my breasts, making my nipples hard and elongated. I opened my legs a little, offering myself to him.

"My turn," James said and grabbed my hands, holding them above my head. He put his mouth on me, licking and sucking my breasts hungrily. He ran his hands down my body. He quickly found my clitoris and circled it slowly with his powerful fingers, making me moan as he got me wet.

"I want to bury myself in you," he said, as I moved beneath his hand. "After I make you come first." He continued to circle my clit, and I rocked against him, getting slick with wetness. I could already feel a tremendous orgasm building inside me. He bit at my nipples, and I cried out, arching my back. He increased the pressure on my sex as I writhed beneath him.

I was fighting my orgasm. I preferred to come when he was inside me, when we were totally connected. Like this, I was completely at his mercy. He was in charge of my body right now, and my body was out of control.

"I can't," I said. "I don't want to… I need you inside me, babe."

He stopped touching me and watched my face. "Do you trust me?" he asked. I nodded at him. "Then let me be in charge. I want to explore your sweet, tight body," he said. He got on his knees and put his lips on me, and his tongue circled my swollen sex. He was in control, and I had to ride the waves of pleasure that were crashing through my body. I had no choice.

He pulled back for a second. "When I'm ready, I'm going to fuck you. Deep and hard." He took my clitoris in between his teeth and bit it gently, and then continued to suck and nip at me. I threw my head back and cried out. He continued to lick me, and suck me, and play with my body until I shattered beneath him, an orgasm ripping through me. Completely out of control, I screamed his name as my body spasmed.

"James," I panted as it started to subside.

"Are you ready for me now, baby?" he asked. He stood up and put his long, hard cock against me, rubbing it against my slit as I was still shaking from my orgasm.

"Yes," I whispered. "Please." I was desperate to feel him inside me. He didn't make me wait; he was so hard he was about to burst. He stood at the side of the bed and entered me like that, almost immediately, all the way to his hilt. I moaned as he filled me, and I looked up at his glorious, tanned, and muscled body. His cock was enormous and hard inside me, and my body fit around his tightly, as if I'd been built for him.

He thrust into me once, twice, deep and sharp. I ran my hands down his muscled lower torso as pleasure ripped through me. He was in deep, like he promised, and it felt so good. I felt complete.

I wrapped my fingers around the base of his shaft as he continued to drive into me. I let my hand stroke his base with each thrust, wanting to increase his sensation and his pleasure. It worked. He threw his head back and was riding me hard, his hands gripping my hips. "Holy fuck, Audrey."

He was in deeper than I'd ever felt him. I felt the familiar pleasure build inside of me, and I started to come, all of my senses overtaken by him. He buried himself into me, over and over, fucking me through my orgasm and finding his release. His powerful arms wrapped around me as our orgasms shook the bed.

Afterward, he collapsed next to me. "Damn," he said and pulled me against him. I nestled there happily, feeling content and completely connected to him. I was waiting for him to say something more—then I watched as he promptly fell asleep with a smile on his face.

"I love you," I whispered.

He opened one eye and looked at me, that happy smile still on his face. "I love you too, babe."

I WOKE UP A few hours later with sun streaming through the windows. James was up, wearing his Wharton T-shirt and some sweats. He was pacing around the room.

"What's wrong?" I asked.

"Nothing," he said. "I got you your coffee." He motioned toward the nightstand.

"Thanks," I said. I sat up and took a sip, eyeing him warily.

"You're pacing for a reason, James. I'd like to know what that is."

"We're back home from the trip. Our two weeks are up. You've fulfilled your contract." He ran his hands through his hair.

My heart clenched, and I put the coffee down before I spilled it. "Is this the part where you fire me? Again?"

"Not if it's the part where you quit. Again." We just looked at each other for a beat. "No, Audrey—we've reached the end of our mutual agreement, is what I'm saying. There's nothing but free will going on here."

"Okay," I said, a nervous pit forming in my stomach. "When you asked me to move to California with you… that was free will, right? So has something changed?" I asked nervously.

"No," he said. "Yes." He ran his hand through his hair again. "Being with my family these past two weeks has had me thinking. And all of this horrible stuff about my mother and Danielle—it's made me realize some things."

He paused for a beat. "Do you remember what I told you Todd said to me? Right before the wedding?"

"No," I said. I looked at him blankly. "Was it something like, where the hell is Audrey running off to? 'Cause that's when my mom showed up." He was scaring me, and I was just babbling, afraid to hear what he had to say.

"No," he said and sighed. "That wasn't it. It's something that's been bothering me."

"Okay," I said again. I braced for whatever was coming next.

"He said that when you finally figure out what you want in life, you're pretty ready for forever." James came and sat on the bed next to me. He reached for my hand. "Like I said, these last two weeks have had me thinking. About family. About what I want… for *my* family."

I held my breath.

"Audrey, it's taken me a very long time to find you. And we haven't been together very long. But I've *finally* figured out what I want. And I am pretty ready for forever."

He got off the bed and knelt by me. He pulled a small black box out from his pocket, and I was pretty sure I was no longer holding my breath—I'd just stopped breathing. He opened the box, and inside there was an enormous, square-cut diamond, fit for a princess.

"Are you?" he asked.

I was stunned. I just blinked at him. "Am I what?" I asked stupidly.

"Ready for forever?"

I blinked at him again.

"I don't want to wait anymore," he said, watching my face. "I love you. I want you to know that I mean it forever."

I couldn't speak. I couldn't find my breath.

"Audrey, will you marry me?"

Finally, comprehension dawned on me and I nodded my head up and down.

"I'm going out on a limb and guess here—is that a yes?" he asked hopefully.

"Yes," I whispered, finding my voice. And then I threw myself at him. "Yes, yes, yes."

# JAMES

The next two days passed in a blur. We'd gone to the police and given statements. We'd also given them my parents' flight information; the detectives said they would be waiting at the airport when they arrived. They wouldn't tell us if they would make an arrest, but we knew they would at least question both of my parents. That was something.

I was still having a hard time adjusting to my new reality. This was real. My parents were involved in Danielle's death. I let the shock, betrayal and disgust course through me as Audrey and I went about our other business. This was my new reality, and it was going to take some time getting used to it.

My parents had always been difficult, but now I found them abhorrent. No matter how distant we'd become, that wasn't an easy thing for a son to feel.

Audrey and I went to New Horizons, and I'd finally met Tommy. "This is James," Audrey told him. "I love him, and you will, too. He wants us to move to California with him."

"What about Mom?" Tommy had asked.

Audrey had shrugged. "She'll probably come out and visit, even though I don't want her to. Because she's Mom."

They both laughed at that.

Then we paid a visit to East Boston. Because before we got to *my* horrible mother, we had to deal with Audrey's. We had to make sure she was completely on board with my proposed agreement. She had to promise not to blackmail us and/or communicate with my mother, in exchange for my private investigator's silence on her ongoing parole violations and a large sum of money being wired into her bank account.

Mrs. Reynolds was wearing an old Pour House T-shirt and hadn't bothered to clean her apartment, but she did say she was happy to see us.

"You're happy to see *me*?" Audrey asked, flabbergasted.

"Mostly him," Mrs. Reynolds said, lighting a cigarette and jutting her chin out at me.

Audrey gave me a quick look and turned back to her mother, her brow furrowed. "Didn't that investigator come over here?" she asked. "And tell you about his file?"

"Yeah," her mother said, exhaling in Audrey's face. "He didn't bother me none. I mean, once he told me what I was gonna get."

I pretended to study my phone while Audrey gave me a scathing look.

"What exactly *are* you going to get?" she asked her mother.

Mrs. Reynolds looked at me too, possibly waiting for some sort of direction. I continued to study my phone, not wanting to admit anything. Audrey sighed. "Never mind, Ma," she said, resigned. "I'll get it out of him later."

It was quiet for a beat. I looked up just in time to see Mrs. Reynolds holding her hand over her chest, clutching at her heart and staring at Audrey's left hand. "Sweet baby Jesus in the manger," she said, "is that an *engagement* ring?"

"Yes. It is." Audrey sighed again. "James and I are getting married. And I'm moving to California with him. And we're bringing Tommy." Audrey looked defiantly at her mother.

"Well. Huh. Okay," her mother said, agreeably enough, not missing a beat.

Audrey appeared speechless, like the wind had been knocked out of her. "*Okay*?" She looked suspiciously at me again. "How much freaking money did you give her?"

"Enough," I said innocently.

"I know you'll take good care of Tommy," Mrs. Reynolds said, interrupting us. "And I'll come out to visit all the time."

Audrey looked at her in horror, her eyes wide. "Visit… *us*?"

"And stay at a *hotel*, Miss Holier Than Thou. Your boyfriend—I mean, your fiancé—has made all of that possible."

"I thought you didn't like him," Audrey said, jerking her thumb at me. "I thought you said he was prick masquerading as a gentleman."

"Yeah, but things change," her mother said and shrugged. "Except you. You'll always think you're too good for me."

"That's because I am," Audrey said.

Her mother laughed a little, and then took another deep drag. "Well, you *are* holier than thou. And I'm sure as hell not."

"Being holier than thou's not for everybody," Audrey said.

"You don't have to tell me that," Mrs. Reynolds said, through a cloud of smoke.

AUDREY CALLED ELENA from the car and quit. "I'm not coming back to the service, Elena," she said. The relief was evident in her voice.

"You and Jenny *both*?" the madam wailed. I could hear her from across the car. "Jenny already called me from the island. Jesus, it must've been quite a vacation."

"It was, Elena." Audrey said, lacing her hand through mine. She hung up and turned to me. "I'm officially unemployed," she said.

"In this particular case, it's really for the best," I said.

Audrey smiled at me but wrinkled her nose. "I'm pretty young to be retired."

"I'll keep you busy," I said.

"You have to. You promised. Remember the cowboy thing?" she asked.

"Can the *cowboy thing* get retired?" I asked.

Audrey laughed. "Maybe. I don't mind you being the bed, though," she said, and snuggled against me.

"When you put it like that, I guess I don't either." I pulled her close to me, not minding at all.

"I HAVE TO RETURN those clothes to Elena," Audrey said later. We were in her room and she was staring at the formidable closet.

"Nah," I said, "I'll just pay her for them. I'm very fond of that black dress. And I might frame that bikini."

ALL THINGS CONSIDERED, I was happier than I thought I could be. Especially because I was about to meet my mother at the airport with two police detectives and Danielle's parents in tow.

I still couldn't believe that my parents were involved in Danielle's death. And yet, I *did* believe it. What my mother had said to Audrey, and the way that she'd threatened her, confirmed my worst fears. I knew in my heart that my mother had done something terrible, even though I still didn't know exactly what it was.

I also believed that my father knew. Even if he'd done nothing to help my mother, I was certain that he'd done nothing to stop her. And that made him guilty and reprehensible, too.

We didn't know what, if any, charges the police would bring. We didn't know if my father would ultimately be implicated as well. But still. Danielle had been an innocent girl, and her murder deserved justice. For Danielle's sake, her parents', and for mine. If we couldn't have justice, we could at least have some sort of public acknowledgement. Some sort of reckoning.

Danielle's parents, Mr. and Mrs. Anderson, were waiting for us at the airport. I hugged them awkwardly and introduced them to Audrey. They looked tired and strained, but they said they were glad to be there. They wanted to see my mother's face.

"All these years, and we've never made peace with Danielle's death," Mr. Anderson said. His wife blotted her eyes. "I told myself it was because it's so terrible to lose a child. And it is—but it was more than that. It seemed more than just... unnatural. Like it was more wrong than that."

Mrs. Anderson cleared her throat. She had aged gracefully, but there were dark circles under her eyes. She looked hollowed out. "When you called it was like we'd been waiting for that call for twenty years," she said. "We didn't know it, but we had been. Your mother never thought Danielle was good enough for you, James. Danielle used to tell me that. I always thought your mother would finally warm up to her, see what a great kid she really was. Now I know the truth. My daughter never had a chance." She started crying and Mr. Anderson pulled her to him. I turned away.

The two Boston police detectives we'd spoken with were waiting nearby. There was also a reporter from *The Boston Tribune* and a photographer for *Paparazzi*.

"How did the press know about this?" Audrey whispered to me.

"I took a page from your mother's playbook and called them," I said. "I figured that would push Celia right over the edge. Which is exactly what she deserves."

Audrey nodded at me, and I held my breath, watching as the plane pulled up to the gate. I waited for my mother to come out and meet her fate. And my brother. I had to tell my brother the horrible news.

Todd and Evie came first, followed by Cole and Jenny. They all looked surprised by our presence. "What're you two doing here?" Todd asked. "Mother said—"

"Don't believe it," I said, grabbing his shoulders. "Everything's fine. Audrey and I are engaged."

"That's so great," Todd said. He beamed at us.

"But I'm not here for good news," I said lowly and urgently. "I tried to call you, but I couldn't get through. I'm here because of Mom and Dad. Because of something terrible."

"But they're fine," Todd said, confused. "They're right behind us."

"Not something terrible that happened to them—something that they *did*." I gave my baby brother a long look and then I motioned to Danielle's parents. "This is Mr. and Mrs. Anderson. Do you remember my girlfriend from high school? Danielle? These are her parents."

"It's nice to see you," Todd said, shaking their hands. "And I'm still so sorry about your daughter. I was young when it happened, but I remember what a tragedy it was."

Todd turned back to me. "I don't understand," he said, looking baffled. He looked from Mr. and Mrs. Anderson to the police detectives standing behind them. "What's going on?"

I took a deep breath, knowing the blow I was about to deliver. "Mother has been implicated in Danielle's death. She threatened

Audrey in Eleuthera and we started putting the pieces together," I said. "The police are here to bring her in for questioning, and maybe dad, too. And the Andersons are here to see them face-to-face."

Todd went pale beneath his tan. "Are you kidding?"

"No. I'm sorry, I'm not." For the first time, I felt real sadness and regret about our parents, not just the rage that had been coursing through me.

"Come and sit down," Evie said gently. She led Todd to some nearby seats, talking to him softly and rubbing his arm.

"Holy wow," Jenny said, coming up next to us. She must have overheard at least part of the conversation. "I'd say I didn't believe it, if Mrs. Preston wasn't such a c-word. Sorry, James." She turned to Audrey. "She just kept looking at me the whole flight. Like I was going to infect her with hooker cooties, or something."

Audrey gave her an exhausted smile. "I'd say I was surprised, but—"

"Ho my frickin' God, Audrey!" Jenny shrieked, interrupting her. "Is that an engagement ring?" Audrey nodded at her and Jenny grabbed her, jumping up and down. "It's not even a rock! It's a frickin' *boulder*!"

"Jenny," Audrey said calmly, "let's talk about it later. We have some bad stuff to take care of right now."

"Right," Jenny said. She stopped jumping and crossed herself. "But wow. Just wow."

My mother swept off the plane then, in a green polo shirt with the collar turned up, immaculate khakis, and white loafers. Her face managed to move enough to register shock when she saw us.

"James?" she said. "*Audrey?*"

I glowered at her, and she stopped dead in her tracks, my father bumping into her from behind. "Watch it, Robert," she snapped.

"Mother, be polite—we have company," I said, motioning to the Andersons. "You remember Mr. and Mrs. Anderson, right? Danielle's parents? And this is Detective Gordon and Detective Fisk, from the Boston Police Department. I believe they'd like to ask you and Dad some questions—downtown." I smiled as she fought to maintain her icy composure. Just then, the photographers started snapping pictures, their flashes going off.

"And that's the *Tribune*. And *Paparazzi*." I smiled tightly at her while she regained her composure and perfected her posture for the photographers.

"Mother, a couple of other quick things: Audrey's mom is playing for my team now. You can still pay her if you want to. I'm sure she won't object."

I watched as the detectives headed purposefully toward my parents. The Andersons followed close behind, pale and resigned.

"Oh—and one more thing," I said. "Audrey and I are engaged."

"Mr. Preston! You're engaged?" called one of the photographers. "Let me take a shot of the happy couple!"

They published the picture all over the Internet that afternoon. In it, Audrey and I had our arms wrapped around each other, tired smiles on our faces. In the background you could just see my mother, the police converging on her. Her face managed to move enough to look as if she had swallowed a very bitter, very low-class pill.

# EPILOGUE

## Five Years Later

Cole, Jenny and their three kids were waiting for us at the beach. Todd and Evie were just getting their youngest up from a nap; they were coming down to meet us shortly.

"I can't believe you two are pregnant again," I said, shaking my head at Cole.

"I told you years ago that I couldn't keep my hands off her," Cole said and laughed. "This is what happens." He motioned to the baby strapped to his chest in a Baby Bjorn.

"Plus, you should talk, bro." He motioned to my youngest, who was strapped to mine.

"Yeah, but you're pregnant with your *fourth*. That just seems exorbitant. Audrey and I have a respectable three."

"For now," Cole said. "I can still see that emotional boner on your face. If Audrey wants another one, she'll get it."

"That's probably true," I said and laughed.

We'd kept our promise and come back to the Bahamas every year. The only part of the promise that was not intact involved Todd and Evie's children. They had three little boys, and they were indeed screaming and often filthy. They brought home bugs and worms for their mother and made her scream, too. But she loved them, and it let me see another side of Evie—a side that let me know she was sincere in her love for Todd and for their children.

And I loved her and Todd's screaming, filthy little buggers for that.

Four years ago, Audrey and I had been married in a small ceremony at the Gardner Museum. Todd and Cole had been my attendants; Jenny and Evie had been Audrey's. Cole and Jenny had married later that same year. In contrast to our intimate wedding, they rented an entire Caribbean island and had hosted a blowout, black-tie affair, complete with fireworks shot out over the water.

"This is huge," I'd said to Cole at the time, looking around at the celebration.

"Jenny's sort of used to huge," Cole had said, deadpan.

At our wedding, Tommy had walked Audrey down the aisle. She'd looked exactly like an angel, in a long lace dress.

My eyes had filled with tears the moment I saw her. Audrey's mother had tears in her eyes, too—most likely for a different reason. She was probably counting all the dollars Audrey was marrying into, relieved that she didn't have to sweat the annual increases to the Massachusetts cigarette tax.

My mother was crying, too. Probably because she was worried about the dilution of her bloodline, as well as the fact that I was marrying the woman who'd brought her house of cards tumbling down.

I thought of it as poetic justice.

Things had changed irrevocably in my family after the allegations surrounding Danielle's death were made public. No charges were ever brought against my father; there wasn't enough evidence. My mother, however, had been arrested on a felony-murder charge. The prosecution's theory was that she had hired someone to kill Danielle by running her off the road. But there wasn't enough physical evidence for the grand jury assigned to her case to charge her, and she was set free after a preliminary hearing.

Still, she'd been briefly incarcerated, and the tabloids had gone crazy over the story. Her face had been plastered over all the gossip columns online. Her arrest had even been featured as a companion piece to the spread of Todd and Evie's wedding in *New England Brides Magazine*. The Andersons wrote a novel, a thinly-veiled fictional account about what they believed happened to their daughter, that made all the bestseller lists. Celia Preston had been thoroughly and publicly humiliated. Even though it wasn't the justice she deserved, it was still something.

She would deny her involvement until the day she died. I had made my peace with that. But I also made her donate two million dollars to Danielle's scholarship fund and include a healthy bequest to the foundation in her will.

I never wanted to speak to her again, but Audrey convinced me to invite her to the wedding and to at least send pictures of the children on a regular basis. Just like I'd convinced her to invite *her* mother to the wedding and to regularly send pictures of the children.

"They're our family," I'd said, shrugging. "For better or for worse."

"I liked it better when you said that they were dogs. And that we were walking them," she'd said, but she'd sent the invitations anyway.

Audrey now walked down the beach carrying Bella, our two-year-old daughter. Next to her was Jenny, who was pregnant and glowing, holding her daughter Reese's hand. Our three-year-old son, Rhodes, was running around with Cole and Jenny's son, Kyle, both of them splashing in the water and screeching in delight. I had the new baby, Mia, strapped to me. As did Cole. Except his wasn't a Mia—she was an Audrey, named after her aunt.

There were a lot of us to keep track of.

"Weren't we all just here a while ago, single, drinking beer, and snorkeling?" Cole asked, looking at our crew. "Jesus, there are a lot of us now." He looked baffled.

"I know," I said. I looked at Audrey and smiled, wrapping my arm around her.

"You look happy," she said and kissed me on the cheek. "I'm just pointing that out to you, babe."

I beamed at her, the way I always did. "That's what you're here for, Mrs. Preston."

# SPECIAL THANKS

If you'd like to hear about my latest books, sign up for my Mailing List at www.leighjamesbooks.com. I only send emails if I have a new release or want to you to know about a special sale.

Thank you for reading this book! I truly hope you enjoyed it. It means so much to me that you took the time to read this story—I love James and Audrey. I'm rooting for them and I hope you are, too!

I also want to say thanks and send huge love to my mom, who always helps me and is an enormous source of support for my writing. I love you lots.

A special shout-out to W. Myler and A. Warren, my first readers and two of the loveliest, most intelligent, most patient and forthcoming women in the whole world. I would also like to thank my friends at RD and D. Waganer, who is my proofreader and who is awesome.

And always, love and hugs to my husband and my three children. You guys make every day the best.

# ABOUT THE AUTHOR

Photo (c) 2015 Tracey Hanlon Photography

Leigh James is a USA Today bestselling author of contemporary romance. She has a degree in journalism from the University of New Hampshire and a law degree from Suffolk University School of Law in Boston.

She lives in New Hampshire with her husband and three children.

Social Media:
@LeighJames19
Facebook.com/leighjames19author
www.leighjamesbooks.com

Printed in Great Britain
by Amazon